"I own this greenhouse now."

"Right." Adam reached into his pocket, took out the key. "It's the craziest thing—this key to the greenhouse. It takes me back not just to us, but to all the fun, the sharing, the knowledge. And to Frank. This greenhouse was his passion," Adam said.

"I remember the feeling I had when I'd walk through the doors after school. Being here was..."

"Magic," he finished for her as he took her hand, turned it palm up, placed the key in her hand and closed her fingers around it.

Joy sucked in a breath as he touched her.

Energy shot from his hand to hers, filling her with an overwhelming longing to be held by him. Joy couldn't stop this magnetism even if she wanted to. And she didn't want to.

His eyes held hers, not wavering.

It was as if they were in a realm all their own. Maybe it *was* magic that she and Adam had once had...

Dear Reader,

For most of my life, one of the joys of Christmas was visiting the local greenhouses. There I would peruse rows and rows of the most magnificent poinsettias. But eventually the family-run greenhouses closed as more box stores moved in.

In *Home for Christmas*, I wanted Joy Boston to come face-to-face with her past, but also take on the challenges of our modern times. Joy inherits her grandfather's business, which is now closed—until Joy's first love, Adam Masterson, appears. They broke up when she bolted out of town after high school. Joy has moved on to a new life in New York City. Adam moved on as well and has a six-year-old son, Titus. Still, Adam always had a place in his heart for Joy and the greenhouse. Is the same true for Joy?

Home for Christmas will warm your heart and show you that where there is love, there is always hope.

Please write to me at catherinelanigan.com or follow me on Facebook, on Twitter, @cathlanigan, and always at heartwarmingauthors.Blogspot.com. Join Prism Book Tours at prismbooktours.Blogspot.com. Don't forget to watch my movie on the Hallmark Channel: *The Sweetest Heart*, based on my Heartwarming novel *Heart's Desire*.

Catherine

HEARTWARMING

Home for Christmas

—

Catherine Lanigan

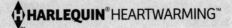

ISBN-13: 978-1-335-51092-1

Home for Christmas

HARLEQUIN®
www.Harlequin.com

Printed in U.S.A.

Catherine Lanigan knew she was born to storytelling at a very young age when she told stories to her younger brothers and sister to entertain them. After years of encouragement from family and high school teachers, Catherine was shocked and brokenhearted when her freshman college creative-writing professor told her that she had "no writing talent whatsoever" and that she would never earn a dime as a writer.

For fourteen years she did not write until she was encouraged by a television journalist to give her dream a shot. That was nearly forty published novels, nonfiction books and anthologies ago. To add to the dream, Hallmark Channel has recently released *The Sweetest Heart*, based on the second book in her Harlequin Heartwarming series, Shores of Indian Lake. With more books in the series and more movies to come, Catherine makes her home in La Porte, Indiana, the inspiration for Indian Lake.

Books by Catherine Lanigan

Harlequin Heartwarming

Shores of Indian Lake

Family of His Own
His Baby Dilemma
Rescued by the Firefighter
Hers to Protect

Visit the Author Profile page
at Harlequin.com for more titles.

This book is dedicated to my parents, Frank J. Lanigan and Dorothy Lanigan, who taught me the meaning of Christmas was love. Their home was always welcoming, warm and generous. No one was a stranger in our home. This is the home I now inhabit, and as my dear friend Vicki Bushman described, "The walls of this house drip love." There is no greater love than the love we have for our fellow man. Merry Christmas to all. God bless us, everyone!

ACKNOWLEDGMENTS

It is true that there are thousands of Christmas stories, but this one is very special to me. Its publication is due in part to my dedicated and insightful editor, Adrienne Macintosh, who instantly saw the eternal connection between Joy Boston and Adam Masterson.

Thanks also to executive editor Kathleen Scheibling and my mentor, editorial VP Dianne Moggy, for believing in the Shores of Indian Lake series. Bless you.

My gratitude and love always to my ever-faithful friend and agent, Lissy Peace.

You are all the very best of gifts that life has to offer. You are always welcome, Christmas or anytime, in my love-filled home.

And to all my readers, without your support and affectionate emails, letters and tweets, I don't know how I would continue on. Your words of encouragement through the dark days after my husband's passing meant the world to me. Your letters are still coming in and I treasure every card and letter. Heartwarming is so very aptly named. YOU are the heart-warmers. Never stop.

CHAPTER ONE

JOY STOOD AT her large office window, watching the Christmas decorating below. A fire truck raced down the street with a Christmas wreath attached to the front grille. She couldn't help smiling. Joy always happily anticipated Thanksgiving preparations. It was the one time of year her grandfather left her hometown of Indian Lake, coming to New York to be with her. The fire truck blasted its siren and Joy smiled, remembering her grandfather always hanging a wreath on the front of his old truck and then driving her around Indian Lake with a thermos of hot cocoa, singing Christmas songs together as they looked at the lights reflected in the frozen lake waters. She'd thought then even the aurora borealis couldn't compare to the beauty and sparkle of Indian Lake at Christmas.

Her view of Manhattan had blurred, and she wiped away her tears. She hugged herself, wondering why her thoughts kept wandering back to her grandfather so much this year. Perhaps it was because this year they wouldn't be spending Thanksgiving together. Her grandfather owned the largest poinsettia wholesale nursery in northwestern Indiana. Though Joy's year-end at Newly and Associates CPA firm was grueling, Frank Boston's Christmas rush was brutal. This year he told her he simply could not break away.

"He's so busy…bless his heart," Joy mumbled.

The rap on the doorjamb was familiar. "Hey, girl," Glory said. "Got a minute?"

Joy turned and smiled. Glory Washington was not only her best friend, but her roommate. They'd met the first week Joy had come to work at Newly and Associates. Glory was a month older than Joy to the day and never let her forget that she had seniority. When Glory wanted something her way, she usually got it. Glory was also the most trusting, generous and brassy person Joy had ever met, and Joy loved her to pieces.

"For you? Always. What's up?"

Glory's smile flashed impishly as she sashayed into the office in high-heeled suede boots, which she'd no doubt bought at one of her favorite resale shops. She wore a faux fur deep burgundy coat, black wool skirt, black cowl-neck sweater and an enormous rhinestone snowflake clip in her blond-black-and-cherry-bark dreads. The woman could wear a potato sack and look stunning.

"I saw you with the old man. You think he's going to make you partner after the wedding?"

Glory was referring to Joy's seven-day-old engagement to Chuck Newly, handsome, successful, ambitious and heir of the two-centuries-old New York Newly family.

She couldn't wait to tell her grandfather, and she was doubly sad that he wouldn't be in New York for Thanksgiving. He hadn't returned her call from a few days ago, and she'd been too swamped at work to call him again. She was giddy with excitement about the announcement, though. She'd call him tonight for certain.

"Glory. Honestly," Joy snorted, "you have a talent for shooting for the moon without any fuel or even the rocket. I'm not marrying Chuck to get ahead in my career."

"Yeah? Why, then?"

"Because he's sweet to me, uh, when we're finally alone. Not always easy. He's smart… and…and good to the employees and he's clearly devoted to his father. His attitude toward family is important to me, you know? His mother must have been wonderful."

Glory folded her arms over her chest, her faux Louis Vuitton purse banging against her side.

Joy frowned. She didn't like that probing, accusatory stare Glory was piercing her with. "And...they've planned an incredible Thanksgiving for us. We'll watch the parade at some friends' penthouse. Then dinner at Le Bernadin."

"Wow. Impressive," Glory groaned and rolled her eyes.

"Liar. You're not impressed."

"Neither should you be."

"What?"

"You already bought a turkey. We were going to have the whole gang over for dinner. Remember?"

"I'm sorry."

"Did you forget?"

"No. Not really. But when Mr. Newly... Dad, I mean, told us of his plans, what could I say?"

"Oh, no. I get that. Alexander Newly is the most overbearing person I've ever met."

Joy smiled. "And that's saying a lot... coming from you."

"Okay. Fine. I admit to being somewhat obtrusive on occasion, but it's for everybody's own good. I like being the mother hen."

"This, of course, is because you're older than I am."

"That's right."

"You're the best roommate in the world. And we still have Christmas."

"Look, I don't mind missing the holidays, if I thought you were happy."

"Don't start. I've told you. I'm happy! What's not to be happy about? I'm engaged to a handsome, up-and-coming guy who—"

Glory cut in. "Whose father appears to love you more than he does."

"That's not true," Joy countered as she fingered a sheaf of papers on her desk. Anytime the truth pinched the edges of her heart, she immediately rebuffed the feeling by moving on to something new. Immersing herself in yet another client's financial fiasco or potential bankruptcy was her forte. She liked saving her clients, bailing them out of hot water, taking meetings with the IRS and pulling their hands off panic buttons. She was good at her job. Very good.

Glory stared at her. "Not true, huh?" She jerked her head toward the open door.

Chuck, dressed impeccably in a new black wool suit, brilliant white shirt and gray-and-black designer tie, breezed into the office, his Bluetooth activated as he spoke with a client. Going up to Joy, he kissed her cheek and smiled, not missing a beat of his conversation.

"Fine. Later," he said and clicked off. "Joy, you gotta learn to take my calls—especially after hours."

She frowned. "Not when I'm working on Nathan Withers's account for you. And not when the only thing you have to talk about is the client."

"Ouch." He grinned, glancing at Glory. "My bad. But you know how I get around the holidays. Forgive me?"

He kissed her lightly on the mouth.

Joy barely had time to pucker her lips before he whirled around, took an incoming call on the Bluetooth and was gone.

Glory glared at her. "I didn't say a word."

Joy opened her mouth to protest and closed it. She didn't like how much truth was in what Glory said. Too many times Joy had wondered why there weren't romantic moments between her and Chuck. He was always like this at the end of the year. Of course, that didn't explain the lack of romance during the summer. There hadn't been a weekend where they took the Staten Island Ferry and just "escaped" the city. No trips to an island beach or even the Jersey beach. Even dinner date conversations revolved around their clients.

Still, she and Chuck had planned a future together. Solid. Secure. Clearly devoted to family as she was to her grandfather. And one day, they'd get around to romance. Wouldn't they?

Glory's smile was too smug. "That guy makes my case for me."

"Forget it. I'm marrying Chuck and that's it. I've got work to do. So do you," Joy finally said.

"I do," Glory replied. "Want a coffee? I need a pot of caffeine myself."

"Is that because you didn't get in till after one last night?"

Joy's cell rang. She looked at the caller ID. "Gish. Another Indiana scammer."

Glory cranked her head around. "How many of those have you gotten in the last few days? Maybe it's not a scammer."

"Right." Joy accepted the call. "This is Joy."

"Joy, thank heavens I got you!"

"Mrs. Beabots? Is that you?"

"You recognize my voice?"

"Yours I would never forget. So, what's up?"

"Oh, Joy, dear. I have the most awful news."

Joy felt her scalp crawl, and her knees weakened. She placed one hand on the desk and lowered herself into her chair. "It's Grandpa."

Glory stiffened, her eyes instantly alert. Quickly, she crossed to Joy. She put her hands on Joy's shoulders.

Joy felt her support and covered one of Glory's hands with her own.

"I'm afraid so."

"Is he sick?"

"He passed away. Last night, dear. Massive heart attack."

"But…" Joy tried to make sense of what she was hearing. Frank could not be dead. He was her touchstone. "He was fine last year at Thanksgiving. I mean, I know he took a couple naps. And when I last talked to him, he said he had to cut the call short because his poinsettia supplier was on the other line." Joy's eyes were full of tears, but she didn't feel them. Her face had turned cold. Her hands shook.

"Frank's attorney tried to call you last night. He said he left a message…"

"My phone was off. Then this morning, my fia—my boss called right when I woke up. He's relentless and he talked to me on the entire subway ride and up until I walked into my office."

"I understand, dear. Now, you have to come

back here immediately and tend to the funeral details. The attorney wants to go over the will with you. His name is Kyle Evans. I'll text you his number. Joy, I'll do all I can to help you with anything you need."

"That's sweet of you. Thank you."

"We all loved Frank, dear. This is a shock to all your friends back home. Call me when you arrive."

"I will." Joy hung up.

Friends? What friends did she have in Indian Lake? None that she knew. There was only her grandpa, and now he was gone and she was alone. She put her phone down and dropped her head into her hands. "I feel sick."

Glory rubbed Joy's shoulders. "I'm so, so sorry, Joy. What can I do?" Glory asked.

"Nothing. There's nothing anyone can do. My grandpa is gone. My only family. I...I have no one."

"Not true. You have me. And—and Chuck..." Glory's voice trailed off.

Joy looked down at the incoming text from Mrs. Beabots with Kyle's phone number. "I have to go back to Indian Lake. ASAP."

"Sure you do, sweetie. But..." Glory glanced out the door.

"What?"

"That'll make your new father-in-law-to-be not so overjoyed."

"The firm can live without me. Chuck is very capable. Even though he puts a lot on my shoulders, he'll be fine," Joy replied firmly. "Grandpa was all I had. Plus, I need to take care of the funeral arrangements."

"How long will all this take?"

"A week, tops. Besides, I have over a month of accrued vacation. Honestly, I can video chat with our clients, and with text and email, no one will know I'm gone."

"Tell me what I can do," Glory said.

"Would you mind going to the apartment and packing a bag for me? Casual stuff. And a dress for the funeral? I'll book my flight now."

"Done." Glory rushed to the door and stopped. "Joy. You know I love you, girl."

"Love you, too. And thanks."

As Glory whisked out the door, Joy dialed the attorney's number.

The call was picked up on the second ring. "Evans and Evans Law. How may I help you?"

"Hello. This is Joy Boston. I need to speak with Kyle Evans. I just received his message that…my grandfather, Frank Boston…" Joy's voice was chopped off by the biting burn of sorrow in her throat. Tears streamed down her cheeks as she dropped her forehead to her palm. "...died..."

CHAPTER TWO

THE AUDITORIUM SEATS at Saint Mark's Elementary School were filled to capacity with parents, grandparents and students who applauded as the final curtain fell on the traditional Thanksgiving pageant. Adam Masterson bolted to his feet and proudly yelled "Bravo!" as his son, Titus, took another bow.

Adam felt his heart swell and his sight blur watching Titus's smile radiate across the expanse. Titus. The light of his life, the motivation that forced him to get out of bed in the morning despite the shroud of grief he wore since his wife, Amie, had died three years ago. "Well done!" Adam shouted, smiling at Titus, who stood next to Timmy Bosworth, dressed in a Pilgrim costume.

Timmy took Titus's hand in his and raised it over their heads. "Thank you and happy Thanksgiving!" Timmy announced to the crowd.

The audience erupted in more applause as the curtain fell for the last time.

"Adam," Sarah Bosworth said, as she hoisted three-year-old Charlotte into her arms, "Titus was wonderful. He recited his lines like a professional actor. I felt like I was right there on Plymouth Plantation with those kids."

Adam couldn't help the rush of pride that shot straight up his spine. "He was good, wasn't he?"

"He was. Timmy told me that he and Titus only practiced three times."

"I'll let you in on a secret," Adam said, bending closer, his hair falling over his forehead. "I think Titus has an eidetic memory. The first time I took him through his lines, he'd memorized everything."

"No kidding?" Sarah's eyes widened. "Wish I had that ability."

Adam glanced toward the stage and saw some of the kids running down the aisle. "He's been reading since he was three. I guess I shouldn't be surprised at anything he does."

"Trust me," Sarah said. "Gifted children aren't easy. I know. Both Timmy and Annie are exceptional, and just last week, I caught Charlotte here sitting at the piano playing with Annie."

Adam chucked Charlotte under the chin. "A prodigy, huh?"

Charlotte tossed her blond curls and laid

her head on Sarah's shoulder. "I like piano." Charlotte smiled up at Adam.

"Dad! Dad!" Titus shouted exuberantly, as he worked his way through the throng of parents leaving their seats. Titus's rented Pilgrim costume was faded but fit well. He did struggle with the black hat, which tended to interfere with his ever-present sport band that held his thick glasses in place. Titus's mom had been myopic, too. But unlike Amie, Titus tended to be quite clumsy, always impatient to race to the next room, the next day and the next adventure.

"Dad! Did you see me?" Titus hurried up to Adam and flung his arms around his waist.

Adam smoothed Titus's thick black hair away from his forehead and looked down into his eager crystal-blue eyes. His son looked exactly like Adam had when he was "nearly six"—minus the glasses. "I did! And you were the best. You did great."

"Thanks, Dad." Titus hugged him again.

Timmy Bosworth rushed up to Sarah, along with his eleven-year-old sister, Annie.

"Mom," Annie said. "Can I take Charlotte backstage to see Mrs. Cook?"

Sarah narrowed her eyes. "Why does Mrs. Cook want to see your baby sister?"

Annie glanced sheepishly at Titus, who had

a conspiratorial expression. "Um. I told her Charlotte could play piano."

Charlotte squirmed out of Sarah's arms. "I can play!"

Annie reached for Charlotte's hand. "Mom?"

"Oh, fine. Go." Sarah acquiesced.

Adam watched as Annie and Charlotte bounded up the stage steps. Titus said, "Charlotte should think about her future career. Like me."

Adam jerked his head back. This was news to him. "And that would be...what?"

Titus looked at Timmy, who elbowed him for encouragement. Timmy and Titus were close, now that Titus was in kindergarten. Timmy had taken Titus under his wing, and when Adam had been immersed in a geothermal energy construction project, or if he'd had to drive to Chicago to meet with a prospective client, Sarah generously watched Titus at her house. Adam didn't know how Sarah juggled three children, a creatively demanding career as a busy commercial design consultant, the summer fund-raising festival for Saint Mark's and volunteer work for the new Indian Lake Community Center.

Too often, Adam was caught spending late-night hours at his computer rather than doing the laundry, making costumes for Titus or thinking about things like Thanksgiving and Christmas holidays. The only thing that broke his focus on work was caring for Titus. His son was his joy.

"I've had a revelation, Dad," Titus said seriously.

Adam crossed his arms over his chest and glanced at Sarah, who smiled at Titus. "Go on."

"I liked working on this pageant and I think I want to go into the theater business."

Adam coughed and held his fist to his mouth. This was not what he'd thought his brilliant son would say. He'd imagined that Titus would want to follow in his footsteps. Become an engineer or a physicist. Titus was smart and quick and liked working alongside him on his local projects. Just last week Titus had gone with him to Frank Boston's greenhouse, where Adam had been installing a new geothermal heating unit.

"Theater? You mean you want to be an actor?"

"No, Dad. Timmy's gonna be an actor. I want to write plays. Like I did for Mrs. Cook."

Adam's eyes snapped to Sarah, who shook her head. "What did you write, son?"

"My speech. I did the research, which was interesting. And enlightening."

Adam mouthed "enlightening." He was continually surprised at Titus's vocabulary. He'd bought Titus a dictionary and thesaurus six months ago. He wondered if Titus had read them both cover to cover. "Well, we'll have to talk about it."

Titus's smile vanished. "You always say that and we never do."

Sarah's eyebrow arched. She put her hand on Timmy's shoulder. "Let's go find your sisters."

"Sure, Mom."

She gave Adam a quick hug. "I'm guessing I'll see you at Frank's funeral?"

Adam had known Sarah and her group of friends since high school. Adam had been the nerdy guy in high school, wading through CAD programs, tinkering with machines and engines.

Adam had never known his parents, who gave him up for adoption to a church-affiliated foster home only weeks after his birth. They'd left him in a car seat at Pastor Flutie's front door with a note giving his birth date and name, which Adam always believed was fictitious. Years ago, Adam had tried to track down information about his birth parents, but the time and money he'd spent were wasted.

Pastor Flutie and his wife, Martha, were

good people and raised him, along with over thirty other children who didn't have parents and had come their way.

Though they'd clothed and fed him, given him attention, Adam had always kept to himself. He didn't voice opinions often, and when he did, he made certain he had all his facts.

Adam had always wanted a family. He'd envied the close-knit Barzonni family and Sarah's loving mother, Ann-Marie, and he'd been there for Sarah when both her parents died.

Sarah had been a good friend to him ever since he'd come back to town, after Amie died of leukemia. Sarah and Luke had included Titus, and their friendship meant a great deal to him. But he was also careful not to ask too much of them.

Sarah touched Adam's sleeve. "Look, I know how close you were to Frank…"

Adam felt the emotion in his throat grow hot. He choked it back. "He was like my own grandfather."

"I know. He loved you, Adam. You did so much for him these past years."

"I should have done more."

"Come on. You were with him when he died. If you hadn't been there… Calling the ambulance. Staying with him at the hospital until…" Sarah's eyes filled with tears. "It's so hard."

Sarah had been through a great deal of grief herself. He touched her hand. It was ice-cold. "I'm sorry, Sarah. All this must remind you of your parents. They were good people."

"The best. They liked you a lot, Adam."

"You don't have to say that. I was such a… dork."

"Stop. Okay?" She looked down at Titus, who watched them both with serious, probing eyes. "I gotta go. Let me know about the funeral. I'm guessing the family will take care of everything."

Adam shoved his hands in his jeans' pockets. "That would be Joy."

"Oh…my…gosh. Adam. I forgot. I'm sorry. Mrs. Beabots called her and broke the news. Have you talked to Joy?"

"Not since she left for college." Ten years ago, Joy had been his girlfriend. Adam had given her a promise ring the day before they'd started their senior year in high school. That same day he'd received a letter from Purdue University that he'd won a full-ride scholarship for engineering. Adam had believed that he and Joy would spend the rest of their lives together. She'd promised to love him.

For a foster kid with no love in his life, Joy had been all he'd ever wanted. He was the one who dreamed of a cottage by Indian Lake with a rose-covered fence. He'd envisioned kids and a dog and a life of happiness.

All that year after school, Adam had gone to the Boston greenhouses to work until supper alongside Joy and her Frank. Frank had been the kind of grandfather Adam thought came along only in fairy tales. He gave Adam a few extra dollars to take Joy to a movie or out for a pizza. He loaned Adam his truck to drive them all out to the beach in the summer. Frank had been father, grandfather, mentor and adviser. Where Pastor Flutie had lacked in practical and business guidance, Frank filled in the blanks.

"He was family to me," Adam whispered, trying desperately not to show the emotion he felt so sharply.

Sarah leaned closer. "I didn't mean to open that wound."

"It's okay. Joy left. She wanted Columbia, her accounting degree and life in New York." He shrugged his shoulders. "And she got it."

"She did." Sarah paused. "When I talked to Mrs. Beabots this morning, she said Joy's coming back here to arrange the funeral."

"Of course. Mrs. Beabots talked to Joy…"

"I know, right? Mrs. Beabots keeps up with the whereabouts of all of us. I suppose Frank had told her where Joy worked."

"Newly and Associates," Adam said.

"Yeah." Sarah eyed him, but continued. "She's flying out of New York today."

"Today," he repeated. His heart shook. Joy, who had told him she didn't want the same things out of life that he did. She wanted to leave Indian Lake and never come back. She wanted a life in New York with hustle and noise and excitement.

She didn't want him.

She'd given him back his promise ring and told him she was going to Columbia University. She never answered a phone call or an email after she moved.

By the end of Adam's freshman year, Frank told him that Joy had made it clear that Frank could visit her in New York, where she'd arranged for internships in the summers, but she never wanted to see Indian Lake, her parents' graves or any of the people of the town, whom she blamed for the car accident that killed them both.

The cut that had hurt Adam the most was the fact that Joy never gave him the chance to comfort her. She never turned to him. The pain of those days was still with him.

Adam had met physicist Amie his senior year at Purdue. She was pretty and bright and they shared common interests. She'd got pregnant on their honeymoon in Chicago. They'd had little money back then, which had bothered Adam. In two years, his midnight "tinkerings" had resulted in patents for his geothermal plans and then sales of the units themselves. Two years after Titus was born, Amie was diagnosed with leukemia. The progression was fast.

"It worked out in the end. I have Titus."

"We all adored Amie. And Titus is a true blessing. I love every minute he's around." She looked at Titus. "I really have, honey."

"Thanks, Miss Sarah," Titus said, slipping his hand into Adam's.

"Speaking of which," Sarah went on. "Why not let Titus come home with Timmy and the girls and me? Miss Milse is making pies for Thanksgiving. The kids can play video games while you get your errands done."

"Are you sure? I mean, I don't want to impose."

"Dad." Titus yanked on his hand. "Please? Can I go?"

Adam had to smile. "It's not much fun hauling cement and nails around, is it, Titus?"

"Not really and the building supply place is so dreary."

"Dreary." Adam grinned. Another new word. He wondered if he shouldn't buy a second thesaurus for himself, to keep up with his brilliant son. No wonder the kid wanted to write plays.

"So? Can I?"

"Sure." He ruffled Titus's hair and dislodged the Pilgrim hat. Titus righted it, smiling at his dad. "Thanks for this, Sarah. I really have a lot to do at the greenhouses. For Frank."

"I know." She held out her hand to Titus. "C'mon, honey."

"Titus," Adam said. "Get your coat and zip it up this time. Don't forget your knit cap. It's getting cold outside."

"Dad. I know." Titus pouted.

"And you mind Miss Milse. Don't poke your finger in the pies, and stay away from her Cuisinart."

"I know, Dad. Sharp knives. Mixers. All off-limits."

Sarah laughed. "He'll be okay."

"I know. I know. It's just…"

"Hard to be mom *and* dad?" she asked.

"Something like that."

"Okay. Let's go find the girls." She started to walk away. She looked over her shoulder. "Just text me when you're on your way to pick him up."

"I will. Thanks again."

"No worries." Titus and Timmy raced ahead of her, both boys yelling for Annie and Charlotte.

Adam chuckled to himself, leaned down and grabbed his sheepskin jacket and slipped it on. Most of the parents and children had left by the front doors to the auditorium. Adam found a couple folded playbills that Mrs. Cook had printed up. He'd come in late, a bad workaholic habit, so he hadn't grabbed a playbill earlier.

As he started up the aisle, he noticed Titus's name in bold print. Above his name was that of Mrs. Mary-Catherine Cook.

Above that was the title: PLAYWRIGHT.

Adam halted. "Titus's teacher gave him writing credit for his little speech." He was both awed and humbled.

His son was growing up far too quickly. And he wasn't ready for it.

He put the playbill in his inner jacket breast pocket and walked out into the November cold.

He wasn't ready for a lot of things. Titus growing up. Frank dying. And he especially wasn't ready to see Joy again.

CHAPTER THREE

JOY HAD JUST deplaned at O'Hare Airport when her cell phone rang. "Hello, darling."

"Darling? Who's that?"

"That would be you, Chuck. Us being engaged and all, I was thinking we should have endearments for each other."

"I don't like it."

"How about 'baby'?"

"Nope."

"Sweetie? Cutie? Chuckie?" she joked.

"Don't go there. Look, Joy. Seriously, talk to me. The Taylor account…"

She shouldered her way into the throng of people moving toward baggage claim. "The Taylor account is on your desk. I sent an email to Lessings Acoustics, too. They'll contact you directly. Until I get back."

"When will that be?"

"I don't know, but not long."

"This is putting a lot on me, you know," he groused.

Joy rolled her eyes. Looking up, she saw

huge Christmas wreaths above the concourse. An enormous Christmas tree with thousands of lights rivaled the Rockefeller tree. Surrounding the bottom of the tree was a sea of lush, tropical poinsettias.

Joy pulled to a stop, her roller bag banging the backs of her legs. She felt the jagged edge of sorrow in her heart as hundreds of loving moments with her grandfather flashed across her mind's eye. Her head dipped, and she let her tears drop to the terrazzo floor. She pulled out a tissue and blew her nose, remembering that Chuck was still on the phone.

"Joy? Joy? What's going on?"

"Sorry. Big crowds." She glanced up at the signs directing her to baggage claim. It would have been easy to fall apart, but she needed, no—had to stay strong now. She couldn't lean on Chuck.

"So, how long till you get to Indian Lake?"

"An hour and a half. I hired an Uber."

"Call me from the car. I have half a dozen more accounts to go over with you."

"Sure."

Chuck hung up without another word. Joy got on the down escalator. She held the phone up to see that the call had ended.

"I love you, too, Chuck."

Joy shoved the phone in her purse and saw

the Uber driver at the bottom of the escalator, holding a sign with her name on it.

She walked up to him. "Hi! I'm Joy Boston."

The middle-aged man nodded. "I'm Roy. Happy to see you. I'll take your bags for you. Do you have more luggage to claim?"

"No, this is it. I won't be staying long."

"Oh, that's a pity," Roy said, as he politely ushered her toward the outer door.

"Why's that?"

"Indian Lake is so lovely at the holidays. So many decorations and activities. The Christmas Concert. The symphony. The children's Christmas pageant. The caroling parties. The Candlelight Tour…"

They walked outside to the cold. "They still have all that?"

"Of course. I take my grandson to the Christmas parade every year, and then we mail his letter to Santa at the Elf Mail Station." They walked to Roy's black SUV, and he put her bags in the back as she got in the back seat.

As much as Joy had struggled to make a new life for herself in New York, with new friends and new holiday traditions, the old days and the old ways of celebrating flooded her.

Just thinking about Indian Lake released anger she hadn't felt in years. Anger toward the townspeople for their apathy—laziness that directly caused her parents' car accident. She hadn't been able to forgive them then or now. The pain of her long-ago scars resonated in her. She would go to town, do her duty, find a buyer for the greenhouse and leave as quickly as possible.

She forced her mind to redirect to happier times.

She remembered her mother and father working alongside her, tending the poinsettias. The week before Thanksgiving, enormous delivery trucks would roll into the parking lot and they'd unload red, pink and white beauties. Just thinking about those gorgeous tropical flowers caused Joy to wish for faraway adventures, sandy beaches and palm trees, places she'd planned to explore with...

"Adam."

She sat up straight.

Adam hadn't crossed her mind once since she'd got the news of her grandfather's death. But there he was. She remembered his wide shoulders, his thick raven hair and how he'd forget to cut it, so it would hang down, nearly covering half his face as he worked furiously on yet another machine that never reached "functionality."

She'd known Adam was smart and was

convinced he hadn't yet found his groove. She'd urged him on, believing his genius would pay off one day. The time when he'd lost the state science fair championship, he'd been despondent and distant, but Joy had kissed away his tears and forced him to envision a golden future filled with success. He said he believed her.

They'd had a romantic senior year together, stealing kisses in the greenhouses. Learning how to cross-pollinate and hybridize poinsettias from her grandfather. Going to summer concerts in the park and dancing at the beach under the stars—with Adam humming a song to her. He'd given her a gold promise ring and told her he wished he was rich enough for a diamond. At the time, she hadn't cared.

I loved him.

Those days with Adam had been the most romantic of her life. Idyllic days—until her parents died.

She looked out the window at the nude maple trees along the interstate. The ground was barren of flowers; the grass was frozen. The sky was the same depressing slate-gray, promising snow flurries or rain.

She felt gray inside without her grandfather, just as she had after her parents' deaths. Grief's fingerprint was a deep one. She wondered if she'd ever feel sunny again.

She looked down at her gloved hands and remembered a winter day once when she'd forgotten her gloves and Adam had walked her to the greenhouses after school. He'd taken both her hands in his, rubbed them until they were pink and warm again, and then he'd given her his too-big gloves to wear. He'd pulled her close as the wind whipped around them.

"I'll always keep you warm," he'd said.

"Ditto," she'd replied.

"In fact, I'd like to be the one who discovers cheap energy to keep all the world warm. No one should go cold," he'd said.

"That's what you want to do? Save the world from freezing?"

"It's a tall order, but it's what I want to do," he'd said and kissed the end of her very cold nose.

"Now, that was very warming," Joy had replied.

She certainly couldn't remember anything memorably romantic that Chuck had done with her since they'd met.

There was never a lack of wine or exotic food, but their dates wound up being work dates.

He'd proposed at the sushi bar they frequented, though she didn't like much on the menu except the California rolls. He'd asked her to be his wife, and just as she'd said "yes" his cell phone rang. He'd looked down at it, but didn't take the call. She'd thought it was a good sign. But after he kissed her and they toasted with sake, which she also didn't like, he excused himself to take the call.

Joy knew that Chuck felt enormous pressure to perform to his father's high expectations. Chuck had a good heart and he was eager to please both her and his father. He was mindful of their long hours and would surprise her with a latte and buttered bagel from the deli down the street. When she complained her back hurt after long hours at the computer, he introduced her to a killer pain-relieving essential oil as he rubbed her neck. Chuck had seen Joy's performance potential on her first interview and hired her on the spot. She gave him credit for that. Because he was her boss, she ignored his excuses to work overtime with her over the years. She pretended not to notice him lingering in her office after client conferences. Chuck had actually gone to his father and discussed his growing attraction to her before asking his permission to pursue a romance. For Joy, their relationship had evolved slowly over the next few years. No fireworks. No adrenaline rush. They were solid and secure. She liked that.

She had to admit, though, that dinner with Chuck was polar opposite from the mac and cheese she used to make for Adam and Grandpa, which they'd share after a ten-hour Saturday working retail at Christmas in the greenhouses.

Joy had been so lost in thought that she'd forgotten that she'd turned off the ringer on her cell phone. She turned it back on and saw that Chuck had left three voice messages and five texts. She answered the texts and replied she would call him when she wasn't with Roy, as some of their conversations were best kept confidential for the clients' sake.

They had driven into town and stopped at the light with beautiful Indian Lake dead ahead. Joy leaned forward.

"Oh, Grandpa."

"Pardon?" Roy asked.

"Sorry. Nothing. It's just that I've forgotten how pretty this place is. I grew up here."

"So, you have family here?"

"Not anymore."

"Sorry."

Roy drove into town, past the red sandstone county courthouse with its one-hundred-and-forty-year-old clock tower and onto Maple Boulevard. They passed houses she remembered, belonging to Sarah Jensen and Mrs. Beabots. Saint Mark's Church. The Indian Lake Police Station. Specters of past, happy days flew around Joy, pulling her back to Indian Lake like magnets. And with each memory, she missed her mother, her father and especially her grandfather all the more.

That was why when Roy drove up to the three glass greenhouses, which her grandfather had built right after World War II, her vision had been blurred by her tears. She couldn't possibly be seeing correctly.

"What is this?" she asked Roy, like a stupefied tourist.

"Boston Greenhouses." He waved his hand across the expanse of the windshield. "This is it."

"No." She shook her head and opened the door, wiping her eyes. The greenhouses were empty. Totally devoid of even one poinsettia. Panes were filthy, cracked or missing from the glass ceilings and walls. The farthest greenhouse was in the worst condition. Its once perfectly maintained and cleaned brick-and-tile floor now sprouted weeds, frozen back from the cold November weather. Joy walked liked a zombie toward the greenhouse. Her father and grandfather had taught her how to clean the tiles with the sprayer. She'd swept the water away to expose the pretty sand-colored tiles. She'd taken a great deal of pride in the glistening glass walls and ceiling. She and her grandfather had pressure washed those panes every month. Their patrons commented on how good the plants had it when they came to live at Boston Greenhouses.

Joy felt her insides twist. Not only was her grandfather dead, but he'd lied to her. He'd told her he couldn't come to New York to be with her because he was too busy. It was going to be his best year ever, he'd said.

She turned to Roy. "How long have the greenhouses been closed, Roy?"

"I'm not sure. A few years."

A few years... Joy's shock turned to a sense of betrayal.

"Grandpa lied to me. And now he's gone."

CHAPTER FOUR

JOY LOOKED BACK at the weeds growing through the tiles.

"Years. Not just this Christmas, but many holiday seasons it's been closed."

She went to the front door, peered through the windows and tried the latch. It was unlocked.

"What?" Why would the door be unlocked? Had the attorney unlocked it? Perhaps when she met Kyle Evans, she'd gain more insight.

She pushed the door and stepped in. She wasn't prepared for the shock.

As if she'd been swallowed by a time warp, she was eighteen again, rushing in on a Saturday morning to see her grandfather already at the cash register, his big Chicago Cubs coffee mug filled with steaming coffee as he counted the money. She remembered her mother, dressed in jeans, a floral blouse and a rubber apron while she watered the flowers and sang to them. Her father whistled while he carried in heavy sacks of humus and fertilizer to sell. She'd forgotten how much she missed his whistling.

As the door swung closed behind her, a numbing chill enveloped her. The sight of empty shelves, dusty counters and cobwebs around the ceiling where garlands and Christmas ornaments once hung was heartbreaking. The walk-in flower cooler was dark and smelled like mold. The carpet needed shampooing. Worst of all, there were no poinsettias, no life, no energy.

"No Grandpa. No Mom or Dad."

Joy walked to the checkout counter, where she used to wrap gold and silver foil around the flowerpots and swathe the flowers with colorful print paper to protect the delicate poinsettias. She and her mom would work the counter together. She could almost smell Mom's rose soap.

Unwinding her scarf, she walked behind the counter and was surprised to see full boxes of ribbons, foil and cellophane, and bolts of wrapping paper sitting in the same spots as they had a decade ago. "Not everything was sold or discarded."

She looked toward the back of the retail gift area. Two French doors led to a smaller greenhouse where specialty orchids, amaryllis and hybrid poinsettias used to be displayed on long wooden tables. That was Joy's favorite area, where her grandfather would test his yearlong projects of coral-and-white-striped poinsettias, yellows, ambers, and try as he might, the absolute impossible task of creating a blue poinsettia. Blue poinsettias didn't exist naturally, and he would dye white ones to please designers in Chicago, but he was a dreamer. He'd often told her he wanted to create a flower that was not only beautiful but timeless. Something the world would never have seen if it hadn't been for him.

Behind the special greenhouse were the storage rooms, where the new shipments of gift items, table linens, Christmas stockings, birdbaths and feeders, scented candles and bath oils and washes used to be delivered and stored until they were put out for display.

"I wonder if any stock is left…" Joy started toward the storage room when she heard a door slam. She halted. "What was that?" She peered through the French doors. Was someone breaking into the greenhouse?

"Hello? Is someone there?"

Peering through the windows, she saw a tall man, wearing a buckskin-yellow suede jacket with a sheepskin collar and lining, jeans, a scarf around his neck and a tan cowboy hat that was pulled down low so that she couldn't see his face. He was carrying a large sack of something on his shoulder as he pushed one door open with his booted foot.

His presence filled the room as if he owned the place and she was the one intruding.

He placed the sack on the cement floor of the greenhouse, then slapped his hands together, creating a cloud of white dust. He pushed the tip of his cowboy hat up and leveled on her the bluest eyes she'd ever seen.

Familiar eyes.

Eyes that probed her in a way that went straight to her heart.

"Adam?" She almost choked out his name, being both stunned and oddly pleased to see him.

"Hey."

He continued to stare at her, assessing her as if she were one of his cogs in a machine he was creating.

"Hi," she returned.

Unsmiling, he said, "I heard you might come back."

"Yes. Of—of course. Why wouldn't I?"

"Been a long time."

Joy didn't like the accusatory tone Adam used. Nor did she like the fact that he'd matured into a handsome man with flashing, mesmerizing eyes. And how was that possible? They were "over" a long time ago.

"He was my grandpa."

"And you came back because he died."

"Excuse me?"

"Sorry. I mean I'm sorry about Frank. He loved you a lot."

"And you know this…how?"

"He never stopped talking about you."

Joy felt a pang of guilt for not being there more for her grandfather. But she didn't like Adam's tone. She glanced through the French door, propped open by the sack of cement he'd deposited. She saw a compressor, metal pipes, PVC pipes, vent apparatus and coils of copper tubing. A toolbox with wrenches, hammers and screwdrivers sat next to the pile of materials.

"Just exactly how did you get in here?"

"Key."

Joy had to consciously halt her eyes from flying wide open. "You? Have access to my grandfather's place of business?"

"Clearly—" he waved his hand across the empty retail area "—it's not a business anymore."

"I was told Frank closed it years ago."

"He did. Five years, to be exact."

Joy put her fingertips to her temples. None

of this made sense. "I don't understand. I flew him to New York for Thanksgiving every year. He told me he had to hurry back here to get the poinsettia shipments in. He said business had never been better."

"He lied."

"I got that, Adam!"

"Don't jump on me!" he shot back, all too quickly and with twice the force.

"Why didn't he tell me the truth?"

"He didn't want to disappoint you," Adam replied, dropping his harsh tone.

Her eyes were tearing again, but she didn't care. "He told you that?"

"He did."

"But nothing he would do could ever, ever disappoint me. I loved him. That's all. The attorney told me on the phone that Grandpa was too proud to ask for my help."

"That, too." Adam glanced down as he asked, "Would you have come back if he asked?"

"I don't know. No. Maybe…if he'd told me how bad it was."

Adam shook his head. "Well, we'll never know."

Adam took off his hat, and as he did, his thick black hair fell over his forehead.

Joy nearly gasped as the movement reminded her of when they'd been in love.

"I know that Frank didn't want to destroy your memories of this place. How it was."

"It was glorious, wasn't it?" Joy felt her first smile creep slowly to her lips as she remembered so much.

"It was," he replied wistfully, still staring at her.

"From the time I was nine or ten, it was my job to keep those tiles clean. I took pride in scrubbing them—"

"Until they glistened," he interrupted. "I remember."

"Adam."

"I remember a lot of things."

She paused, fearing what she wanted to ask, but daring to say it. "Like us?"

"Yeah, like us."

"We were kids."

"I thought we were pretty adult. Planning a life together."

"Well, we're different people now."

"We certainly are," he replied with that dark tone he'd used before.

"You're angry with me. About the past…"

He took a long step toward her. "Not the past, Joy. The present. I was the one who was with Frank when he had the heart attack. I called 911. I was in the hospital with him. I held his hand when he passed."

"Oh, God. I'm so sorry."

"His last thoughts were about you."

"Thank you for being with him." A new wave of guilt and grief hit her.

"I should go." He started to go, then turned back to her.

Joy braced as she felt a wave of heat from him.

"I know Frank lied to you about some things, but it seems to me you could have pried yourself away from your city friends long enough to visit your only living relative. All these years and you never came back. I watched Frank spend Christmas after Christmas alone. He talked about you and the old days. How he loved you. And what did he get? A ten-minute phone call, Joy. A ten-minute phone call."

Adam slapped his hat against his thigh, turned and stomped toward the French doors.

Joy's natural defenses shot to the fore. "I have responsibilities!"

Adam pulled to a stop and marched back to her. His face was nearly nose to nose with hers. "Nothing was as important as Frank and you know it. I would have killed to have what you had with Frank. All that love. All that concern and caring. At least I got to enjoy that after college, when I came back here. Frank befriended me as if not a day had passed. He may have been your blood, but he was *my* family. And I miss him."

"Me, too," she whispered, as she lowered her eyes.

He moved back. "I'm sorry. It's just that I swore when I moved back here that I'd keep myself in check. Getting close to people never worked out for me."

"Like when I left—"

"Like then, yeah."

Joy blinked back tears. Everything Adam said was true, and she felt like dirt. She should have come to visit her grandfather, but she couldn't. It wasn't always college or her career. It was Indian Lake. The place where her loving parents were buried. She couldn't face it. She wouldn't be reminded of the way they died. And the aftermath.

"I'm sorry, Adam. For everything."

"Yeah. Well." He stepped back. "I guess I'll see you at the funeral."

"Yeah."

Deflated, Joy watched Adam walk away before backing up to the counter and slowly sliding to the floor.

Joy pulled her knees to her chin, shivered and looked at the empty space. "I'm sorry. I'm so very sorry, Grandpa. Please forgive me."

CHAPTER FIVE

JOY GREETED THE dark-haired, fortyish receptionist at Evans and Evans Law Firm office and asked if she could leave her luggage behind the front desk.

"Of course. I'll let Mr. Evans know you're here," she said and picked up the intercom. "Mr. Evans is down the hall, Miss Boston."

Joy wheeled her weekender around to the back wall. "Thank you."

Kyle Evans greeted Joy at the door to his office. She guessed him to be in his mid-thirties. He was tall, handsome and wore a well-tailored blue suit. He held out his hand. "Joy. I'm Kyle, and I'm so sorry for your loss." He ushered her into a bright, cheery office, decorated with Danish modern furniture and a wall-to-wall aquarium.

Joy was still mired in confusion. "Kyle, I just went by the greenhouses. I don't understand. Grandpa told me this was going to be a banner year for him."

Kyle held a chair for Joy as she sat. Then

he went around to his side of the desk. "That was a bit inaccurate."

"What's going on?"

"I worked with him when he closed up. I think, though he never said so outright, that he always hoped to reopen them. I told him it would take a miracle."

"And he never told me about any of this."

"Frank was a proud man. And he didn't want you to worry about his failure."

"Failure?"

"The business was too much for him to run alone. Costs were rising and he told me he would never ask you to come home to save him."

"No, he wouldn't," she replied. "I was firm on that issue when I moved to New York."

"He was so proud of you and your career. He talked about you all the time."

Kyle looked down at the papers on his desk. "He left everything to you. The house, the greenhouses, his old truck."

"He...still has that truck?"

"He did. Yes."

"And it runs?"

"Uh, yeah. It does." Kyle folded his hands and put them on the desk. "I'm so sorry, Joy. This all has to be such a shock for you. It was for me. For the whole town."

"Grandpa never told me he was ill," she said, feeling another bout of tears stinging her eyes.

"I understand from his doctor that Frank died soon after arriving at the hospital."

"That's what I heard." She remembered Adam's description of Frank's death. Joy couldn't help her tears now. They came like a torrent. She found a travel pack of tissues in her purse and whisked the tears from her face. "We never talked about what to do if he died. I guess I'm guilty of thinking he would live forever. He was…my grandpa." She wrapped her arms around her middle and leaned forward. "I'm sorry. So sorry. I…I can't help it. I have no idea what to do. All he ever said was that when he died, he would make sure I was taken care of. I thought it was a life insurance policy or something. I'd always cut him off. Talking about death reminded me too much of my mom and dad."

"I remember," Kyle said. "I'm sorry for your loss of them, as well."

She looked into his empathetic eyes and wondered if the caring she saw was genuine or if that was some mask law school professors taught students to wear when dealing with bereaved clients. The minute the thought entered her head, Joy realized it was something that Chuck had said once to her. She cast it away.

"It's fine. And the details are in his will."

"Oh."

"I talked to Father Michael over at Saint Mark's. He's waiting for your call."

"I should have a reception or something after the funeral. At his home." Joy blew her nose in the tissue. "Pardon me."

"Certainly. Olivia Barzonni over at the Indian Lake Deli has offered to cater a lunch for you. If you wish. She and her mother, Julia, are great people."

"Olivia Melton? She's married now, then. Yes, I remember her. She was a friend in high school." Joy brightened a bit.

"And Sarah Bosworth said to tell you if there's anything you need, she's here. Sarah Jensen Bosworth, that is. She—"

"Sarah is married, too?"

"She is. Three kids. I see Luke at the YMCA where we work out with Gabe and Nate Barzonni. Scott Abbott joins us often, as well."

Joy put her hands to her cheeks. "All these names. Talk about a blast from the past."

"Joy. All your friends are here for you. You just have to ask for their help."

She dabbed her tears again. "They are?"

When her parents died, Joy had cut ties with her Indian Lake friends. She'd wanted to run away from her grief. She'd chosen Columbia University and New York as her safe haven, and it had been that for her all this time.

"That's wonderful and so…unexpected. I haven't been back in a long time. Years and years."

"I know." Kyle picked up a manila folder. "This is your copy of the will. This is the key to the greenhouse. Frank's house keys. I assume you'll be staying there? Is there anything else you need from me?"

Joy took the keys. "When I went to the greenhouse, the door was unlocked. I understand Adam Masterson has a key."

"I don't know, but it wouldn't surprise me. He and Frank were close."

And Adam had said he tried not to get close to people. "Well, thank you so much, Kyle." She started to stand and stopped. "Would you be so kind as to get a number for me?"

"Sure. What do you need?"

"The best Realtor in town."

"That's easy. Cate Sullivan Davis."

Joy tilted her head to the left. "I don't remember that name."

"You wouldn't. She's only been here a few years."

"But you trust her? She's good?"

"Very. And her husband is a detective. Trent Davis. He's famous in these parts. Took down a huge drug ring. It was in all the papers."

"Grandpa told me about that. He's her husband?"

"Sure is. And she's really smart. You'll like her."

"Thanks," Joy said, rising to shake Kyle's hand.

Once she'd gathered her luggage, she stood on the sidewalk watching the passing cars.

"I forgot. I'm not in New York."

There were no cabs. No subways. No mass transit of any kind. Joy had sent Roy away thinking she wouldn't need him. Fortunately, he'd given her his direct number in case she needed him while in town.

"I'm so not in Kansas anymore." She punched in his number. "Roy. I need a favor."

"Sure. What is it?"

"I forgot there are no cabs in Indian Lake."

"And now you're stranded. I'm at Cupcakes and Cappuccino. About three blocks from you. Where do you want to go?"

"Is there a car rental in Indian Lake?"

"Of course. I'll take you there."

Joy hung up and sighed. She'd been away a long time. And she couldn't wait to leave.

CHAPTER SIX

ADAM HAD PICKED up Titus from Sarah's house and stopped for groceries. Tonight was grilled chicken tenders on angel hair pasta with pesto sauce and salad. The one thing Amie had insisted that Adam do for their son was to feed him a balanced diet and organic foods. She'd been a good cook and taught him how to prepare food. Adam found the process enjoyable. So did Titus, who liked to share in the kitchen action.

When Adam had gutted the kitchen last year, he'd equipped it with everything he would need to make meals for himself and his son. He'd been sure to include a small appliance "garage" that was under lock and key so that Titus couldn't get to any sharp knives, mandolins or the Cuisinart. Titus had been curious nearly from birth, so teaching him to be careful was important. And the fact that Titus's impaired vision caused him to trip or bump into things worried Adam.

Angel, their four-year-old golden retriever,

sat on the whitewashed wood plank floor watching her two masters cook. Angel was pregnant, a planned union with Sarah's golden, Beau. According to the veterinarian, Angel would have Christmas puppies. Titus was curious and anxious about the coming blessed event. Their trips to Grandy's Groomers to buy a new bed, puppy food and toys were numerous. Titus was overjoyed and so was Adam. He and Titus decided they would draw names from all the people who wanted a puppy, after Sarah and Luke had their pick of the litter, of course.

"So, Dad," Titus said as he dipped thin chicken tenders in a mix of flour, chili powder, granulated garlic and black pepper, "do you think we should ask Mr. Boston's granddaughter over for Thanksgiving dinner?"

Adam stopped pouring the olive oil into the frying pan. "How do you know anything about Joy Boston being in town?"

"Mrs. Beabots. She came over to Timmy's house and made oatmeal cookies for us."

"Oh, she did? And how many did you eat?" Adam asked, hoping to change the subject.

"Only one and a glass of milk. Organic, of course," Titus answered, finishing the last tender. He looked at Adam. "Miss Sarah said that you knew her in high school."

Adam grimaced. Deflecting the probing questions of a smart kid was not an easy task. Since the day Titus had learned to talk at nine months, the boy hadn't shut up. "Of course I knew Sarah. You know we've been friends forever."

"Dad," Titus huffed. "I meant Joy Boston."

"Oh." Adam placed the tenders in the oil. He lifted the lid of the boiling water, added salt and then reached over and stirred the pesto sauce.

"Miss Sarah said you were boyfriend and girlfriend."

Adam rolled his eyes. This was going from bad to worse. "And why would she say that?"

"Because I asked her a lot of questions about Joy Boston," Titus said proudly. "Like what kind of person she was and if she liked flowers as much as old Mr. Boston...and you."

Adam nearly burned his fingers as he turned the tenders. "And what did Sarah say?"

"That you guys worked together for Mr. Boston when you were in high school."

"We did."

"And you thought you were going to marry her."

Adam coughed. He put his fist to his mouth. "Sarah said a lot, huh?"

"Dad! Think about it. I coulda been her son!"

"Not exactly." Adam put the angel hair in the boiling water. "But things have a way of working out all for the best. What I want to know is why Sarah told you all this."

Titus hemmed a bit and glanced away.

Adam stopped stirring the pesto. "Titus…"

"She didn't exactly say all that."

"What?" Adam put his hand on his hip. "What's going on here?"

"You know how it is. I asked a few questions. Put some things together. Like you asking Joy to marry you."

"So, this is something you deduced all by yourself."

"Deduced? What does that mean?"

"Figured out." Adam turned another tender, knowing fully that Titus had used the word *deduced* over a month ago. His son was stalling. Adam had him on the run and the idea pleased him. But only a little.

"I did." Titus smiled sheepishly. "But I needed confirmation."

"Which I gave you."

"Yes." Titus lifted his chin proudly.

"You know, Titus, I don't think you should be a playwright."

"No?"

"Clearly, you have the makings of a lawyer."

"Hmm." Titus went to the sink, stepped onto his step stool so that he could reach the faucet and washed his hands. Then he rinsed the lettuce. "I have to think about that. But about Miss Joy—"

"Son," Adam began, taking a deep breath. "Joy is leaving soon. She's not going to be part of our lives. Okay?"

Titus wiped his hands on a paper towel. "Okay, Dad."

AFTER DINNER, ADAM helped Titus make pinecone turkeys, which he wanted to gift to all his friends. After gluing and glittering feathers to the pinecones, Adam watched as Titus nearly fell asleep at the kitchen table.

"C'mon, sport. Let's brush your teeth and wash up for bed."

Titus yawned. "Okay. But I want the *Star Wars* pj's tonight."

"I would never have guessed," Adam said as they walked down the hall, Angel at their heels. Adam went into the bedroom, with its slate-gray walls and white trim and *Star Wars*, *Star Trek* and *Avengers* posters covering every inch of the space. From the dresser, Adam pulled out the desired pair of pajamas as he heard Titus in the bathroom using his spin brush.

Adam sat on the edge of the bed and looked at the stainless-steel reading lamp and the overflowing bedside bookshelf. Titus had been only four when he joined a reading group at the library. The kids declared how many books they would read over summer vacation. Titus always set high goals, so when he announced he'd read one hundred books, Adam hadn't doubted him. Most kids' books were only twenty pages long, after all. But Titus sailed through the picture books meant for early readers. Titus liked to read chapter books. He didn't reach one hundred, but he did read over twenty chapter books. His kindergarten teacher told Adam that Titus had the reading comprehension of a sixth grader.

"Yeah. Sixth grade going on high school," he muttered to himself. "Mozart was six when he started composing. Young prodigies aren't unheard of."

"What's unheard of?" Titus asked, coming into the room, yanking his shirt over his head.

"Genius showing itself at a young age," Adam said proudly, holding out the pajama top. Titus pulled it on.

"Were you a genius?"

"Hardly. Some thought I was a failure. I couldn't make things work."

"You do now," Titus said as he put on the pajama bottoms and climbed into bed. "You just needed education."

"I did. How did you know?"

"Mrs. Cook tells us that all the time."

"Ah! Wise woman." Adam chuckled. "So, what do you want me to read tonight? *War and Peace*?" Titus screwed up his face. "Sorry. Just a joke."

"I'm too tired. Tomorrow. Okay?"

"Sure." Adam leaned down to kiss Titus on the forehead. Titus lifted his arms and hugged him.

"I love you, Dad."

"I love you, Titus. You sleep with the angels."

Angel jumped up on the bed. Titus hugged her neck. "I always sleep with my Angel." Titus smiled. "So, Dad, when Angel has her pups, can I help?"

"I'm hoping the vet will take care of that."

Titus propped himself up on his elbow. "You think we'll have warning?"

"I hope so. Usually, dogs try to make a nest and find a warm place."

"Like her doggy bed?"

"Not necessarily. She might like it in front of the fireplace on her rug."

"Yeah. I could see that," Titus agreed and lay back down. "It's gonna be a great Christmas present to have puppies."

"Remember what I told you. Puppies are a lot of work in the beginning. I have to get a pen ready for them in the basement."

"And buy more space heaters and blankets and collect newspapers for their pee."

Adam laughed. "We need to do all that."

"Okay," Titus said as he lowered his sleepy eyes. "I'll help."

"Night, son."

"Night, Dad."

Adam walked to the door, turned off the light, and the glow-in-the-dark planets and constellations on the ceiling shone.

He walked down the hall and past the living room of his 1920s refurbished bungalow. Five years ago, the house had been a steal. He'd put a lot of work and money into it, and the results were worth it. The living room was furnished in comfortable charcoal-gray twill sofas that faced each other on either side of the fireplace. A maple-and-stainless-steel coffee table was heaped with books and magazines, most of them Titus's. Under the large picture window was a long desk with two laptops, a desk chair and a small file cabinet. On top of the file cabinet were a half-dozen framed photos of Adam, Amie and baby Titus. A large TV hung over the fireplace. The dining room table was midcentury modern, made of bird's-eye maple, and the chairs were covered in a deep blue twill.

He walked out to the front porch to check the mail he'd forgotten earlier. He shuffled through the utility bills, then pulled out an envelope with a familiar return address. It was the company that bought his wind turbine invention. His smile was broad. "Thank goodness for royalty checks."

Back inside, he went to his computer and pulled up his email.

Adam worked freelance for Jacobson Corporation out of Indianapolis. The pay was satisfactory, but it was his private, solely-owned creative patents that he hoped would one day boost his income. The best part was that he only had bimonthly trips to Indianapolis, and his weekly meetings with think-tank managers and engineering interns were via Skype and phone conferences. Adam had made it clear that Titus was his priority. Adam was an asset to any firm and Jacobson knew it. Adam worked at night on the computer and held conferences in the early morning with his team.

Scanning the emails, he replied to his team and then saw the one he'd been waiting for. "Halstead."

Halstead Industries had finally replied to the proposal and project renderings he'd presented to them in California in October. Adam's engineering genius had flourished at Purdue. He'd made good money over the years, and his works-in-progress would bring even more. His future was financially stable. Titus's college fund was solid. Sometimes, it seemed as if his high school days had happened to someone else.

"In more ways than one…"

He didn't share his successes with others. He didn't like to brag, and creative ideas were easily stolen. Not until his patents were secure, the contracts signed and executed, would Adam talk even to Frank or Mrs. Beabots about his work.

It's better that way, he thought. Keeping distance was his operative.

He opened the email as he heard Angel walking down the hall—his sign that Titus was sound asleep. Next to his desk was a new red-and-black-plaid doggy bed, which she curled up on.

"Look at that, Angel. I finally sold my wind turbine. Wait till my patent comes through on the geothermal unit. Not to mention a few other propulsion irons I have in the fire." The latter ideas for antigravity drapes and futuristic propulsion had been pipe dreams decades ago, but now he was being taken seriously.

Angel yawned.

"You'll see. It'll be thrilling."

Angel closed her eyes.

"Okay. Not so thrilling for you. But for a guy who never had much, this is a victory. I should celebrate."

Angel didn't stir as Adam went to the kitchen and took out a bottle of beer from the Sub-Zero.

"Now, where did I put that opener?" He opened the utility drawer where he kept spatulas and spoons, then went back to the desk in the living room. He dug around a few drawers, moving papers and old birthday cards. "Where is it?"

In frustration, he started pulling papers out of the far-left drawer. In the bottom, he found an old photo album, one he hadn't seen since he'd moved back from Cincinnati. "Aw, jeez."

The first photo had been taken well over ten years ago in the greenhouse. It was Christmas. He and Joy were surrounded by red poinsettias. Joy's head was on his shoulder, his arm around her waist. What captured his attention was the look of love and contentment on both their faces.

So long ago.

He glanced at the album photos of Amie. They'd been happy and thrilled about Titus. But the truth was that, initially, Amie had kept her illness from Adam and he'd never quite forgiven her. His feelings for Amie were different from the love he'd once had for Joy. Back then, Joy had lived up to her name. She'd lit up the world for him. And when he'd kissed her, he'd felt as if he were connected to the moon, the stars, the entire universe.

He raked a hand through his hair. He'd been hard on her today. He realized now that she was mirroring all the confusion and pain he'd felt when Amie had finally told him the truth about her leukemia. He'd felt lost. And betrayed.

Adam loved Frank. The old man had been his friend and mentor. But there had been times when he'd counseled Frank to tell Joy the truth, and Frank wouldn't do it, because of his pride.

It was a wasteful thing. It kept people from doing the one thing they should do. Love.

Adam opened the middle drawer and put the old photo album on top of the sheaf of papers. As he withdrew his hand he felt the bottle opener.

He opened the bottle and tipped it toward the photo album. "You were such a nerd, Adam. With no guts."

He took a deep swig. "And no glory."

Angel lifted her head and gave a low snuffle.

"Oh, you think so, too, huh?"

She snuffled again.

"Great. Thanks for the vote of confidence."

He sat in the desk chair and stared at the photo. "But that was then. What do I do about now?"

He closed the album and eased the drawer shut.

CHAPTER SEVEN

JOY LOOKED UP at the old rooster-shaped clock that hung against the kitchen wallpaper that had been put up before her birth. Her father often joked that he'd hated the wallpaper when his mother had chosen it. Joy didn't think it was all that bad with its depictions of antique coffee grinders and coffee cups and saucers. It was homey. It was Grandpa's house, where her father had grown up. Because Frank had purchased a large section of land after the war, there was enough acreage for Bruce and Jill to build their own house on shortly after their wedding. As a child, Joy always felt she lived in both houses.

The light wood cabincts were just as old, and they needed to be replaced as much as the wallpaper and vinyl flooring. The Formica-topped kitchen table set should have been tossed years ago, but Joy knew that her grandfather put his money into the greenhouses. Not into personal comforts.

Her cell rang, breaking her thoughts. "Hi, Chuck."

"So, how goes it?"

"What part?" she asked, as she opened the cabinet over the old electric stove and pulled down a box of crackers. Then she went to the cupboard on the other side of the kitchen and opened it. It was as it had always been. Peanut butter. New jar of grape jelly. Sack of potato chips. And a brand-new bag of chocolate candies.

Some things never changed. Blessedly.

"All of it. I tried to call you earlier, but I guess you were busy."

"I have been. I spent the afternoon on the phone planning the funeral and the luncheon at the house here afterward. It's tomorrow, so that was fast work."

"All funerals are… At least my mother's was."

"I'm sorry, Chuck. All this probably brings back sad times for you, too."

"It does, but don't worry about me. What did the attorney say?" He sounded rushed. "You're going to sell the greenhouses and the house, right?"

Joy was about to respond when she heard his office phone ringing. "You're still at the office?"

"Yeah. Dad and I are working late. Listen, I gotta take this. I'll call you tomorrow. Can't wait till you get back and we can have Thanksgiving together. Love ya."

Thinking back to this afternoon and the heat of Adam's anger, she realized she might be doing Chuck an injustice. Sure, he wasn't all that romantic, but he was *there* for her. He'd called to check on her. He would call tomorrow after the funeral. She could count on him.

She picked up the peanut butter jar and noticed it was organic, low sugar. She found a knife and sat at the table to eat crackers and peanut butter. It wasn't cracked crab or medallions of beef like she'd have with Chuck. The clock ticked loudly. She got up and went to the thirty-year-old side-by-side harvest-gold refrigerator and found a carton of milk.

"Organic."

She glanced at the table, at the chair where her grandfather always sat. She half expected to hear him say, "I love you, pumpkin. Don't ever forget it."

JOY GUESSED THAT as far as funerals went, her grandfather's was well attended. Father Michael's eulogy revealed his deep friendship with her grandfather. Joy had written a short piece, but when she got to the pulpit to read it, she spoke from her heart instead, admitting her fault in not returning to Indian Lake to see Frank, remembering how their Thanksgivings in New York were her happiest moments. It was difficult not to tear up, not to lose her words in her chaos of emotions, but she made it through and thanked everyone for being present for Frank. As she walked back to the front pew, she saw many compassionate, familiar faces. Faces she'd forgotten.

Afterward, on her behalf, Father Michael had invited everyone to Frank's house for a luncheon.

Now they all stood three deep, around the dining room table, admiring the bounty. Joy had covered the table with her mother's Irish linen cloth. Olivia and Julia Melton had set up the buffet while Joy and the rest of her friends had been at Saint Mark's. Huge crystal bowls held seafood salad, chicken salad with red grapes and walnuts, a pasta salad and a green salad. A large hammered pewter tray held two large planks of grilled salmon topped with capers and lemon slices. A honey-baked spiral ham and candied yams filled the end of the table. On the sideboard were plates, napkins and silverware.

A second, round table, skirted in white linen, was set up with hot and cold drinks.

Sarah hugged Joy before introducing her husband.

Joy shook his hand. "I'm very pleased to meet you, Luke. Sarah was such a good friend to me in high school."

"Then you two should pick up where you left off," he said, putting his arm around Sarah and kissing her cheek. "*Best* is the word to describe her."

Joy watched as Sarah smiled up at Luke. He touched her cheek and kissed her lips. They couldn't take their eyes off each other.

Joy got the distinct feeling she was intruding, but as she moved to the drink table for iced tea, she saw Maddie Strong, who had been another close friend in high school. "Maddie? How wonderful to see you!"

Maddie hugged Joy. "I'm sorry it's under these circumstances, but I've missed you, Joy," she said, not letting go of Joy's hand. "So much has happened since you left, but you look like not a day has passed."

Just then, Dr. Nate Barzonni walked up and slipped his arm around Maddie. "Joy, it's good to see you," he said, smiling. "I'm sorry it took this…to bring you back. I have to say, New York looks like it's working for you."

"She looks fabulous," Maddie agreed.

"So do you," Nate whispered in Maddie's ear, but it was loud enough for Joy to hear.

"The lovebirds are at it again," Gabe Barzonni said as he walked up with his wife, Liz, and their three-and-a-half-year-old son, Zeke.

"Look who's talking." Maddie chuckled. "You said you were bringing Joy some wine. Where is it? I brought cupcakes for everyone."

Gabe grinned mischievously and shot his thumb over his shoulder. "It's in the kitchen. Olivia is uncorking a couple bottles."

Joy glanced from Nate to Gabe. "So, Gabe, you're not running the family farm anymore?"

"Nope. I gave it up when I fell hopelessly in love." He kissed Liz soundly on the mouth.

Liz shook her head and placed her hand on his broad chest. "The truth is, Gabe always wanted to be a vintner. He fell for me and my grapes."

"Not a chance," Nate said, butting in. "That'd be like me saying Maddie plied me with cupcakes."

"Hey!" Maddie retorted. "I did."

Nate put both his arms around her. "Did not."

"Did, too." Maddie laughed and kissed Nate. Joy excused herself and continued around the table, receiving condolences from Nate and Gabe's mother, Gina Barzonni. Joy had always liked her when she was in high school. Joy was stunned to discover that Gina had recently married Liz's grandfather, Sam Crenshaw. She shook hands with Rafe Barzonni, congratulating him on his marriage to Olivia Melton. "She's amazing, Rafe. She put all this together in one day."

"And wait till she shows you the photographs. She took photos of your table and the flowers. With your permission, maybe— and she'd do this as a friend. She thinks the world of you, by the way. If you'd want some candid shots of the guests, she'd snap a few. Nothing intrusive. Memories, you know? It's up to you."

"Really?"

"She's gone pro. And been published in a few magazines. I'm really proud of her," he said, looking from Joy into the kitchen, where pretty Olivia was walking out with a silver tray filled with Maddie's delicious cupcakes.

"I owe her a great deal for all her help."

"She was happy to do it for her friend, Joy."

"Yes, Grandpa was an amazing man."

He leaned a bit closer and said, "I meant you."

"Oh."

As Rafe walked over to his wife, Mrs. Beabots walked in with Adam, who was holding the hand of a little boy.

Mrs. Beabots walked straight up to Joy and hugged her tightly. "Joy, I'm so happy to see you. Though losing Frank is hard for all of us."

"He was a good friend to you. I'm so glad you're here. I missed you at the church."

"I was in the back. I don't drive anymore, so I must rely on others to cart me around. Though when the weather's nice, I walk everywhere."

Mrs. Beabots had always been part of her life in Indian Lake, especially when she was in high school. It was Joy who filled orders for Mrs. Beabots's fall bulb list. Her Christmas poinsettias and amaryllis. Joy had loved delivering flowers to Mrs. Beabots, who always invited her in for tea or pastries. Or if she got lucky, a piece of sugar pie. Since Sarah lived next door to Mrs. Beabots, she and Maddie would often meet at Sarah's house and then the three of them would barge into Mrs. Beabots's kitchen, help her with dishes or put away groceries and be rewarded with something special right out of the oven.

The clutch at Joy's chest came from too many memories she'd shoved away and tried, successfully for years, to replace with exciting New York.

"Now, Joy. Tomorrow you must come to my house for dinner."

"Oh, I couldn't impose."

"Too bad. You have a great deal to do here," Mrs. Beabots said.

"How do you know that?"

"You forget my reputation for knowing what's happening in this town?"

"I did. So, who told?"

"Why, Adam, of course."

"Figures."

"Well, it wouldn't be your attorney. That would be immoral. Or something." She waved her hand.

Joy couldn't help but chuckle. "I bet you kept Grandpa on his toes."

"Frank was a sucker for my peach cobbler. So were you."

"I was."

Mrs. Beabots touched Joy's arm. "I need to check on something in the kitchen. You probably need to see to the rest of your guests."

She winked and looked over at Adam, who was standing near the kitchen doorway.

Just as Mrs. Beabots turned, Joy asked, "Wait, is that—Adam's son?"

"It is…" Mrs. Beabots walked to the kitchen.

The shocks kept coming. So, Adam was married? Where was his wife? Had they both been at the church? The funeral was already a blur to her. She barely remembered anything.

A pretty woman about Joy's age with striking aqua eyes came up. "Joy. I wanted to introduce myself. I'm Cate Davis. Kyle Evans told me to give you a call, but since I knew Frank so well, I thought this might be better."

"Cate? The Realtor?"

"Yes."

"I'm so pleased to meet you."

"Kyle said you were anxious to list the greenhouses."

"Yeah. I have to get back to New York by Thanksgiving."

"That's…only six days away."

"I know. Is there a lot to do?" Joy asked.

"We're fine. Tell you what. I'll meet you there tomorrow morning at, say, nine o'clock? I'll take some photos, work up some comps.

I'll do my best to get back to you by the end of the day or Sunday afternoon."

"Gee, I hate to take up your weekend."

"I'm a Realtor. We're used to it. And we do have some work to do, this being a commercial property. What about the house here?"

"That, too," Joy said, feeling a sharp pang through her middle. Now that she'd said it out loud, she suddenly wanted to hang on to the house. But she lived in New York. Her life was in New York. Wasn't it?

Joy saw Adam now standing at the fireplace in the living room. His son was still by his side. The boy had picked up the fireplace poker. She excused herself from Cate and walked toward Adam, overhearing their conversation.

"What's this, Dad?"

"Titus, put that down. It's dangerous."

"But what's it for?"

"To move the logs around so air gets to the fire."

"We don't have one."

"We have gas logs. They're safer."

"Oh," Titus said and looked up as Joy smiled at him. "Hello."

"Hello." She stretched out her hand. "I'm Joy. What's your name?"

"Titus Masterson. This is my dad. But I know that you already know him. From high school," Titus said, pushing his glasses up the bridge of his nose and smiling broadly.

"Titus…" Adam used that same warning tone he'd used with Joy.

"Thank you for coming, Adam," Joy said. "I'm sure Frank would appreciate it."

"I'm sure he would."

Titus rocked back on his heels and tugged on his blue blazer. "We were good friends with Mr. Boston. He let me eat peanut butter and crackers in the kitchen."

"He did?" Adam and Joy chorused.

"Uh-huh. And grape jelly."

"I suppose the milk was for you, too?" Joy asked.

"Yep. Organic."

Joy smiled. "I can see why my grandpa liked you, Titus. You're quite the charmer."

"Thanks." Titus grinned.

Joy looked back to the kitchen. "Is your mother coming to the luncheon?" she asked.

"No," Adam replied sharply.

"She died. She's in heaven with Mr. Boston," Titus said matter-of-factly. "When I die I get to see them both."

Adam put his hand on Titus's shoulder. "That's right."

Joy knew she was blushing with shame. "I'm so sorry. I didn't know."

"It's okay," Adam said, not to Joy but to Titus, who was looking up at him. "It's been three years since Amie died. Titus and I are doing better."

"That's right, Dad. We are." Titus looked at Joy. "So, is it okay if I have a cupcake?"

"You can have anything you want, Titus. Please. Enjoy."

"All right!" Titus nearly sprinted away.

"Titus! Slow down! You might trip on that throw rug," Adam warned.

Joy watched Adam as he stared after Titus. "He's wonderful."

"He's like his mother."

"He's like you," she said, feeling a long-remembered warmth flood her. "He looks just like you."

"He does. Poor kid."

"Adam, you are incredibly handsome. I always thought that."

"I was a nerd."

"I like nerds," she countered. "Though you aren't one."

His blue gaze bored into her face, and for a moment, she was back there with him, in the potting shed where no one could see them and he was about to kiss her.

He jerked away and turned to the photos on the mantel. He picked one up. She looked at the picture.

"That's us at prom. I forgot we had this one."

"I remember. It was the night I proposed. You forget that, too?"

"No."

"You said 'yes.'"

"Adam. We agreed. We'd wait till after college… You had a scholarship to Purdue. I had a scholarship to Columbia. We grew up."

"We drifted apart."

This time when his eyes met hers, she saw sadness and regret. Not the sadness of mourning, but the kind she'd seen when she looked in the mirror after their breakup. She'd lost her parents. Adam. Her town. It had taken every ounce of courage to go to her classes and keep her grades up so that she didn't lose her scholarship. But she'd done it. And she'd done it alone.

"We did."

"Can I have this?" he asked.

She thought it an odd request. He had a son. A life and recent past she knew nothing about. But he wanted their prom picture. "Sure. Uh, Frank would want you to have something."

"Frank—" Adam started to say something but Joy's cell phone rang.

"It's New York. I have to take this."

"I better go. I'm truly sorry about Frank."

"Thank you, Adam. I know you are."

Adam walked to the dining room. She noticed that all the Barzonni brothers came up to him and slapped him on the back. Sarah hugged him. Maddie and Liz did, as well. They were all friends and they carried their affection for each other well.

Her cell phone rang again. She answered it. "Chuck. Sorry. I was just saying goodbye to a guest."

"I didn't know the luncheon would still be going on. I lost track of time myself. So, did you get the flowers?"

"I did. They were huge. Thank you very much."

"Dad thought it was a good idea. They're from both of us."

"Please thank him for me."

"I will. I tried to order them from your grandfather's greenhouse, but the line was disconnected. You closed it down fast."

Joy worried her lip. "Uh, actually, Chuck, it's been down awhile now."

"What?"

"It's a long story. My grandpa and I always used our cells and texts. I never called the greenhouse, where he'd be too busy to talk. Personally, I think he was expert at intrigue. Probably, all those old mystery movies he watched, because he kept his secret well. Even his deteriorating health was a secret. No one knew. Not even in town. Bottom line for us is that I'm meeting with the Realtor first thing in the morning."

"Great. Thanksgiving is less than a week away."

"Miss me that much, huh?"

"I'll say. The work has stacked up like crazy since you left."

"The work…"

"Yeah. Oh, and Dad said to say hi."

"I gotta run. My guests, you know."

"Oh sure. Absolutely. Kisses."

"Kisses," she echoed, as Chuck hung up.

Joy stared at her cell. "Work."

Olivia walked up and put her arm around Joy's waist. "You okay? Could use a hug, I bet."

"Yeah."

"This has been a shock for you," Olivia said. "We've all been missing the greenhouses since Frank closed them up. But knowing that someone else will be buying them. It's so… final, you know?"

"Yeah."

"Frank was the best guy. It's a shame he had to close down. Christmas isn't the same without his poinsettias all over my deli. I miss that magic…"

"Do you know why he closed?"

"Not really. I thought he might've had health issues."

"He never told anyone why?"

Olivia's expression was thoughtful. "He was a private man. But if anyone would know, it would be Adam."

"Really?"

Olivia nodded. "Adam was like a son to him. When he moved back and his wife was ill, Frank was there for him. They've been inseparable since Amie died."

"I didn't know."

"Really? Frank didn't talk with you about Adam?"

"No."

"That's odd. But like I said, Frank was a private man."

One by one, Joy's guests came up to give her last hugs. They all begged her to call them for whatever help she would need. But all Joy needed was to put the greenhouses on the market, sign the papers, fly back to New York and let Cate take care of the rest.

It was a good plan.

Her life would go on. She'd be out of Indian Lake and out of their minds. Once again.

CHAPTER EIGHT

JOY WAS PLEASED with Cate's professionalism as she took the photos of the greenhouses. She walked every inch and took measurements. She'd gone to the county recorder to find the original title to the land, the survey and early construction blueprints.

This was Joy's first opportunity to assess the property.

They walked around to the back of the buildings and saw deep open trenches filled with PVC pipe that ran from the greenhouses to a small building Joy didn't recognize. It looked newly constructed of white vinyl siding and had a green roof that matched the other buildings.

"What's that?" Joy asked.

"I have no idea." Cate snapped a photo on her iPhone.

"Looks like new plumbing to me. Was Frank considering reopening? Because these materials aren't cheap."

Cate and Joy stepped between mud puddles, frozen ground and another stack of pipe toward the new outbuilding.

Cate checked the door, which had a padlock on it. "Did Frank leave a key for this?"

"Not that I know of. I better ask the attorney." Joy walked a few feet over to the old potting shed. The wood siding was peeling and beginning to rot at the joints. The roof needed new shingles and the little window box to the right of the barn-style door had nearly disintegrated. Everything needed repair. Lots of it.

Cate continued taking photographs. She turned to Joy. "I think I have what I need."

They started back toward the front parking lot. Joy stomped the mud off the bottom of her boots as they walked along the stone walkway.

"This is so strange for me," Cate said. "I haven't been back here since Frank closed. I had no idea it was in such disrepair."

Joy swallowed hard. It wasn't good that Cate, the expert, had misgivings. "So, you're saying…"

"Honestly, Joy, I don't know how much all this will sell for."

Joy felt the earth move under her feet. This was so far removed from what she'd expected.

And Chuck thought the place would bring over a million dollars?

"I mean…" Cate started and then looked up at the greenhouse. "You can't be blind to the situation, Joy."

"I know, I know. It's been more than a shock. Grandpa always believed this was my future. He thought it was a gold mine."

"Look. I don't know the reason he shut down, but it had to be a good one. His heart was in every flower he sold."

"My entire youth was spent here. Feeding the flowers. Watering them. Watching each cutting grow. I thought it was magic."

"You loved it."

"Adored it. I was with Grandpa every day after school and all weekend long after my parents died. He was my world."

"And he wanted you to have this place."

Joy scanned the cracked glass panes, feeling hopeless. It was as if she could sense her grandfather's disappointment at closing the business. "So, what do we do?"

"I'm going to find some comparable locations that will help us, not hurt us. This old place, all glass… It's one of a kind. Maybe someone will be interested in the retail unit."

"For what?" Joy asked. "I mean, you can't turn it into a B and B."

"No, but you might want to consider fixing it up. Replace these broken glass panes and clean it up to amp up the value. Curb appeal is paramount. I'd clean up the interior, get the lighting up to par. That kind of thing."

"Good advice. But to do all that, I'd have to oversee the project, and I'm due back in New York pronto."

"A dilemma for sure."

Joy rubbed her neck—a tic whenever she considered alternatives.

"And what about Frank's house?" Cate asked, pointing across the drive. "That, at least, will be a snap to price it out and list. I could put the sign up today. Despite the fact that it's nearly Thanksgiving, I'm betting I could have a buyer quickly."

"But it needs updating," Joy said. "I noticed the faucets all need replacing. I haven't checked the roof, but…"

Cate shot her a skeptical look. "Are you saying you don't want to list the house?"

"I'm that obvious?"

"Uh-huh."

Joy sighed. "It's all too much, Cate. I mean, losing the business is one thing, but that house… Yesterday with all my old friends there, it— I don't know. I felt so much love there, as if the walls were hugging me."

"You know, as a Realtor, I go into house after house, and most are lovely. Some are staged. But only a few have real, loving warmth. Frank's house is one of those that speaks to me when I walk inside. If I didn't have the perfect bunga-low for Trent, Danny and me, I'd be interested."

"The house *is* like that. Suddenly, I can't bear the thought of losing it."

"Leave it for now. There's no rush. Maybe you should keep it. So that you have a place to come home to."

Come home to? What in the world was Cate talking about? Indian Lake wasn't her home anymore.

Cate gave her a hug. "I'll call you later."

"Thanks for everything, Cate."

Joy's shoulders sagged with the weight of her dilemma as Cate drove off. A little over two days and she was already feeling the pull of her old life here. A life she'd thought she'd long since buried.

She opened the door to the retail area, went inside and closed the door behind her.

Bam!

The noise from the back of the space sounded as if something had fallen. *Which shouldn't be a surprise. Probably another glass pane break-ing.*

Joy walked past the empty display area to

the French doors. Not seeing anyone in the greenhouse area, she shrugged her shoulders and turned to go.

Bam!

"What's going on?"

This time, she marched through the retail area, through the small tropical greenhouse area, to the back-storage area, and flung the door open. Standing in the middle of the cement floor was Adam, both his arms filled with PVC pipe.

"Adam!" she shouted.

He jerked, and when he did, the pipe went rattling out of his arms and onto the floor. "Jeez, Joy! You scared me."

"Now you're stealing my grandpa's pipe?"

"What? This is *my* pipe," Adam countered, hands on his hips, eyes blazing at her.

"Since when?"

"You'd know if you came back to Indian Lake more than once a decade."

"If you'd get off your high horse and tell me what's going on, then maybe I wouldn't be so suspicious about you."

"Suspicious?"

"Yeah. Like why are you loitering around here all the time? And by the way, I want that key back."

"It's my key."

"I own this greenhouse now." She'd stand her ground and she'd get some answers out of him if it took her all day.

He glared at her. "Right."

He reached in his pocket, took out the key.

She stared at the key, suddenly not wanting it back. She heard his breath intake as if he didn't want the surrender either.

"It's the craziest thing—this key to the greenhouse. It takes me back not just to us... but all the fun, the sharing...the knowledge I soaked up from your parents and Frank. He couldn't wait to show me the newest hybrids being displayed at the horticulture convention at McCormick Place."

"I remember those..."

"This greenhouse was his passion," Adam said.

"You're right. He was so passionate about his hybrids. Grandpa was such the dreamer. I remember the feeling I had when I'd walk through the doors after school. I couldn't wait to water, feed, stock shelves, I didn't care. Being here was..."

"Magic," he finished for her as he walked closer, took her hand and placed the key in her palm. Then he closed her fingers around it.

Joy sucked in a breath as he touched her.

He used to kiss her with a tenderness she hadn't experienced since. She'd forgotten that.

Energy shot from his hand to hers and filled her with a longing to be held by him. She couldn't stop this magnetism even if she wanted to. And she didn't want to.

He didn't want to break the moment, either, she noticed. His eyes held hers, not wavering. Not blinking. It was as if they were in a realm all their own. Maybe it was magic that she and Adam had once had.

But that had been teen love. Young. Inexperienced and not to be trusted to bring about a lifetime of happiness.

"Adam," she murmured, finding it nearly impossible to speak. All she wanted was for him to hold her hand. "Talk to me."

Then he did let go of her, shoving both hands in his jeans' pockets to create a barrier between them.

"Why?" he asked. "You're gonna sell this place and hightail it back to the Big Apple. What do you care about Frank's dreams?"

"Dreams? He shared that with you?"

"He did."

All these years that she'd been gone, she didn't realize that he had dreams beyond what he'd shared with her for enjoying his greenhouses. That was all they'd ever discussed.

He'd always be there for her, he'd said. But then he hadn't told her about shutting down.

Adam toed his boot on the floor as if hesitating to share the truth with her. Perhaps he felt he was betraying Frank by sharing this very private information with Joy. Maybe Frank had sworn him to secrecy, since it was obvious to Joy that Frank trusted Adam.

And not me.

"He wanted to reopen the greenhouses."

"Do you know why he closed them?" she asked.

"Yes."

"Really?"

"I was here, remember?"

Adam was still accusatory, and she was getting tired of it. "Can we call a truce here?"

Silence as he glared at her.

"For Frank's sake," she added.

The wave of softness across Adam's face tore at her. Adam did care about Frank. For that, she was grateful.

"Sorry. You're right," he answered.

His hand came out of his pocket and reached for hers. She looked at his hand, big and strong. The kind that had tinkered on impossible-dream-idea engines, that had melted her heart. That had cared for a baby boy after his wife died.

"What?"

"Come on," he said, a thin smile breaking across his lips, but it was the flash in his eyes that stole her attention.

"Where're we going?"

"Out back."

"I was just there. It's all muddy. Grandpa had some kind of plumbing problem going on. I thought maybe the sewer broke but didn't want to say anything to Cate. Something like that could bring the property value down. More."

Releasing her hand, Adam held the back door open for her as she passed in front of him.

"Not a plumbing project," Adam said. "Frank told me never to tell you why he closed...not until I proved myself out."

"I'm so far beyond confused here."

"He closed because the price of gas skyrocketed a few years ago. He couldn't make any money. Probably, when we were kids, we didn't realize there were things like energy bills and heating costs. Anyway, at just about that time, I came back to town and helped him finish closing up."

"I didn't know. Thank you for that, Adam."

"Frank always believed in me and my silly, unworkable inventions."

"Those inventions were why the kids in school made fun of you."

"Yeah. Adam the skinny nerd."

"I never thought so," she replied, giving him a direct look. He didn't take his eyes off her.

"You believed in me…for a while."

He tore his eyes from her and continued before she could answer. "I came up with the idea to install a geothermal system to heat the greenhouses. My system is much more efficient than any in use."

"Because…"

"I put the pipes even deeper in the ground and I used a smaller pipe so that the water doesn't have a chance to cool by a single degree."

"And you've been doing this work here?"

"I have. And working with Frank to create that salmon-striped hybrid poinsettia he'd always dreamed of." Adam smiled broadly.

"No way!" She was astonished. So much had been going on in Indian Lake. Adam had had a child. Seen a wife through illness and death. Done all this work with her grandpa. And he was still pursuing his dreams.

"It's true," Adam said. "All those summers working here with you and Frank, I got the horticulture bug."

"You are full of surprises."

"I hope so," he replied, with a longing she hadn't heard in anyone's voice except…except his on the day she broke up with him.

She felt a fluttering in her chest, but that could only be from nostalgia. It wasn't real. She was a victim of shock and grief, still trying to grasp that the greenhouses had been closed and that they might not sell for much. She wasn't having new feelings for Adam.

Nothing was as she'd thought it would be when she flew in from New York.

New York.

"Adam, look. This—" she waved her hand toward the half-buried pipes "—is all wonderful, but…"

"You have to sell," he finished for her.

"And go home."

"I thought this was home."

"Not anymore."

He looked down at the pipes. "Yeah. That's what I thought you thought."

Without another word, he walked away, past the potting shed and the new little generator building. He got in his truck and, without waving to her or looking back, drove away.

Joy felt a chill and didn't understand why she felt alone now that Adam was gone. When he was around, it felt like the ground was more solid. She looked down at the key in her hand, then closed her fingers around it, making a fist and pulling her hand to her heart.

Adam and Grandpa had planned for a new beginning, to reopen the greenhouses. Frank would have had a chance to create his hybrid and Adam would have been part of making his dream come true. But it was not to be.

Once she sold the greenhouses, her grandpa's dreams would be buried with him.

But that was the way it was with death. Things ended. Including dreams.

CHAPTER NINE

JOY PUT HER phone on speaker as she held up an old red cable-knit sweater she'd found in the bureau drawer. The last time she'd worn it, she'd gone ice-skating with Adam, Sarah, Nate and Maddie at Craven's Pond. She'd also worn jeans, her work cowboy boots and had pearl studs in her ears. Pearls that Adam had just given her for Christmas. She'd kissed him to thank him, and he'd pulled her to his chest and hugged her so close, she could feel his heartbeat even through the sweater.

"I love you, Joy, forever and always," Adam had said and kissed her again. She'd thought then that no one could kiss her with the depth of emotion as Adam.

They all used to hang out there on cold winter Saturdays. There was always an impromptu and often vigorous hockey game between the Barzonni brothers and Isabelle Hawks's brothers. Despite the teams being unbalanced in number, the lack of helmets, padding and equipment and even nets, Joy rooted for all her friends. The city provided old oil drums filled with burning wood where they would warm their hands. The Barzonni brothers shaved the ice with home-made, long-handled blades resembling rakes to keep it smooth for the skaters. From time to time, old Mr. Marsh would trundle down from his house on the hill with his hot dog wagon, which he brought to the Fourth of July parade, the Santa parade and to the county fairgrounds. Mr. Marsh's steamed Chicago-style hot dogs with relish, peppers, celery seed, mustard and onion were delicious. And memorable enough to cause her mouth to water now.

It had been a long, long time since Joy had put on a pair of skates. *Not since I left Indian Lake.* Ice-skating was a thing of the past.

"Did you hear what I said?" Chuck barked into the phone.

Joy blinked and came back to the present. "Are you talking to me?"

"Sorry, no. That was Glory. Just a sec, Joy."

She'd call Glory tonight after Glory was home. Not while Glory was at work and couldn't *really* talk.

"Chuck," she said, putting the red sweater on the bed and smoothing out the arms. "Why don't I call you later when you're not busy?"

"I'm good," he said. "So, what happened with the Realtor?"

"She's gathering comps." Joy paused. She needed to tell Chuck the truth and she didn't know why she had held back.

Waiting for a miracle?

Joy had never been one to skirt adversity. Dealing with it was her job, after all. People came to her with accounts that were in the red and expected her to fix everything. Sometimes overnight. They paid a great deal for her expertise.

Fixing this greenhouse situation was precisely what Joy's education and years of experience had taught her how to do.

"Chuck, I don't think you're going to like this."

"What?"

"My grandfather has been keeping the truth from me for years. His business was on a decline, so much so that he closed the greenhouses five years ago."

"So—this isn't a recent development?"

Now she had Chuck's full attention.

"No."

"Give it to me straight."

"I can guarantee there won't be any blue-sky money. The Chicago florists and local markets have long since switched suppliers. That revenue stream has dried to bedrock.

Therefore, there's no business to sell. Only the property and the buildings."

"I see."

She could tell he didn't see. Chuck had been born and raised in Manhattan. He was fourth-generation Newly. Even if he never worked another day in his life, the family had money. Chuck lived and worked for his father's approval, and to earn respect from his father's friends and their community. She admired his sense of responsibility.

"You're disappointed," she said.

"Surprised."

"I was shocked. I still am. All this time my grandfather never told me what was going on. He never asked for my help."

"Was it his health?"

"No, Adam told me it was the rise in heating costs that shut him down."

There was a long pause before Chuck asked, "Who's Adam?"

"Oh." She cleared her throat, wondering why explaining Adam should be a problem. "An old friend from high school. He worked with my grandfather for the past several years."

"I thought the greenhouse was closed."

"It…was. I meant, they had a special friendship. Adam said he used to come over and tinker," she replied, her hand going to the red sweater and smoothing the rounded neckline.

She remembered Adam's loving smile when she'd last worn the sweater.

Chuck's tone was pointed. "Tinker? What does that mean?"

"Adam was always inventing things in high school. He's an engineer now."

"An engineer."

"Yeah."

"Working for your grandfather. That doesn't make sense. What was he doing?"

"They were just friends. Apparently, his little boy was close with Grandpa, too."

Chuck exhaled loudly enough that Joy heard it. "A son. Well. That's nice."

"Yeah. Titus is darling." She smiled, thinking of the little boy dressed up in his blazer at the luncheon. "Smart, too. Probably grow up to be a CPA."

"So, when can you get the property listed and get back here?" Chuck was back to business.

"Tomorrow, I guess. Cate said she'd call me later today if she had anything. I'm going to Mrs. Beabots's for dinner tonight."

"Who's that?"

"An old friend. You'd love her. She's elegant, funny. Knows everything about everyone, practically before they know it. And she's mysterious."

"C'mon," he groaned.

"It's true. No one knows where she came from when she moved to Indian Lake in the 1960s. But she was married back then. Her husband died, I don't know, about twenty years ago. They had a grocery store on Rose Street for years. But there's all these interesting stories that rumble through the town about her. Supposedly, she lived in Paris at one time and worked for Chanel."

"She's wealthy?"

"I think so, but you'd never know it by her actions. She's as sweet and caring a person I've ever met. She's a love."

"Maybe she needs an estate planner. Do you have any of my cards with you?"

"Chuck!" She laughed. "I'm not going to solicit for business on this trip."

"Why not?"

"This is personal."

"You're right. You're right. Look, text me when you get the quote from the Realtor. Dad and I are meeting with the board at the Met tonight. I have a brunch tomorrow morning with the committee for Feed the Hungry for Thanksgiving and then I'll be back at the office probably until midnight working."

"Can I ask you a question?"

"Whazzat?"

"Do you ever take a day just for you?"

"And do what?"

"I dunno. Just breathe?"

"Look who's talking," he countered. "I'm running. Love you."

"Love you."

Joy hung up.

She was just like him. Time alone had not been a good thing since her parents died. Time to breathe meant she'd be visited by the memories of seeing her mother's face bloody, covered in glass, her hair matted with blood, lying on a gurney in the ER, gasping for air and calling for Joy. Joy had held her mother's hand as she took her last breath. By the time Joy left her mother's side and rushed to the abutting ER bay where a cardiac doctor and his team were trying to revive her father, it was too late.

She would never forget the look on Dr. Caldwell's face as he turned away from her father, who'd been a friend, his eyes meeting Joy's as he said, "Bruce is gone." He'd stared down at the defibrillator paddles in his hands. "I'm so sorry, Joy."

Joy couldn't recall what was said or if she'd said anything after that. What she did remember was sitting at the kitchen table that night as her grandpa spoke to a stream of friends who came to give their condolences. Joy had stared at the melted marshmallows in her cocoa. She felt as if she'd been hollowed out. There was nothing inside her, not even marrow in her bones. No thoughts in her head, no emotion in her heart, and even her breath had frozen in her lungs.

The police chief—Williams, she thought she remembered—had stood at the sink slugging back coffee while her grandpa filled the carafe with water and started the third round of coffee.

"Frank," the chief had said, "Dead Man's Tree is a blight on this community."

"It shoulda been cut down years ago. Now my son is one of its victims."

Joy had raised her head and listened.

"I can't tell you how I've battled the Green Preservation Committee to get rid of that tree," the chief had said. "But Wilma Wilcox won't budge, and you know how she can sway city council."

"Wilma is over ninety years old. She's rich, opinionated, stubborn and self-centered. She's run everything from the school board to city council and most of the charity organizations. When we were growing up, she even ran roughshod over the high school athletic coaches."

"How could she do that?"

"Money," Frank said. "If they danced to her tune, she donated money for equipment or a new baseball field. The old high school was in the middle of town, near the library. Built in 1920. Ever wonder why the new high school is out there off Anderson Road?"

"Don't tell me."

"Wilma donated the land to the city. And then paid for the football field attached to it."

"She's some philanthropist."

"That money always came with a price, if you ask me," Frank said. "For the town's sake, Wilma needs to be booted off that preservation board and keep her trap shut. Let the young folks deal with these issues. That tree is a killer. Bruce and Jill aren't the first to die by that tree." Frank had banged his fist on the counter. "But by God, they will be the last!"

"You've been here all your life, Frank. Why is she so adamant about keeping that darn tree?"

"All that area, the golf course on either side of Anderson Road, the fire station, even the new housing developments up the hills and the new office buildings, are all built on her family's property that goes back to the Civil War. Over the years, Wilma has sold off parcel after parcel. Anderson Road is named after a brother who died at Normandy Beach.

What remains there were of his body, and his dog tags, are buried next to that tree. That's why she won't let anyone cut it down."

"Anderson Wilcox's grave," Chief Williams had mused. "I understand. It's kinda spooky when you think about it. That tree being a grave for her brother and then other people dying because of the tree."

"Well, it's gonna stop," Frank had said. "I'm going to start a petition like this town has never seen. I'll get every last person in Indian Lake to sign if it takes me all year. That tree is done causing pain and sorrow."

Joy came away from that night with bitter hard facts. The town of Indian Lake and its authorities had known of the dangers about Dead Man's Tree for years and had done nothing about it. Wilma Wilcox's wealth, social prominence and political clout had caused Joy's parents' deaths and the deaths of others before them. Indian Lake had been paying dearly for Wilma Wilcox's money. Blood money.

Joy not only blamed Wilma Wilcox, she blamed all of Indian Lake for killing her parents.

If the townspeople had stood up years ago, decades ago, her parents would still be alive. So would others.

There was no excuse for their deference to Wilma Wilcox.

She vowed at that moment to leave Indian Lake at her first opportunity. She had less than a full semester of high school remaining, and her hopes for winning a scholarship to Columbia University were high.

She loved her grandpa, but she couldn't face the townspeople, who knew full well the dangers of Dead Man's Tree and had done nothing to rid themselves of the menace.

There was no excuse for apathy.

Joy had always been a hard worker both in school and at the greenhouse. Infused with a passion for poinsettias and the desire to become a successful accountant so that she could help her parents and grandpa, Joy didn't understand how anyone could stand aside and let a bully ruin their lives.

JOY TOOK THE red sweater and carefully folded it up. Since arriving in Indian Lake, she'd removed only her quilted toiletries bag from her suitcase and put it in the bathroom. Her clothes were still in the suitcase. Even the dress she wore to the funeral she'd folded and put neatly back in the roller bag.

"Ready to bolt," she said aloud.

Subconsciously, she couldn't wait to leave

town. Her anger at the people in Indian Lake had not diminished, even though Frank had carried through with the petition to have Dead Man's Tree cut down. Grandpa had told her it took nine months to get the signatures, and though Wilma Wilcox was still on the city council, she'd been overruled. The tree had come down before the year was out.

But it hadn't brought back her parents. Too little too late. Joy had been robbed of her mother's hugs and laughter, her wisdom and her father's eternal optimism. From him she'd learned no task was too small or too mighty if you looked at work as play.

Forgiveness wasn't something she could give. The pain was still as fresh as it was all those years ago. Perhaps it was intensified by Frank's death, sealing her into a tomb of loneliness.

Her tears fell on the sweater and she stared down at it.

Eventually she put the sweater to her nose and inhaled. It was faint, but the scent of the perfume she'd worn in high school was there. She closed her eyes.

If she breathed, all she could remember was a teenage haunting of kissing Adam.

"Dangerous territory, Joy," she scolded herself.

She walked to the bureau and opened the

drawer. She was about to place the sweater inside, when she quickly closed the drawer, turned and placed the sweater in her suitcase.

Perhaps some memories were worth revisiting.

CHAPTER TEN

CATE WAS AS good as her word and returned late that afternoon with a folder filled with comps, contracts and computer printouts of commercial properties in the area.

Joy scanned the comps. "Is commercial property depressed here?"

"Yes, but it's on the rise with so many people moving in from Illinois to get away from the property taxes there."

"So, you're saying I should wait?"

"I don't know what your situation is. If you need the ready cash, then we should list now and see if we can sell the house by the end of the school year. The greenhouses... I'm not sure how long that will take."

"It's not that I need the money." Although Joy couldn't help thinking about the fact that she didn't own anything, really. She rented an apartment that she shared. She didn't have a car. Most of her furniture had come from re-sale shops. Was it possible that in the back of her mind, her grandpa's house and these greenhouses had always been her safety net? "I mean, who doesn't need security, but that's not the thing."

Cate pulled her coffee mug closer, wrapped her hands around it and asked, "Then what is it?"

Joy found the question hard to answer. Another thing that wasn't like her. Joy was always quick with responses. Chuck always said her mind was lightning fast.

Since she'd come to Indian Lake, her thoughts were muddled. All she did was rehash the past. Revisit and stall.

Like she was doing now.

"Let me look these over tonight."

"Take your time. It could take a couple weeks to line up crews to do the work that's needed. My recommendation remains. I'm confident that if you fix the place up, you'll bring a better price."

"Good advice."

"Plus, you've barely cleaned up from the funeral luncheon. Give yourself a break."

"I feel torn. I should get back to New York, though I know they're doing fine, but I also know I owe Grandpa my best efforts here." Joy rose from the chair and went to the refrigerator. She pulled out a container of pumpkin-flavored creamer. Her eyes went to the pumpkin pie on the label.

Thanksgiving. It would never be the same without Grandpa. She put the creamer down and covered her face. "I feel so ashamed."

Cate was on her feet in a flash. She put her arms around Joy and hugged her.

"I feel so alone. And it's not as if I don't have a fiancé."

"I know, Joy. But where is he?"

"Yeah." Joy nodded. "Not here."

"I understand that he has to work, but Frank was your only family."

Joy wiped away the tears, then grabbed a tissue from the counter. "Chuck and his father are very close. When Chuck's mother died, it was hard on them. This funeral would have been difficult for Chuck to deal with—at this time." Joy blew her nose. "You know how it is."

Cate stared at Joy, skepticism written all over her face. Joy didn't blame her. There was a lot about Chuck's actions and attitude she didn't fully understand. If she'd been in Chuck's position she would have insisted on being in Indian Lake with her.

Cate went back to the table. "I'll leave all this with you. You gonna be all right tonight?

I mean, maybe you shouldn't be alone. You could come to my house for dinner."

Joy forced a smile. "That's so sweet, Cate, and thanks. But I'm going to Mrs. Beabots's for dinner. I'll be fine."

"She's the best, isn't she?" Cate picked up her purse. "I can't wait to hear what she wears tonight. Take note of her ensemble. If I know Mrs. Beabots, her outfit will probably be vintage Chanel."

"That's right. I remember those stories now." Joy swatted the air with her palm, dismissing the comment.

Cate swung back around. "Oh, trust me. The stories about her are true. That woman's closet is not to be believed. The first time she took me in there… I think I was with Isabelle and Sarah that time," she mused. "I was speechless. Chanel suits. Louis Vuitton purses. Couture gowns and dresses. Museum stuff."

"I heard vague rumors when I was in high school, but I never saw that closet."

"Sarah told me the same thing. Apparently, she kept everything packed up until Luke, Sarah's husband, built her that new closet. Now she likes sharing with all of us."

"I wonder if she's a collector?"

"Nobody knows. She drops hints here and

there about the origins of the clothes. Sarah and I have figured out she must have lived in Paris back in the early sixties. But other than that…" Cate shrugged her shoulders.

"Better keep my spidey senses alert."

"And then some." Cate hugged Joy. "I gotta run. Call me."

"Promise," Joy replied, then held the kitchen door and waved as Cate walked to her car.

JOY PUT ON THE same black sheath she'd worn at the funeral, adding a three-quarter-length-sleeved black sweater and black heels. Because Glory had packed for her—in a hurry, no less—there was no jewelry other than the practical small gold hoop earrings she'd worn to the funeral, and her engagement ring.

She arrived at Mrs. Beabots's three-story Victorian house promptly at six. The front steps were decorated with pumpkins and gourds, and around the beveled-glass front door was a garland of wheat and raffia. A gold-brown-and-green-plaid ribbon swirled around the raffia.

She remembered that in Indian Lake people "competition decorated" for every season. It was one of the traditions that kept the register ringing at the greenhouses. Joy had forgotten how much she'd once loved it. And people like Mrs. Beabots, Sarah and her mother, Ann Marie, when she was alive, kick-started each holiday by hoisting up seasonal wreaths, vines around lampposts and baskets of colorful flowers suspended along porches.

Joy twisted the antique pewter doorbell in the middle of the door. The tinny ring was familiar, and once again her mind wafted back to the times when she, Sarah and Maddie would visit Mrs. Beabots.

Remembering her conversation with Cate, Joy thought it funny, in all those years, she hadn't paid attention to what Mrs. Beabots wore. Not that she would have known Chanel from Banana Republic.

The door swung open. Instead of Mrs. Beabots, Titus was there. "Hi!"

Joy smiled at Titus. "Good evening," she said, shifting the white orchid she'd bought as a hostess gift to her left arm. She held out her hand. "How are you, Titus?"

"Very fine, thank you," he replied, pushing his glasses to the bridge of his nose, then shaking her hand. "My dad's in the kitchen with Mrs. Beabots." He stood back, holding the door.

Joy walked in, glancing around the huge foyer, at the library table with its Tiffany lamp and a pair of sterling silver deer that held up an enormous silver-edged bowl filled with pinecones.

"I didn't know it was a party," Joy said.

"It's not," Titus said, stomping past her and then beckoning her to follow him. "It's just us."

"So, you come here a lot, do you?"

"Uh-huh. Timmy and I help Mrs. Beabots bake cookies after school."

"I'll bet you do." She chuckled as her shoes sank into the thick-cut Chinese runner in the hall. She passed the front parlor to the left, which opened by way of massive pocket doors to the library, where a fire was crackling in the fireplace. The familiar portrait of beautiful Mrs. Beabots hung over the mantel. Joy slowed for a moment to peer at the painting. The dress she wore was elegant and clearly something Audrey Hepburn would have worn in Paris.

"Hmm."

"C'mon," Titus urged.

Joy could hear laughter and the clatter of pans in the kitchen. She saw Adam first. He was wearing a sky blue banded collar shirt with the sleeves pushed up, exposing taut muscles, as well as black dress slacks, black dress shoes and a ruffled pink-and-white apron. He paused in taking a sip of red wine when she walked in.

"Hi, Adam," she said cheerily.

"Hello."

Mrs. Beabots pulled a casserole dish from the oven with oven mitts on her hands. She placed the casserole on a brass trivet. "Oh, Joy. How lovely you look."

Joy knew the woman didn't mean the first word she said. Joy felt particularly frumpy compared to her hostess. Mrs. Beabots was wearing a cream-and-gold Chanel short jacket with looped edge braid along the bottom and up the placket. The cream straight skirt to match was paired with cream hose, winter-white leather pumps and five gold-pearl-and-crystal chains around her neck. Gold logo earrings peeked out from her thick silver chin-length hair and danced in the light from the overhead Venetian crystal lamps.

Joy knew the earrings were new because she'd seen them advertised in the *Vogue* magazine she'd picked up at the airport. The rest was vintage—and real. Cate was right. She was exquisite. Which made Joy feel not only underdressed but shabby.

"Thank you for inviting me," Joy said.

Titus climbed up on a wooden stool. "She brought you a flower," he said to Mrs. Beabots.

"It's an orchid," Adam said.

"It's real pretty." Titus reached out to touch a petal, leaned too far and started to fall.

"Titus!" Adam shouted.

Joy quickly flung her arm around Titus's middle, then scooped him off the stool while still holding the orchid securely. She lowered him to the floor. "There ya go," she said proudly, looking at Adam, whose scowl was sharp enough to leave permanent markings on his face. "He's fine."

"I see that." Adam glared at Titus, who paid no attention and continued looking at Joy.

Mrs. Beabots smiled broadly and closed the oven door. "Adam. Why don't you pour our guest some wine? I could use a glass, as well, while I finish up here."

"Sure," he said and went to a silver tray with different-shaped wineglasses. He held up the bottle. "Red?"

"That's great."

"I'll have the chardonnay, Adam," Mrs. Beabots said.

Joy put her purse on the side counter, where she noticed another silver tray filled with more wineglasses. A second brass tray held colorful cut crystal cordial and Irish crystal brandy balloons. "Thanks," Adam whispered as he handed her a glass. "Titus can be, er, clumsy sometimes."

"He's a kid," she said.

"And you're used to kids?" he asked, reaching behind her to take a wineglass.

"A bit. Glory and I volunteer at a family shelter a couple weekends a month—but not during tax season. Mostly it's babysitting, but I love the kids."

His arm brushed hers. She kept her eyes on him, though she made no attempt to move away. She couldn't help inhaling the woodsy scent of the soap he still used. Some things didn't change over time, she thought.

He held up the wineglass. "White wineglass...for the chardonnay."

"Of course."

He poured the wine for Mrs. Beabots. Joy held up her glass. "To your good health," she said.

"And yours," Adam and Mrs. Beabots chorused.

Titus lifted a mug shaped like a turkey with both hands. "Clink with me," he asked Joy first.

"To your good health." She smiled and watched as he drank what looked like cocoa. "I like that mug."

"Mrs. Beabots has mugs for Annie, Timmy

and Charlotte next door," Titus replied. "Then when I started coming over after school, we went to the antiques mall and found Halloween, Thanksgiving and Christmas mugs." He put his palm to his mouth to shield his words from Adam and Mrs. Beabots. "They were only a dollar, so she bought a whole set so Danny Sullivan can have one, too."

"And don't forget Zeke," Mrs. Beabots added.

Titus's mouth rounded. "You heard me?"

"You aren't exactly quiet, Titus." Adam beamed at his son and winked. "I like that about you."

Titus shot his arms straight up in the air. "I know! I like being happy!" he shouted.

Everyone laughed.

Impulsively, Joy put her hand on Titus's little shoulder. "I hope you always feel that way, Titus. We need more people in the world like you."

"Thanks, Miss Boston."

"You can call me Joy," she said, looking down into the same charismatic blue eyes as his father—magnified by the glass lenses. Joy didn't know what it was, but a distinct warmth filled her just looking at Titus. She seriously had to resist the urge to hug him, as if his happiness would infuse her somehow.

"No," Adam said. "You call her Miss Joy. It's more respectful. Just like you do with Miss Sarah."

Titus turned from his father to Joy. "Is that all right?"

"It sure is."

Titus whooped with joy and picked up his mug with both hands again and drank.

The timer on the oven pinged.

"The chicken is ready," Mrs. Beabots said, putting her wineglass down and picking up the oven mitts.

"Here," Adam said. "Let me do that. You ladies take the wine out to the table and I'll bring the meal."

"Well, thank you, Adam," she replied, then walked around the granite-topped island and took Joy's arm. "Shall we?" She winked. "It's not often I get treated like a princess."

"Queen," Adam corrected, as he pulled the stuffed chicken breasts out of the oven.

Mrs. Beabots sat at the head of the table closest to the kitchen. Adam was to her right and Joy to her left. Titus sat next to Adam on a pillow to raise him up.

Joy noticed that as Adam brought the dishes to the table and placed them on trivets, Titus slipped the pillow out from under him and let it slide to the floor.

As Adam sat, Titus glanced at Joy. She looked down to the floor to let him know that she'd seen what he'd done. He pursed his lips and gave the slightest shake of his head. She knew he didn't want her to squeal on him. She nodded and gave him a slight smile. His smile grew wider.

Titus looked at the chicken breasts. "What's inside them?"

Adam held the plates while Mrs. Beabots served the scalloped potatoes, glazed carrots and chicken. "Cream cheese, Parmesan cheese and spinach." She halted. "Titus, you do like spinach, don't you?"

"I do. My dad introduced it to me last year. It's very healthy. Organic, right?"

"Oh, yes. And I cook gluten-free now. I don't think I'll ever be dairy-free, however. Thank goodness I'm not lactose intolerant." Mrs. Beabots laughed.

Adam placed Titus's plate in front of him. Titus sniffed the food. "Smells good."

"Garlic." Mrs. Beabots smiled and handed Joy her plate. "Do you like to cook, Joy?"

"I do, though I don't get much chance, especially this time of year. We work quite late from now until tax season is over."

"I can only imagine," Adam said, cutting the chicken.

"Once we hit January my days last till midnight. I make it a practice to pack several green salads and fruits for the day and night."

Titus had finished all his carrots before tasting anything else. Joy noticed he moved on to the potatoes and still hadn't touched the chicken. "I like to cook," Titus said between bites.

Joy looked at Adam's pride-filled face. "I'm surprised."

"Dad taught me." Titus kept eating, not looking at anyone.

Adam sipped his wine. "Raising a healthy child is an enormous responsibility. Thank goodness for the internet—"

"And," Mrs. Beabots interrupted, "pie-making lessons in this kitchen."

"I love those!" Titus said. "Are we having pie for dessert?" His eyes looked like saucers in his face.

"Of course," Mrs. Beabots said.

"What kind?"

"Titus, that's not polite to ask," Adam said, placing his hand on Titus's forearm.

"It's okay," Mrs. Beabots said. "Dutch apple. I believe that's your favorite, Titus."

"It is." He looked up at his father. "Dad likes them all. Especially that chocolate-and-peppermint-candy one at Christmas."

"That's my favorite," Joy said. "I made that for you at Christmas."

"Our junior year," Adam said, without looking at her.

"My mother made it every year. It was her mother's recipe."

Joy didn't take her eyes from Adam. Neither did anyone else at the table.

"I told her I'd never had anything that sweet." Adam lifted his eyes to Joy.

Joy wasn't sure what she saw in his expression. Though he wasn't smiling, his eyes gleamed with caring, fondness and—hope. Her heart skipped.

Mrs. Beabots looked from Adam to Joy and she caught the glance out the corner of her eye. "Adam's Christmases back then were…"

"Hollow," he finished. He lifted his chin as if courage had come to his rescue. "Then I met Joy and her family. And things changed." He looked at Titus, who was still silent. He ruffled Titus's thick hair. "I promised myself that if I was ever lucky enough to have a kid, I'd make sure every Christmas was special."

"Blowout, Dad. You said we'd have a blowout Christmas this year," Titus said happily.

Joy put her fork down. As delicious as the food was, the conversation was far more intriguing. "And what exactly does that mean?"

The excitement on Titus's face hit mega wattage. "We're gonna have the biggest, bestest tree ever! We're going out to Pine Country Tree Farm, where you can ride out to the groves and pick any tree you want. They cut it down, unless you wanna do it yourself." He tilted his head up to Adam. "You gonna do it again this year, Dad?"

"Probably."

Titus turned back to Joy. "Then we ride back and they bundle it up and put it in our truck. I want a really, really huge one this year."

"Wow," Joy replied. "Just how big is that?"

Adam chuckled. "Titus's imagination is always a bit over the top. Our living room ceiling is only eight feet."

"I know," Titus groaned. "Not like here. Right, Mrs. Beabots? Last year we got her a really, really big tree. Timmy and I and Mr. Luke and Dad went out to get the tree."

"Yes, but I go in November and pick my tree out. Tagged. Purchased and bailed by the time they get there," Mrs. Beabots added.

"What's your tree like, Joy?" Adam asked.

"I don't have one."

"What?" Titus shook his head. Adam nearly choked on his wine. Mrs. Beabots clanked her fork against the plate.

"You, of all people, don't have a tree?" Adam said.

Joy bristled. "What's that supposed to mean?"

His tone softened as he said, "You and your family, your parents, Frank—you were the heart of Christmas for this town. For someone like me with no family, when I found yours and worked at the greenhouses during Christmas, and saw how beautiful you made everything, it was…magic."

"Magic?" Titus's eyes widened.

Adam nodded. "What happened to you?"

Joy's defenses rose. "Life. Work. You wouldn't understand how crunched for time we are at the firm. That's why I loved having Grandpa with me in New York for Thanksgiving. If you ever came to New York at Christmas, you'd understand. The entire city is decorated. I never felt the loss of not having decorations of my own. New York is amazing. And as far as a big tree, Titus, the one in Rockefeller Center is truly 'blowout.' I'd love for you to see it."

"Cool! Can we go to New York sometime, Dad?"

"Maybe."

Joy's hand traced the scalloped edges of the spoon to her right. "You're right, Adam. The greenhouses were part of Christmas for a lot of people in Indian Lake. But they've been closed for a long time. Certainly Titus didn't get to experience them." She took a deep breath. "It seems they died long before my grandpa."

Adam leaned forward. "What do you mean?"

"Cate worked up the comps and did some digging for me today. She says the greenhouses are worthless."

"That doesn't sound right," Adam retorted.

She shrugged her shoulders. "I mean, the land has value and she says the house might sell before the end of the year. But it's far less than what I'd thought it was worth."

Mrs. Beabots reached over and placed her hand on Joy's arm. "Do you need money, dear?"

"I'm not destitute, but I'm not wealthy by any means. My job pays well. But it's the craziest thing. I feel like I'm giving away my legacy—as if I failed by not knowing that Grandpa was in trouble. And I don't like this feeling."

"Then fight it," Adam said. "The green-houses were a thriving business until the heating costs skyrocketed. I'm sure Frank kept all the old revenue reports and tax returns that show how successful it had been. The man kept everything, he told me. And now my geothermal system is nearly finished. If you were to fill those greenhouses with poinsettias, stock the shelves with garlands, ornaments, decorations, candles—all that stuff he used to sell—and then, after a successful season, put the greenhouses on the market…you'd have a viable business. That's the plan Frank and I had."

"Adam, I can't possibly do anything that foolhardy."

"My idea is foolish?" He frowned.

"It doesn't make good business sense. The cost of buying the poinsettias will be huge…"

"I'll help," he said quickly.

Joy was astonished and she knew it showed on her face. "Adam, I couldn't ask you to do that."

"You didn't. I offered. There's a difference," he ground out with finality.

Titus turned his wide eyes from his father to Joy. He couldn't be more intense if he'd been watching a scary movie.

"It's impossible," she countered.

"Nothing is impossible," Adam shot back, leaning toward her, his eyes stern and determined. "You're just chicken."

"Am not."

"Are, too."

"Dad!"

Joy and Adam looked at Titus, who was smiling at them both.

They all burst into laughter.

"What are we doing?" Joy asked, covering her mouth with her hand as she laughed harder. When she calmed down, she looked at Mrs. Beabots.

"You need to think of the bigger possibilities, Joy," Mrs. Beabots said. "If the property was improved and potential buyers saw the activity of the business…"

"I'd get a better price," Joy surmised.

"And you wouldn't feel like a failure," Mrs. Beabots said.

Joy looked from one excited friend's face to the other. "But it's nearly Thanksgiving and we have to clean the floors, replace the broken glass…"

"So?" Adam jumped in. "We have lots of friends here. I'll help clean up."

"Me, too!" Titus chimed in.

"Joe Peterson over at Quality Glass could

get that work done in two days. You handle calling the suppliers in the morning. Get the orders going. I'll supervise the cleanup and construction. What do you say?"

"I say it's crazy." She shook her head at the red flags she recognized from her years in accounting and business. "Absolutely not. Besides, I have to be back in New York."

She watched their faces fall. For a moment she'd actually felt excited. The possibility of fulfilling her grandpa's dream was thrilling. She could almost feel Frank in the room, egging her on. Begging her to try. But her penchant for reality, the stuff of bottom lines and profits, was enough to squelch even an angel's dreams.

Still—

Could she do it? For someone who didn't know the ropes of her business, it would be daunting, but she did recall the suppliers, part-time workers, even cottage industry owners who filled the shop shelves with homemade quilts, jams, honey and Christmas cookies.

Adam was right. The greenhouses had been a retail outlet for local craftspeople. They built their hopes and aspirations on Frank's store.

"Joy," Adam said softly, "you have something I never had."

"What's that?"

"Legacy."

Chills shot up Joy's spine, and the smile that came to her lips was from a place of pride and love. Her mother always told her to listen to her heart. "I'll do it."

"Does that mean you're gonna stay here?" Titus asked.

Joy knew from her emails and texts to Glory and Chuck that they'd been handling the clients. The office was fine. This was the perfect time and cause to use her accrued vacation days.

"I can—at least until closing on Christmas Eve. I have nearly a month of vacation days I've never taken. Fortunately, our most challenging client I took care of before I came back…" She stopped and looked at Adam.

"Home?" he finished for her.

"Here. I was going to say 'here.'" Her eyes locked on his and he didn't look away. He held her to her momentary promise. Initially, she saw hope shine in his eyes, a hope she'd seen before. Then a cloud passed over the light and he shut her out. As he should. She wasn't staying for good.

"Yay! You'll be here!" Titus thrust his arms into the air. "It *is* gonna be a blowout Christmas."

CHAPTER ELEVEN

JOY WASN'T SURE if her Christmas was going to be a blowout or a dud. Her plan to reopen the greenhouses sounded exciting and doable at Mrs. Beabots's dining table, but in the cold light of morning, not so much.

Her first phone call of the day was to Chuck. After he exploded with anger that she would miss the parade and dinner with his dad, she didn't have the courage to tell him about reopening the greenhouses—which would mean she wouldn't be back to New York until Christmas Day.

"I'll tackle that one later," she'd said to herself, swiping her palm across her brow. Her cell rang.

"Oh, no," she groaned, seeing the Newly office number on her caller ID.

"Hey, girl!" Glory said excitedly. "What's your ETA? I'm gonna be so glad to see your face!"

"Um, Glory. There's something I have to tell you."

"Honey. Anytime you say, 'Um, Glory,' I know I'm not gonna like this."

"I hope you're okay with it."

"Spill."

"I just got off the phone with Chuck. Did he tell you anything about what's going on here in Indian Lake?"

"I try not to converse with your fiancé, other than topics pertaining to clients. It's safer for him that way."

"Thank you for that."

"You're welcome. So, what *is* going on and why won't I like it?"

Joy took a deep breath and rushed on. "I'm not coming home for Thanksgiving. In fact, I won't be home till Christmas Day. Though I didn't exactly break that part to Chuck…yet."

"Run that by me again."

"Grandpa's business has been closed for years. The Realtor says it's nearly worthless. Actually, the greenhouses are a deterrent to a sale. Frankly, I had hoped to ask Grandpa for a loan to help me with the wedding. My savings aren't all that, er, substantial."

"Independently wealthy, you are not. You wouldn't have a roommate if that was the case."

"Oh, Glory, we'd probably live together even if we were millionaires."

"No offense, honey, but I was hoping for a clone of Michael B. Jordan for my next room-mate."

Joy laughed so hard she fell back on the bed. "Oh, how I miss you. I needed that."

"So, what are you going to do?"

Joy propped herself up on her elbow and picked a small white feather off her jeans, which she assumed had come from the down comforter. "I'm going to reopen the green-houses and stock them with as many poin-settias as the supplier can provide. Fix it up. Glam it up and…"

"Make your grandpa proud?"

"Yeah."

"I think that's great."

"You…do?" Joy was astonished. Glory was about having fun, going out, living it up, es-pecially over the holidays. Her friend seldom seemed to take anything seriously. But Glory understood her. And that was comforting. "You really are the best of friends, Glory."

After a pause, Glory said, "Joy. Do you have any idea what you've done for me?"

"What are you talking about? I haven't done anything."

"If it weren't for you going to bat for me with Newly and Associates, I wouldn't have gotten my promotion three years ago. Until I finish my courses and get my degree, the rest of the world considers me an assistant. Another gofer in the world of office gofers who used to be called secretaries."

"But you're only a semester away from that degree."

"That's right. Thanks to you. Helping pay for my courses—which, by the way, is *why* you don't have a fat bank account. You're always helping others out. I've never met anyone as generous and thoughtful as you. You cook for me and my crazy artistic gang. You let Jensen sleep on the couch all through October when he lost that gig up in Buffalo. He would have been homeless if you hadn't agreed. And we both know you pay three-fourths the rent on the apartment. Sad digs as it is."

"It's affordable and in a safe area."

"Yeah. Security. Your middle name. That's why this out-of-the-box, pie-in-the-sky venture of yours doesn't sound like you."

"Except for the fact that this is what my grandpa wanted."

"And you loved him."

"I always will," Joy replied, wishing her throat didn't close up so much at the thought of Frank.

"Joy," Glory said, her tone serious now.

"How are you going to break this to Chuck? All he talks about is the parade at that penthouse. The guy is practically counting the hours till you come back."

"Funny, isn't it? I couldn't care less about the parade without Grandpa. It means nothing to me now. There's not a penthouse in the world that can replace his happiness watching the parade."

"Best to get it over with quickly."

"My thought exactly."

Joy pressed her fingers to her temple. She could already feel a stress headache coming on. Then she heard the rumble of trucks driving up outside her bedroom window. She rose from the bed and pulled back the white eyelet curtains.

Three construction trucks had pulled up. She saw a pickup that had tall racks in the bed filled with glass panes. Four men took out tool kits from the back of the second truck. The third truck was a cherry picker with a long lift built into the back with a bucket on the end.

"Hey, I've gotta go. Talk soon. Love ya."

"Love ya." Glory hung up.

Joy slipped her cell phone into the back pocket of her jeans. She grabbed her old high school jacket from the closet and raced down the stairs and outside.

Adam drove up in his truck, got out and walked over to a tall, good-looking man with black hair and dark eyes. The guy had wider shoulders than Adam, if that was possible.

Joy walked up. "Good morning, Adam."

"Mornin'." Adam smiled. "Joy, this is Joe Peterson. He owns the glass company I was telling you about."

When Joe smiled at her, Joy seriously thought his black eyes flashed. If Glory was looking for a clone for Michael B. Jordan, he was right here in Indian Lake. Joy shook his hand. "I'm so pleased to meet you so soon."

"Pardon?"

"I mean, I'm so lucky you're here. Already."

His eyes tracked to Adam.

Adam slapped Joe on the back. "I emailed Joe last night and he had a cancellation for a job he was due to start this morning. So, I jumped at the opportunity."

"Fortuitous," she said, wondering how much this crew was going to cost. She'd barely processed the idea of opening the greenhouses, much less the cost. Kyle Evans had given her Grandpa's checking and savings accounts information. Fortunately, there was enough money to cover the basic repairs and the cost of the wholesale poinsettias, but that was all. Grandpa's living expenses were covered mostly by his social security benefits.

Adam was smiling as if he'd just won the state science fair. "We have to make every minute count, Joy. We don't have enough hours in the day to do all we want to do."

"That said," Joe interjected as he took a step away, "I better get to it. Nice meeting you, Joy. And can I take this moment to say what a great thing this is that you're doing, bringing the greenhouses back?" His genuine sincerity shone in his smile. "My guys will pressure wash all the glass after the panes are installed. You'll be sparkling by the end of tomorrow."

"That's all it takes?"

"Yep."

Joe walked over to the crew, who were laying tarps on the ground, while one man was busting out broken wall panes.

"They don't waste a minute," she said to Adam.

"Joe and his guys are the best." He looked back at her. "What did the supplier say?"

"I put in a call first thing this morning, but haven't heard back. I did get emails from the scented candle company and a local woman who makes quilts and Christmas stockings."

"Hattie?"

"You know Hattie Pottington?"

"Sure. What did she say?" His eyes flashed with delight. If she didn't know better, she'd say he was enjoying this more than she was.

And why shouldn't he? It was his idea. He was all in.

Joy had the impression that when he looked up at the buildings, he was seeing the completed work. Adam had always had that vision that she supposed geniuses possessed. They rushed into a vacuum and created something out of nothing. But they saw creations in their heads.

When she was a teen, she'd been filled with imagination. She was surrounded by beautiful flowers every season. She'd been immersed in the world of black and red numbers for so long she'd lost that sense of wonder. She'd forgotten how precious each moment of life could be under these glass ceilings.

And she'd forgotten what it was like to spend them with Adam.

"She's bringing product over this afternoon for me to choose."

"That's a good start."

They walked to the front door and Joy unlocked it. As she entered the showroom, she said, "I suppose I should give you back your key."

"I suppose."

She pulled the key from her pocket and gave it to him. Odd. It felt natural to give him back the key to the greenhouse that her grandpa had entrusted to him. And to her. Adam had been part of the dream to reopen. Together, they might make this place shine on for years. But for a new buyer and a new generation of owners.

A wave of sadness hit her.

"Thanks," he said, looking down at her hand in his. "I need to get started on the heating system. And you—" he pointed at her "—take that phone and call the poinsettia supplier again. Don't wait."

She shrugged off her dour thoughts, saluted him and said, "Aye, aye, Captain."

He leaned close, his eyes peering into hers, and said, "Frank was the captain. We're shipmates. Taking this dream to the moon."

She held her breath, seeing the image in her mind's eye. Adam had always been able to catch her attention, zero in on the thought that stopped her cold and get her to look at the possibilities from a new perspective.

They were sailing a ship of dreams— together.

For the time being. Joy would be a fool if she allowed herself to waver from her path.

She hadn't counted on the easy feeling she had around Adam and his adorable son, who was quite good at stealing her heart. She couldn't hurt Adam again, and she would when she sold the greenhouses and went back to New York.

He was right to keep up his barriers. Because, in the end, Joy could never, ever live in Indian Lake. Her anger was still firecracker hot.

"I better go." The velvet tones of his voice shattered her thoughts.

As he walked away, Joy was far too aware of his confident gait, how his shoulders squared with the ground as if everything about him was balanced, and no matter what burden life put on him, he could handle it. He'd always been like that. Sturdy. Sure. And sexy enough to keep her attention.

"Hey." He spun back around, killing her thoughts. "I forgot to tell you. I hired a cleaning service for the showroom. They should be here any minute."

"I thought we were doing the cleaning."

"We'll do the hard stuff…like those tiles in the greenhouses. This area needs to be cleaned in a hurry. You're going to be stocking shelves by the end of the day."

"Anything else I should know?"

"Yeah. I asked Maddie if she'd put up one of her display cases and we'd sell some cupcakes here to kick-start things." Then he scratched the back of his neck. "And I ordered a couple coffee makers online. They'll be here this afternoon, along with the coffee, sugar, creamers, sweeteners."

"Guess you thought of it all."

"Uh, not quite." Again, he pointed to her back pocket. "Get on that phone. Without poinsettias, our ship is dead in the water."

Joy grabbed her cell and held it up. "I'm on it."

"Yeah? Show me."

She went to her Recents and hit the number of her grandpa's major supplier. "Hello!" She smiled at Adam.

Adam winked at her and left through the French doors to the back.

"Hi, this is Joy Boston of Boston Greenhouses in Indian Lake. I'd like to place an order. A very large order."

CHAPTER TWELVE

HUSTLING FOR POINSETTIAS only days before Thanksgiving wasn't easy. Most suppliers were committed to their regular retailers.

But Frank Boston's name carried clout. When she told the supplier in Greenback, Tennessee, that Frank had died and she'd returned to Indian Lake to reopen the greenhouses, the man agreed to send a half order of red poinsettias, one full truck of white poinsettias and a half truck of pink. In eight days, they would send another truck of red.

Adam had come in from working on the compressor and saw the dark look on Joy's face. "What's wrong?"

"I need more red poinsettias."

He took off his work gloves. She watched as he Googled a number on his iPhone.

"Ah! Here it is. Nancy Jessup's Wholesale Nursery."

He punched the number. "Hello! This is Boston Greenhouses up in Indiana. I'm in desperate need for red poinsettias. What do you have left?"

He paused for a moment. "I understand that you don't deliver to Indiana, but what if I were to take all those off your hands? Great. Then I want to place a second order for the same or similar. When can we come back and pick those up? Eight days. Excellent. My driver will be there tomorrow."

He hung up.

Joy's eyebrow hitched up. "What driver? I can't leave here and neither can you. You have a heating system to finish. Otherwise the poinsettias will die."

He grinned at her again.

Joy's eyes narrowed. Adam was in his element, flying by the seat of his pants, banking on fate to align all his spinning plates so that Joy could bring a good price for the greenhouses.

And return to New York.

And Chuck.

"Hey!" Adam said when his next call was answered. "What're you doin', man? I've got a job for you, if you want it. I need you to drive down to Dallas and pick up a load for me and drive it back here to Boston Greenhouses."

Joy mouthed, "Who are you talking to?"

Adam held up his palm. "And when you

get back, since your regular business is slow this time of year, how about a part-time job helping out at the greenhouses taking care of the poinsettias for us?" He paused. "Oh, yeah. I forgot about the lights. Well, just the Dallas trips, then."

"Who is that?" Joy whispered, narrowing her eyes as Adam ignored her.

"I'll make the arrangements for the truck. Thanks, man."

Adam clicked off. "You can thank me later." He chuckled, apparently enjoying her frustration.

"Who. Was. It?"

"Lester MacDougal, a local landscaper and friend of Sarah's and mine. Obviously, he's slow this time of year and welcomes extra work. And we'll need him. He works in large holiday lighting jobs. Trees, garlands. Stuff like that. He does the courthouse lights. The firefighters do the downtown trees. But he's perfect for us."

"I don't remember him. Did we go to school with him?"

"No. Actually, he walked here from Kentucky when he was fifteen. Sarah's mom was still alive then and he literally walked up to Ann-Marie when she was planting bulbs in the boulevard in front of Sarah's house. He told her that he liked diggin' in the dirt. She put him to work, fed him, clothed him, and Maddie rented him his first apartment. Later, Sarah and Maddie helped set him up in business. He got a horticulture degree online. He's good people."

"Why did he leave Kentucky? Didn't he have family?"

"Not the kind of family I'd wish on anyone. His father abused him. Regularly. He said the day he fought back, he walked out and kept walking till he met Ann-Marie."

Joy put her hand on her heart and felt it throbbing with compassion. "In so many ways, I was lucky to have my parents and grandpa as long as I did."

"Yeah," he said, looking away. "You were."

She saw the judgment in his eyes. "Don't say it."

"I wasn't."

"I feel terrible about not coming back. I do. I wish I had spent more time with Grandpa. I just thought…"

"He'd always be around. Yeah. I know how that is."

"You do?"

"Uh-huh. I thought the same thing, too. I thought I could wish him alive."

"Oh, Adam, it had to be so hard—what you

went through, being there when he died. It…
it probably brought back memories of Amie's
death."

"Yeah." He slapped his gloves against his
palm.

She saw his blue eyes glisten as he lowered his head.

"I was with my mother…" She gulped back
a sob. She hadn't talked about her mother's
death to anyone in all these years. Yet one
more buried painful dragon to unearth. "The
doctors couldn't save my dad. I was holding
her hand and looking at the doctor, and I felt
her hand go limp." She paused and cleared
her throat. Joy smelled the pungent hospital
smells, heard the monitors beeping, then the
monotone flat line. "I couldn't save her."

Adam raised his head. "I couldn't save
Amie, either. I was so…helpless…"

"I know… I know…" She exhaled and felt
hot breath escape her lips, heated from her
long-held anger.

"Joy…" He reached for her hand. "I tried
so hard to be there for you, but you pushed
me away. Why?"

"Oh, Adam. I…I couldn't take it. I was
losing everything. I thought if I pushed you
away, I wouldn't have to deal with losing you
in the future, too."

"But I loved you."

"And I loved you." She reached up and smashed her tears with her palm. "I'm sorry. I shouldn't have said that."

"Why not? It's the truth, isn't it?"

"It is."

He inhaled deeply. "No, you're right. That was the past. We can't change any aspect of it. Not death or what was between us. This is now."

She forced a smile, watching his barriers rise up. Again.

"I better get to it if we're going to make this enterprise happen," he said slowly, as if it was difficult to speak each word.

But as he walked off, she saw him sweep his fingers under his eyes. Of course, Adam believed in miracles. He had to, she thought. The alternative was unacceptable.

Joy's heart bubbled with compassion for him and grief for her own loss. What would have happened if she hadn't run away? Would they have stayed together? Would that teen love have endured? This was now, he'd said. She had a purpose being in Indian Lake at the moment and that goal needed tending.

Joy gathered her strength and went back to organizing the front counter. She found clippers, floral tape, wire, pipe cleaners, floral foam, boxes of iridescent marbles and glass stones in the storage room, plus old garland and Christmas picks with frosted pinecones, tiny decorative wrapped presents and silk poinsettias they used to use when wrapping gifts or in the bows around flowerpots.

Though the cleaning crew was due within the hour, she knew how she wanted the counter to look. After wiping it down, she covered it with a long red brocade tablecloth she'd found in her grandpa's linen closet. The end of the counter was covered in white plank wood, which she kept clear for the wrapping of poinsettias.

She ordered three rolls of printed floral paper and three rolls of iridescent cellophane from the floral supplier, along with other designing supplies she would need to make wreaths, door swags and floral arrangements.

It was after three o'clock—and another twenty calls to various gift suppliers and showrooms for ornaments, tree skirts, place mats, napkins, Christmas china and cookie jars—when Sarah drove up with four children in her SUV. She held Charlotte's hand while Annie led her brother, Timmy, and Titus inside.

The cleaning crew had left and the first shipment of lit faux garland had arrived. Between phone calls, Joy had hung the entire perimeter of crown molding with the lit garland and plugged it in.

"It's already a fairyland, Miss Joy!" Titus exclaimed.

Joy hugged Sarah. "Not even one day in and we're moving like a bullet train."

"I thought I'd give Miss Milse a break while she puts dinner together. The kids were excited to see your progress."

"Did Titus tell you?"

"Mrs. Beabots told me the happy news."

She watched as the boy touched every empty shelf and investigated behind the counter. "He's so curious." Joy looked at the shiny object in Titus's mitten-covered hand. "What you got there?"

"Ornament. Miss Milse was showing us how to make Santa faces on our glass ornaments with cotton and glitter." He took off his mittens, switched the ornament from hand to hand as he put the mittens in his pockets and then held it up. "Pretty, huh? I'm gonna make a whole tree full!"

Joy sighed. So many simple things about Christmas she'd pushed out of her mind when she left Indian Lake. *When Mom and Dad died.* "I bet you don't know how to make a donkey and a reindeer."

"Uh-huh. Out of clothespins and Popsicle sticks."

Joy looked at Sarah. "They still sell those?"

"At the craft store," Sarah whispered.

"I need to remember that," Joy said, grabbing her pad and jotting down the reminder. "Seriously, Sarah, my head is spinning. And my credit card is beat up."

Sarah leaned in. "I think it's valiant of you, what you're doing, and I want to help."

"That…that would be great."

"You know I'm a designer now? I could set up the displays for you. Section things out like I do for my retail commercial clients. When people come in the store, they naturally veer right. So, we want to put your most spectacular tree, gifts and florals right by the door. Then we can create a winter walkway for them to follow, taking them past all the decorations and gifts. You'll need baskets for them to put their goods in."

Joy snapped her fingers. "We have those! In the storage room."

"Perfect. Then we take them to the back, where we'll put the food. Jam. Honey. Cookies. And then end up at the checkout counter, where they can eat a fresh baked cookie while they get their poinsettia wrapped."

"What cookies?" Joy asked.

"The ones Mrs. Beabots has volunteered to bake for you."

"No way." Joy shook her head. "I…I can't believe this. And you are too busy to do so much."

"My work is nearly nonexistent in December. We just wrapped on the unit north of town. I have some drawings to do, but I don't present the mock-ups and blueprints until January 15, when the client returns from Italy. So, see? I have time on my hands. Miss Milse will watch the kids. It's done." Sarah put her hands on Joy's shoulders and smiled broadly. "Just say yes."

"Sarah…" Joy pressed her lips together, thinking that would stifle a grateful sob, but she failed. She hugged her friend. "I forgot— so much. I forgot how wonderful you are and how much you mean to me. I'm so…lucky…"

Sarah sniffed and grinned, fighting her own happy tears. "And you are so far behind."

"I know. The first poinsettias arrive in forty-eight hours. Half the inventory will be shipped in the morning and a great deal arrives tomorrow afternoon."

"So, I'll be here first thing in the morning to start setting up the trees."

"What trees?"

Sarah laughed. "Oh, the ones Luke went to

cut down at the tree farm for you today. He'll be here in an hour or so."

Joy exhaled in amazement. "You think of everything."

"Everything except the heat you're going to need by tomorrow," she said, hugging her arms around her middle.

"I know. Adam's working on it. I should check on him." She turned back to Titus, who was inspecting the bins with frosted pine-cones. "Titus, let's go see your dad."

"All right!" He jumped up exuberantly. "I gotta show him my ornament I made." He picked up the Santa face and rushed to the back.

Something made the hairs on the back of Joy's neck prickle. "Titus. Not so fast!" She rushed after him.

But Titus had pushed through the French doors to the back greenhouse. He raced past the wooden tables that would soon be filled with colorful poinsettias and toward the back door.

He was fast, but so was Joy as she caught up to him. "I'll get the door," she said.

Titus ran out. "Dad! Dad!"

Adam was on the opposite side of the trench, filling it in shovel by shovelful of dirt. The long trenches from the compressor building were covered over with the dirt, but up here, close to the greenhouse building, there was still over ten feet left open.

Adam had told her that the key to his geothermal design was to bury the pipes deeper than most systems. She hadn't realized until young Titus rushed up to the very edge, dangling his glass Santa face in front of him for his father to see, just how deep that trench was.

Titus's boot had stopped short of the edge, but the dirt was loose. Joy saw bits of rock crumble under Titus's foot.

"Titus!" Adam yelled, as he dropped the shovel.

Without thinking, Joy bolted up to Titus, threw her arms around his middle and yanked him backward. She fell on her rear and Titus landed on top of her.

"Titus! Son!" Adam raced down his side of the trench to the end and up the other side.

In the process of falling, Titus's bare hand had smashed the glass Santa ornament.

"Oh, no!" Titus wailed.

"Son! Are you hurt?" Adam asked as he ran up.

"No."

Joy lifted Titus and scrambled to her feet.

As she did, she noticed that Titus's hand was bleeding.

"You're cut," Joy said.

"My ornament," Titus cried. "I made it for you, Dad. Now it's broken."

Joy inspected his palm. "There's still a piece of glass in his hand. Let's get him inside."

Adam swooped Titus into his arms. "I don't care about the ornament. I only care about you."

Joy followed them. They went through the greenhouse and up to the front retail area, where Sarah and her kids waited.

"What happened?" Sarah asked.

"Titus fell."

"I broke my ornament," he moaned.

Sarah went behind the counter, grabbed her purse and took out her makeup tote. "Put Titus on the stool there, Adam. I have tweezers, Band-Aids…"

Titus sat on the stool. Timmy, Annie and Charlotte hovered around, wanting to see the wound.

"You'll be okay, Titus," Timmy said and patted his back.

Adam started to reach for the tweezers in Joy's hand.

She pushed him back and said, "How many times have you tweezed your eyebrows?"

"Huh? None. Why?"

"I'm aces at this." Joy leaned down, placed the tweezers gently around the delicate glass and eased it out. "There."

"It didn't hurt." Titus looked at her with amazement.

"Okay, now to clean it up." She reached for tissue and a bottle of alcohol she'd placed under the counter and swiped the wound. "Adam, you apply the Band-Aid."

Joy cleaned up the blood and Adam opened the bandage and put it on Titus.

"Next time you make ornaments, let's buy the shatterproof balls," Adam said.

"I should have thought of that, Adam," Sarah said. "But the kids raided an old box of ornaments I'd put out for the tree Luke is bringing home."

"It's okay," Adam said, ruffling Titus's hair. Then he hugged his boy. "Maybe we should call it a day, huh? Go home and feed Angel?"

"Okay, Dad." Titus hugged Adam back.

Joy walked with everyone to their cars. She hugged each child and thanked Sarah again.

"Luke just texted and said he's on his way over. He'll help you put the trees up."

"He doesn't need to do that."

"The farm people put the stands on them. All he does is prop them up and cut the bailing. I'd put some plastic sheeting down if you have it. Then it's easy to haul them out after Christmas."

"I think I saw some in the storage room." Joy beamed.

"See you in the morning."

Sarah drove away.

Adam waited by the side of his truck. Titus was in his car seat. "I'll finish up the trenches in the morning. I've tested everything and we should be good to go."

"Thank you so much, Adam."

"Sure." He opened the door. Then looked back. "Listen. I appreciate what you did for Titus. But he's my son. I'm responsible for him. Okay?"

"Yeah. Sure. But…"

He lowered his voice, she guessed so that Titus couldn't hear him. "He shouldn't have been anywhere near those trenches. I haven't allowed him out there since I started this project. Next time, if he's in your presence and I don't know about it, keep him close. Don't let him go running off. And trust me, I'm very, very good with tweezers."

He got in the truck, buckled his seat belt and drove away.

The sun had dropped; the air had turned cold. A wind kicked up and lifted her long hair off her shoulders, chilling her back. She hugged herself as she rushed to the green-house.

Only hours ago, she'd felt the warmth of Adam's friendship. Now there was only this bitter cold.

CHAPTER THIRTEEN

ADAM SAT AT his laptop staring at his inbox. He hadn't answered email in days because he'd got caught up in Joy's world.

His world.

The world of the past, when the greenhouses had been thriving. Life had opened up to Adam when he'd met Joy in speech class. He was having a hard time finding happy subjects to write about. Joy was the best of them all. She was always bright and happy. His childhood was not filled with growing flowers, change of seasons and twinkling Christmas lights like Joy's. When she spoke in speech class, describing life as she saw it, she made him believe that everyone should have a happy ending. Everyone loved her. He loved her from afar.

Pursuing Joy was the first leap of faith he'd ever taken. He wanted to learn more about this girl who hummed to herself as she dug in her locker for her other gym sock or smiled at everyone she saw in the halls between classes whether she knew them or not. He wanted to know what it was like to have friends that made her face light up the second she saw them.

He'd watched her walk out the front doors to the high school that day on her way home, he'd thought. He'd plucked up his courage, rushed up to her, and before he could ask if he could walk with her, she said, "I see you, Adam Masterson."

"Good. Because I really want to walk you home."

"Why?"

"Because I want to spend time with you."

"Why?"

"Because I want to see the world through your eyes."

With her staring at him with eyes so piercing, he'd felt her gaze to the pit of his belly. "You do?"

"Uh-huh."

"Then you should know I'm not going home. I'm going to work."

"Work? You're only sixteen."

"I've been working since I was ten. Eight? Yeah. Eight."

She'd started to walk away. He'd stared after her, shocked really. All the time he'd been admiring her, he assumed she lived like a princess.

"Adam Masterson, are you gonna just follow me or walk alongside me?"

"Alongside."

"Good. I'd like that." She smiled.

She'd taken him to the greenhouses, and that day her father and grandfather hired him on the spot to help clean the glass, sweep floors and restock the tables with new plants.

Adam had been right. The world through Joy's eyes was brighter, more colorful and filled with love and friendships he hadn't known existed.

It was through Joy he got to know Sarah Jensen and the Barzonnis. Maddie Strong. Olivia Melton. Isabelle Hawks and all her brothers. Liz Crenshaw. The list seemed endless back then. Joy knew everyone. And she loved everyone.

"And why not?" He drummed his fingers on the mouse pad. "She's so full of love—and lovable."

Until the accident, the February before their high school graduation. Adam had always blamed the fog for the fact that Bruce didn't see Dead Man's Tree. After the funeral, all through March and April, Joy kept pulling away from him. Or pushing him away. He'd gone to the greenhouses after school to help get the place ready for spring, always hoping to get a kiss or ten from Joy, but she was too busy. She'd taken over her father's job of keeping the books and ordering supplies. She took over her mother's job of tending the plants. Frank had told him to give Joy space.

But that hadn't worked.

On prom night, Adam pushed the envelope and asked her to marry him. Since he didn't have an engagement ring to replace her promise ring, Joy didn't take him seriously. She'd said they were too young. They both had college. Days later when he'd pressed her again, she brusquely told him that she was leaving Indian Lake and she never intended to come back.

He'd believed she'd change her mind. That she'd miss him once she left. But that didn't happen.

For years he'd rationalized that they'd drifted apart, but that wasn't true. Her staying away was intentional.

"But she never said she didn't love me."

He rubbed his forehead.

He rose from the chair. "I'm an ass." He rubbed his forehead again. "Maybe I should apologize. I could send her flowers. Duh. Jeez, Adam. Be original, wouldya?"

He knew he shouldn't have pounced on her the way he did, but he'd always had a problem with being reactionary, especially when it came to Titus. He acted first. Thought last. He needed to switch that around.

But when he'd seen Titus on the edge of the deep trench, he panicked. Adam had been on the wrong side of the long trench and couldn't get to him as quickly as Joy did.

The glass in Titus's hand had scared him. He saw blood and imagined visits to the ER. Stitches. Tears. Antibiotics.

Adam was terrified of any kind of injury to his little boy. He meant it when he told Joy he wanted her to keep Titus close. Maybe it was Adam's fault for not fully explaining to Joy, who had no children, how accident-prone Titus was. Plus the fact that Titus had double dosed on curiosity from the day of his birth. He was forever investigating. It was as if Titus wanted to discover the entire world in the next ten seconds. The kid never walked into a room; he rushed. He flung his arms around Adam; he didn't hug. He kissed a dozen kisses, not one.

Adam didn't want to diminish any of Titus's traits. In many ways, Titus reminded him of Joy. Or at least the girl he'd known in high school.

That was the thing. She'd changed. Grown up and taken on responsibilities of her career and life in New York. And yes, she was grieving over losing Frank.

But it was something else.

He'd had to push her to see the possibilities in front of her. To see that the greenhouses could flourish again. The old Joy would have been the one urging him to try new things. Find a different way to make his inventions work. To test them against other inventors. To go for the prizes and awards.

It was as if that girl had died along with her parents. Life had dealt them both a rotten hand. They'd lost the ones they loved the most.

Frank wasn't coming back. Amie wasn't coming back. He and Joy had figured out how to cope. Maybe their mechanisms for dealing with pain weren't all perfect, but they'd worked.

Adam thought he understood her better now that she was home. But he was surprised by his reaction to her now.

One minute he remembered what it was like to be in love with her. The next, he was unsure and his defenses hardened to granite because he'd taught himself to keep his distance from others. Though he had friends, that wasn't the same as a romantic relationship.

"Except that…"

Joy was engaged, and from what Adam had observed so far, she didn't seem as in love with this Chuck guy as she had when she'd been Adam's girl.

Maybe that was because they were kids. Teenage love was nothing but romance and moonlight and had little to do with the hard lessons in life.

"And death," he whispered, thinking of Amie.

Had he been right to encourage Joy to stay in Indian Lake and reopen? Or had his motivations been purely selfish? Admittedly, he wanted to show Joy that Indian Lake could be a safe harbor for her.

Above all, he wanted to prove to Joy that Indian Lake was separate from the pain and sorrow she felt. Her real friends were anxious to help her in many ways. If he could show Joy how so many people cared about her, wanted the best for her, perhaps she would finally be able to quell her burning anger.

That anger was directing her actions and life choices.

"Choices…" Adam had to admit it *was* a gamble doing what they were doing, but Adam believed in Indian Lake. Once people knew the greenhouses were open, he believed they would swarm to the reopening.

"Oh, jeez," he said, pulling the chair out and sitting down again. He'd started a new website for Boston Greenhouses last night. He would take photos once the place was decorated, but for now, all he needed was a "coming soon" banner and a lot of stock photos of poinsettias.

He made a note to order Candy Cane and deep burgundy poinsettias. Tomorrow he'd take the graphics he made and have flyers made up at Image Printers in town. Lou's Diner always allowed flyers. So did Olivia at the deli and Scott Abbott at Book Shop and Java Stop. It was good to have helpful friends.

Then he emailed Mary-Catherine Cook, Titus's teacher at Saint Mark's, who also worked on the weekly church bulletin. She'd put the banner in the bulletin and he'd make a donation to the church.

Adam didn't have Joy's permission to advertise, but they needed to work fast. This was not the time to stand on protocol.

He could only hope that Joy would appreciate his effort and possibly forgive him for snapping at her earlier.

He turned off the laptop, flicked off the

lamp, swiped his fingers across Amie's photo the way he did every night. "Thanks for our son, Amie. I'll take good care of him."

He rose from the chair and started up the stairs.

With each step he wondered if other widowers felt like he did. Each night was emptier than the last. Some days it was hard to greet the morning sun. Others passed by in numb awareness. With the holidays approaching, life decisions seemed weightier.

Second chances, do-overs, were one of those things Adam thought were only for fairy tales.

Was there magic in Christmas? Or in the promise of the New Year?

He looked in on Titus, who was sleeping soundly with a *Star Wars* stormtrooper figure clutched in his hand. Adam didn't disturb him. Maybe the stormtrooper helped Titus to feel protected.

As he entered his bedroom, he thought he'd been luckier than most guys. Though his time with Amie had been brief, they'd been happy and they'd both been giddy over their baby. Adam couldn't imagine his life without Titus.

If he hadn't broken up with Joy all those

years ago, he would never have married Amie or had Titus.

Perhaps his love for Amie was giving him courage to open his heart…one more time.

CHAPTER FOURTEEN

IT WAS THE day before Thanksgiving and Joy hit a level of anxiety she'd never experienced. She'd been up before dawn and cleaned the last of the old tile floors and the wooden poinsettia tables, and had started unboxing her first shipments. Whenever she'd felt apprehension, she'd learned to throw herself into work, either mental or physical. Unfortunately, neither was working for her today.

"I gotta be nuts to do all this."

She second-guessed every decision she'd made, starting with the massive poinsettia orders when she didn't know if Adam's heating system would actually work.

He'd said he'd tested it. She was still working with only space heaters in the retail area. The geothermal system was designed to heat the greenhouses. Not the front sections.

She wanted to believe Adam. Believe in him again like she once had.

"And now he's mad at me because I saved his son."

That wasn't actually the case. She'd interfered and Adam had shown his possessive side. Again. Not being a parent, she didn't have anything to compare to Adam's emotions and choice of actions. She had to believe that if she was Titus's mother, she would want him to explore the world. She wouldn't want to stifle his natural curiosity.

But she was not Titus's parent or even a guardian. Not even the babysitter like Miss Milse.

Adam probably wasn't all that much out of line when he'd chastised her.

A cold chill swept across the room as the front door opened. "Hey, girlfriend!"

Joy looked up, almost pleased it wasn't Adam. "Sarah." She rose from the floor. "I didn't expect you so early."

"Are you kidding? I've already been to the wholesale craft store," she said, walking in with arms loaded with massive plastic bags.

"What is all this?"

"Snow. Well, polyurethane faux snow. I also have wood slatted and knotted walkways I've used at home shows and convention booths. We'll put the walkways down, make a path and then mound the snow around them. I found some old candy-cane poles that my mom used once at the church for a Christmas bazaar."

"You are amazing!"

Sarah beamed. "My head is spinning with all kinds of ideas. And once your stock arrives, we'll have a blast putting this together." She thrust the light but voluminous bags at Joy. "Here. You take these. I'll go to the car and get the walkways and candy canes."

Joy put the bags aside. "I'll come with you."

As Joy and Sarah unloaded the car, Adam drove up in his truck. He parked the truck, got out and helped carry the decorations inside.

He smiled warmly at Joy as he held the door for her and Sarah. He followed them in with a box filled with Christmas lights.

"You two have your work cut out for you," he said.

Joy put the bundles of wood slatted walkways down. She was surprised at his mood. Maybe he wasn't mad at her any longer. She liked him better when they joked around or bounced creative ideas off each other. Helpmates.

"You have the biggest task," Joy said, tilting her head to the rear of the store. "I need heat."

From outside they heard a rumble of a semitruck. Joy's eyes swung to the front window.

"Oh, my gosh! The first shipment of poinsettias is here!"

Adam didn't waste a second as he bolted toward the rear of the showroom. "I'm on it."

Joy watched as he jogged up to the breaker box he'd installed at the back of the smaller greenhouse. Through the door's glass she saw him smile at her. He threw the breaker.

She heard a hum. Then a thrum. She saw Adam thrust his arms in the air in victory. He rushed back to the showroom.

"It's on!"

Sarah clapped her hands to her mouth. "This is so exciting!"

Joy turned to Sarah. "I have to help unload those flowers. Do you mind getting this started?"

"I have the whole thing in my head." She tapped her temple. "Go!"

Joy and Adam rushed out the front door. Joy signed for the shipment. Adam directed the driver to the first greenhouse as Joy opened the door.

But it was when the driver parked the truck, opened the truck's back door and exposed the sea of poinsettias he was delivering that she felt chills of glee.

Adam stood beside her staring at the flowers. "Incredible."

The driver began handing flats to Adam and then to Joy. They filled roller carts and then wheeled them into the greenhouse.

With each cartload, Joy saw the greenhouse come to life. Table after table was filled. One all red. One pink. And two tables of white poinsettias.

After the driver left, Joy turned to Adam. "It's only two-thirds full and it's a dream come true already," she gushed. "I don't know how to thank you for—"

"Acting like an idiot. I'm sorry. I was outta line yesterday."

She stared at eyes filled with apology and sincerity. "It's okay."

"No, it's not," he said, stepping closer. "It's just that I—"

"Was scared?"

"Yeah. I saw Titus on that edge and I panicked. I should be thanking you, not jumping all over you."

She put her hand on his forearm. Like she'd done so many times in the past. And like she wanted to do now. Touching him felt so natural. She didn't know what he thought of that, but oddly, she needed to touch him. Feel his warmth beneath her fingertips.

For a long moment, he said nothing, but she'd seen that look in his blue eyes before, as if he was diving into her. That look that caused her to think of nothing in the world, not her career, her future, just this moment with the two of them.

"Joy…"

His lips brushed hers and she was stunned. She couldn't have stopped her arms going around his neck if she'd tried. She remembered every embrace they'd ever shared, the longing she'd felt after missing him during the day at school. The years melted away. She didn't think. She only felt as his lips pressed hesitantly against hers. Then captured her lips with an eagerness she'd never expected. He pulled her close.

She was losing all perspective. All logic, but she would be a fool to end this.

It was Adam who withdrew. "I think it's warming up in here quite nicely."

She opened her eyes to his gentle smile. That smile that had pried her heart open once before and was accomplishing the job again. "It is."

"I think the flowers will flourish."

She let go as he released her. "That's due to the genius who invented a new heating system for this old place."

"Oh? That what you call me?" He chuckled.

Sarah rushed into the room. "Guys! Come

look. There's, like, four delivery trucks out here and I don't know where it all goes!" she said excitedly as she raced back to the showroom.

Joy felt light-headed and not quite ready to slip back to reality. "I guess we better get back to work."

He tapped the end of her nose. "Guess we'd better."

SARAH CONTINUED CREATING a winter fantasy with the display shelves, the walkways, faux snow and lights under the polyurethane batting as Joy unboxed product.

When the second shipment of poinsettias arrived, it was enough to fill the remainder of the first greenhouse and all of the second. Joy was beginning to feel their efforts would bear fruit.

"All this is fantastic," Adam said, as Joy put a lit angel on the top of one of the Christmas trees.

Joy stood back and looked at the area. Sarah's design of "walking" the customers through a winter wonderland of live Christmas trees decorated with the ornaments she'd purchased from a wholesaler, glittering faux snow, lit garlands and shelves of cinnamon- and pine-scented candles, hand soap and diffusers, tree decorations, linens, cards, and on to the wall shelves filled with area honey, jams, coffee cakes, cookies and breads was enchanting. "It's a thousand times prettier than anything I've seen in New York."

"You're kidding," Sarah gasped. "I figured you'd think it hokey."

"No way. This is what it should be. And then they go out to the greenhouses. This really is Christmas."

Adam stuck a hammer in his tool belt. "I still have wreaths to hang outside," he said. "We have to double down on our advertising efforts. If we don't get the word out, we're sunk."

Sarah looked from Adam to Joy. She mouthed "We're?" to Joy. She smiled. "I agree."

"Good," he said and reached in his back pocket. He pulled out a folded flyer. "So, what do you think of this?" He opened up the flyer. Joy and Sarah looked down at the colorful photo of the old Boston Greenhouses at Christmas when Frank was alive.

"That's how it looked when we were kids." Joy smiled.

"Our senior year. Yeah," he said. "Do you like it?"

"I do," Sarah replied. "'Grand Reopening

for a Limited Time.' And these silver bells on the corners."

"I like it, too," Joy said, looking up at him.

Adam pocketed it. "Good, because I'm off to pick up five hundred of them to distribute around town. I also got an email from Mary-Catherine Cook at Saint Mark's that this ad will post in the Sunday bulletin," he said proudly.

"You must have been pretty sure I'd like it." Joy grinned.

His eyes fell on her face and she could feel the blush to her toes. "I was and I am."

Sarah looked from Joy to Adam, taking in their pensive gaze. "Okay. Well." She clapped her hands together. "My work is done here. I have to check on the kids. Get to the grocery."

Jolted out of her thoughts, Joy said, "Sure. Sure. I should get us some lunch," she said to Adam.

"Sounds good to me," he said.

Sarah picked up the empty bags, duct tape and scissors she'd brought. "I'll call you." She pointed at Joy. "Bye, Adam."

"Bye," he said.

As the door closed behind Sarah, Joy thought she heard a meow. "What was that?" Then another meow.

"Oh." Adam smiled. "That's Pye."

"Pie?"

Adam walked to the corner behind the counter. "Frank's cat."

"Grandpa had a cat?"

"She's feral, but there's been a recent development."

Joy went around the counter and saw a makeshift bed of blankets for a caramel Manx cat who had three kittens suckling her. "Oh, my gosh! Three little kittens!" Joy immediately sat down and picked up one of the newborn kittens, who instantly licked her face.

"Just like the nursery rhyme," Adam said.

"They're darling. How long have they been here?"

"She's been out in the potting shed with the space heaters. But once I got the heat going in here, I thought I should bring her in. That's where I was a minute ago."

Joy petted the cat. "How are you, Pie? What a funny name for a cat."

Adam harrumphed. "I can't believe you're saying that. You forgot your favorite Christmas movie? *Bell, Book and Candle*?"

"Jimmy Stewart. And the cat's name was Pyewacket."

"Right." Adam picked up a kitten. "So, why don't you go down to the deli and get us some sandwiches. And pick up a can of cat food for Pye?"

"Done." She smiled. "This is so lovely," she said, looking down at Pye.

"You don't have a pet in New York?"

"No. The building doesn't allow them."

"Oh. Too bad."

"You?"

He nodded. "Her name's Angel. Golden retriever. She's about to have pups. Christmas Eve, the vet says."

Joy dropped her jaw. "That's wonderful!"

"Titus thinks so. He's boning up on midwifery." He laughed and continued petting the kitten. "So, you and Chuck? Gonna have kids?"

"It hasn't come up."

"Really?" He put the kitten down. "I should think that would be a first things first."

"Yeah, well." She glanced around uncomfortably. "I better head out. I'm famished."

"Uh, yeah. Me, too." He scratched the back of his neck. "So, I'll get those flyers and meet you back here in half an hour. I want to hang those wreaths up. And the lights around the windows."

"Uh, sure." She walked away and grabbed her coat off the counter. She took her keys out of her purse. "Back soon," she said, hurrying out the door.

She hadn't realized how superficial her relationship with Chuck was. And it had taken only a few days in Indian Lake to see it.

CHAPTER FIFTEEN

JOY TAPPED HER finger on the counter as she waited for Chuck to pick up on the other end.

"Joy? That you? Are you at O'Hare?"

"No. That's why I'm calling. Chuck…" She drew in a breath. "I'm not going to be back for a while. Possibly not till Christmas Day."

"That's a month from now! Are you crazy? Missing Thanksgiving was bad enough. I'm dyin' here."

"Chuck, you can handle a lot more than you think."

"It's better when you're here."

"I'm sorry."

There was a long pause on his end before he said, "What's going on? Really?"

"I should have told you earlier this idea to reopen the greenhouse was percolating. Now it's a juggernaut. I made my decision yesterday. I have nearly a month of vacation days accrued, so I'm due the time off. Glory can help you. And Nathan Withers is not a problem."

"Forget Nathan. And everything else. You sound—different. Does any of this have to do with that engineer guy you told me about?"

"Adam?"

"Yeah."

"Not really." Skimming over the truth had more bite than she'd expected.

The second and even longer pause on Chuck's end told Joy more about herself than she'd faced since the day she first saw Adam. He had a great deal to do with her decision. She was feeling something, but her emotions were raveled with grief, anger and regret.

She was a mess.

"Joy, I have to ask. Are you having second thoughts about us?"

Joy paused, caught off guard by his question, but she owed him the truth. "I'm not sure."

"Really? I didn't expect that."

"I need time here to figure some things out. It's been difficult for me with Grandpa's death. The greenhouses… Please try to understand."

Silence.

"Chuck?"

"I don't like any of this. I'll give you time. However, I'm not the patient kind, which you know all too well."

"I do. And thank you." She started to ask him to come to Indian Lake to help her, but realized that besides the fact that he would refuse, it being year-end in the accounting business, she didn't want him in Indian Lake. Chuck was right. She was having second thoughts.

"Chuck, my life has become a jumble of emotions and I'm rethinking a lot. I've discovered I have a lot of friends here I'd forgotten."

"And they're more important than we are?"

"No. I don't know. But I need to figure it out. Please understand."

"I'm trying, Joy," he said. "Until you figure this out, maybe we should consider our engagement on hold."

"Maybe we should."

"Fine," he said, and the line went dead.

JOY STOOD IN line at the Indian Lake Deli. Every table in the place was filled.

"Hi, Joy." Olivia smiled. "What can I get you?"

"Turkey with guacamole for me. Reuben for Adam, and do you have a can of tuna for Pye?"

Olivia paused as she rang up the total. "Adam? Pye? What's going on?"

"Adam is helping me reopen the greenhouse. Pye is my grandfather's cat, I've just discovered."

"Seriously, we need some girl time. But as you can see, we're swamped, and you're obviously very busy."

Olivia handed Joy her change and Joy went to stand off to the side till her order was ready.

"Joy!" Mrs. Beabots shouted across the room and waved her over. She was sitting with Liz and Maddie. Joy walked over and hugged everyone.

"I thought you'd be back in New York by now," Liz said.

"Joy is reopening the greenhouses!" Mrs. Beabots said triumphantly.

"Really?" Liz and Maddie said in unison.

"I am."

"We need to spread the word. Advertise like crazy." Maddie beamed.

Mrs. Beabots smiled broadly. "This is so exciting. Tell us your plans."

"I wish I had time, but Adam and I are under the gun."

Liz looked at Maddie. "Adam?" They both scrutinized Joy.

"Uh-huh. He's full of ideas."

"I'll bet he is." Mrs. Beabots winked. "Now, listen, Joy. I understand you both have a lot of work to do, but you have to eat. Tomorrow is Thanksgiving. Come to my house. Be my guests."

"Great idea," Liz said. "You can work afterward."

"I won't take 'no' for an answer," Mrs. Beabots cajoled.

"I can't speak for Adam, but I'd love it. That's sweet of you."

"And tell Adam no excuses. He has nowhere else to go."

"He doesn't?" Joy was surprised.

"Why, no, dear. Frank was his only family these past years."

"Oh."

"I'm sure Frank's passing has been nearly as hard on him as it's been for you."

"It has. It…has…"

"Joy! Pickup!" Olivia shouted across the deli.

Joy raised her hand. "I gotta go. See you tomorrow and thanks for the invitation."

Joy thanked Olivia and waved to her friends as she rushed out the door.

JOY HURRIED INTO the greenhouse, noticing that Adam's truck was back.

"Adam! I'm back! I have lunch," she shouted,

not seeing him in the retail area. She took off her coat.

Adam walked through the French doors. "And I have another surprise for you," he said. He was carrying a large moss-filled basket.

"More kittens?"

"Better." He put the basket on the counter.

Joy looked in the basket and saw a salmon-and-yellow-striped hybrid poinsettia that her grandpa had been cultivating.

"Grandpa's poinsettia!"

"Know what I think? We should take it to the growers and see if they can produce them."

"But that would mean…"

"Yeah. A trip to talk to them. Follow-up calls. Possibly a future for…"

Joy didn't know where Adam's head was at. She was puzzled. "You know I'm going back to New York after I sell the greenhouses."

He didn't miss a beat. "It would mean a lot to Frank. This was his legacy. Well, the flowers and you. So, c'mon. What should we call it?"

"You mean…give it a name?"

"Yeah."

"It's timeless, isn't it? Almost magical."

"Eternal. Like Frank…"

"Frankincense!" She blurted the word naturally.

"That's it!"

Adam took the basket to the round display table in the middle of the room. Joy walked over to admire it with him. He put his arm around her shoulders.

"Frank's proud of you."

"You think?"

"I know."

Adam was looking at her with that suffused gleam in his eyes that caused her knees to weaken along with her resolve. She turned away from him and pointed at the counter.

"We should decorate the counter. Maybe put the prettiest flower next to the register."

"I agree," he said, grabbing her around the waist playfully and hoisting her onto the counter. "Yep. The prettiest."

As she looked at him, he had that dreamy look he got whenever he wanted to kiss her. "Adam, you need to know that my engagement is on hold."

"On hold? What does that mean?"

"That I'm confused. I spoke to Chuck earlier. We're giving each other space. Well, the truth is… I can't be engaged to him when I still—do have feelings for you."

"I see…" Adam reached up, cupped his

hand around her neck and gently pulled her closer. Joy's cell phone rang.

"Leave it," he said, skimming her lips with his.

The cell rang again. "It might be…" she started.

"New York." He released her. "Him. Apparently, his space didn't last long."

Joy looked at the caller ID and sighed with relief. When of course she shouldn't have felt there was need for relief. "It's Glory."

"Ah! Your roommate."

Joy slipped off the counter as Adam backed away, picked up empty cardboard product boxes and took them out back.

"Glory. How's everything?"

"Not spectacular," Glory groaned. "Chuck just told me you're not coming back till Christmas, which of course I knew, but I didn't let on."

"True. So, tell me, how's he taking it?"

"The usual when you're not around. Unhinged."

"Poor Chuck," Joy commiserated. "But there's more to it than that. Our engagement is on hold."

"Girl—" Glory sighed "—what is going on?"

"Just about everything in my life is in turmoil. I feel like I'm bouncing on air and yet grounded for the first time in a long time. But I'm not sure if the feeling will last."

"That *is* a bomb," Glory gushed.

"I know," Joy said, looking up as Adam came through the doors with one of the kittens.

"Joy," he said. "Give us a pet." He held up the kitten to Joy's smiling face.

"Who, may I ask, is that?"

"My new best friend." Joy petted the kitten, and Adam took their closeness as an excuse to kiss her ear.

"Sounds like it. No wonder you're not coming back," Glory grumbled.

"Glory, my intention is to come back. I'll figure it all out, but for now, I have to do this."

"Gotcha," Glory said. "Call me later. After your new *friend* leaves."

"I will." Joy hung up and continued petting the kitten. Adam touched the kitten, and when he did, their fingers met. He encircled her fingers with his.

"Nice," he said in a low voice.

She couldn't take her eyes from him if she tried. He'd suggested they take Frank's hybrid to a producer. And if that producer could recreate Frank's discovery, they truly would create an everlasting legacy for Frank. It would be a miracle that would erase the fact that her grandpa had died a failure.

Joy didn't want that.

She wanted everyone in Indian Lake to remember Frank not only with fondness, but reverence. She wanted the Boston name to mean something. This was her inheritance.

She felt it was not only her duty, but her privilege to dust off their dreams—as impossible as the task would seem to someone like Chuck.

"I'll get a poinsettia for the counter," Adam said. "The biggest and the best."

"And I know just who'll buy it," Joy replied.

"Yeah?"

"Mrs. Beabots," she answered.

"Not Katia McCreary? Gina Barzonni? Liz? Maddie? You've been away too long."

This time when she looked at him, she didn't feel guilty. She didn't feel sad. She felt rejuvenated and hopeful. "That I have."

CHAPTER SIXTEEN

"ARE YOU SURE we have time for this today?" Joy asked Adam as he drove them out of town. "I mean, there's still so much to do to get the rest of the quilts up on the rack. The stockings aren't hung. And the order for the cut flowers—"

"Didn't come in yet and won't until Friday morning. I took a call a bit ago."

"Oh," she said, looking down at Frank's hybrid in the moss basket.

"You're nervous," he said, glancing at her in bewilderment.

"Yeah." She inhaled deeply.

"But you were always the courageous one. Couldn't wait to tackle the world. New York, no less."

"You know the real reason I left. The accident."

"I do. But you have to admit, not everyone takes off to tackle New York City."

"I guess I did seem fearless back then."

"You still are. I'd go nuts living in a city

that never sleeps. I need peace and calm. And no rush hour."

"Yeah. Don't have that in Indian Lake at all." She forced a smile, but it faded quickly. Looking at the apricot-striped poinsettia, Frank's last contribution to the world, should have filled her with excitement. Even hope. But it didn't. It was another chance for her to fail.

As if reading her thoughts, Adam said, "Look. The worst that happens is they say no."

Her heart thudded in her chest, the weight of her guilt too much for it. "That's just it! I don't want to disappoint Grandpa," she said, feeling a rush of emotions. She held up her palm. "And don't say it. I know. I already did."

"When?"

"Every year I didn't come back."

"I was wrong, okay? Being so rough on you. I see now you had a lot going on."

"Not that much." She turned her face toward the window so that Adam couldn't see her tears.

They pulled up to All Seasons Organic Growers Farm. Adam parked the truck. The place was busy, with workers loading poinsettias onto trucks. She saw wooden trays with

Norwegian pine trees, flats of white carnations, white lilies, white roses, and boxes of spruce and pine for garland making.

Joy's heart leaped at the traditional Christmas florals. How she'd loved working with her mother filling baskets and vases with Christmas flowers and pines.

There's so much to remember. So much I've forgotten.

A middle-aged woman with flaming red hair came up to them. She was wearing a dress, sheepskin denim jacket and cowboy boots. "Joy Boston? Is that you?"

"Daryl! How wonderful to see you!" She hugged her old friend.

"When Adam called me and told me about Frank, I couldn't believe it. I'm sorry we missed the wake." Daryl's green eyes, suffused with sincerity, began to well.

"It's okay." Joy put her arm around her. "I believe he feels your thoughts even now."

"Thank you for saying that." Daryl dabbed her eyes with the edge of her sleeve. She sniffled and said, "Adam says you have a surprise for me." Daryl looked over Joy's shoulder as Adam withdrew the moss basket from the truck.

As Adam joined them, Joy said to Daryl,

"This is the Frankincense Poinsettia. Grandpa's…"

"Gift to the world," Adam finished proudly, holding it up.

Joy caught Adam's anticipation. This was one of the moments in life that should be savored. She'd never asked anyone for a favor for her grandpa. Frank had been capable and self-reliant. And he worked with nature's most glorious productions—flowers. Today she knew better. Frank was just a man, doing what he loved for those that he loved.

There was not a better life to have lived.

More than ever, she wanted this poinsettia, this Frankincense, to live on. "What do you think, Daryl? Do you think you can grow it?"

"It's fantastic. Such an unusual tangerine color. And this yellow. It's got more depth than most salmon poinsettias I've seen."

Adam reached inside his jacket for a notebook. "These are all of Frank's notes and research that I could find. I believe it's detailed enough to create new plants. I know they'll help."

"Tell you what," Daryl said. "I'll read these notes over and then call you. I don't want to promise something I may not be able to deliver."

"That's wise," Adam said.

"I couldn't ask for more," Joy said. "It would mean so much if this works out."

"I know, honey. And I'll do my utmost to make it happen." Daryl held up the flower and turned it in her hands. "There's something quite magical about it. Tropical, summer and autumn mixed, and yet people will buy it at Christmas. This tangerine blends well with reds and pink and warms up an arrangement rather than clashing with traditional Christmas colors." She beamed at Joy and Adam. "I'll see if I can make it work."

Careful not to damage the poinsettia, Joy hugged Daryl. "Thank you so much."

"He was a special man, Joy. Loved by so many."

"He was, wasn't he?" Joy replied, as Adam took her hand and squeezed it.

Joy squeezed his hand back. Such a small gesture of support.

Support.

When was the last time she'd felt any kind of support from a man?

"We gotta go, Joy. Get back to work," Adam said.

"Sure."

Back outside, Joy observed all the activity around her. She watched as a worker closed the roll-down door on a truck filled with dark burgundy poinsettias, corals and yellows. Another florist van had been stuffed with paper whites, amaryllis, tulips and chrysanthemums. A woman with an armload of seeded eucalyptus, blue spruce, cedar sprigs with their blue-green berries and mounds of vibrant green holly walked over to a florist's van.

A young man, his arms sticking straight out, walked with green pine wreaths stacked from his wrists to his shoulders and whistled a happy tune as he carried the wreaths over to yet another van.

The bustling scene with its colors and fragrances and sounds brought back flashes of her childhood and teen years with her parents and grandpa. Only this time, her tears were happy ones. She'd led a fortunate life up until her parents' deaths. But they had loved and nurtured her. There *had* been happy days. Days of shared interests. Her mother guiding her, teaching her about flowers. Trees. New hybrids. Living things making happiness for so many. She had so much to be thankful for.

As Adam backed the truck up, honked the horn and they waved to Daryl, Joy's smile spread across her face.

What was wrong with a life like this that brought smiles and uplifted spirits to others?

Nothing.

Absolutely nothing.

THANKSGIVING MORNING, Joy woke early, dressed in jeans and one of her grandpa's old sweatshirts that still smelled of his spicy, woodsy cologne.

Joy clipped her long blond hair up and whisked on a bit of blush, eye shadow and lip gloss before shoving her feet into her work boots and dashing out the kitchen door.

The predawn hour was dark, and as Joy turned on the greenhouse lights, she gasped at the garlands, wreaths, trees and twinkling white lights under the polyurethane "snow."

"It's positively enchanting!"

She stood still for a long moment, tilted her head and realized it was just as warm in here as it was at her grandpa's house. "Toasty warm." She smiled as she went to the counter.

Tomorrow they would be open for business. Sarah, Maddie and Liz had all volunteered to help with sales and stocking shelves when they could, but they'd all be cooking and baking for Thanksgiving dinner today.

Joy had promised Mrs. Beabots she'd bring her special candied yams, which she'd prepared the night before and would put in the oven around noon before going to Mrs. Beabots's house at two o'clock.

The old greenhouses' phone number had been reconnected. She'd opened a commercial bank account and picked up change for the float. The counter area was just about ready.

She'd set up an old shelving unit behind the counter and stocked it with ribbons, gift cards, bolts of snowflake-embossed cellophane, scissors, glue guns, glue sticks, copy paper, toner, pens and pencils. The old register still worked for cash, and Joy had set up a point-of-sale app on her tablet, along with a dongle that would take credit card sales. She'd still write up each sale on a carbon receipt pad just like she'd done all those years ago.

Maddie had brought over a countertop bakery display case that she'd filled with gourmet cupcakes. Next to it was a second glass case with three shelves for cookies that Mrs. Beabots baked for Joy to give free to visiting children.

"And some moms and dads, too." Joy smiled.

She'd found an unopened box of receipt pads, letterhead and envelopes, invoices and business cards that Frank must have had printed prior to closing. It was all she needed to look professional.

"Thanks, Grandpa," she said, putting the business cards in the stocking-shaped card holder he used to use. Her fingers traced the red-and-white-striped colors of the stocking.

"These insignificant reminders…" She touched her heart, feeling as if it swelled in her chest. With each box of candles, soap or ornaments she opened, she felt her grandpa's presence.

She wiped away a tear. Then the pads of her fingers slid to her lips as she remembered Adam's kiss.

That kiss was real and from the present, not only bringing back the past but making her rethink every decision she'd made. Like moving away.

She hadn't left town. She'd raced out of town.

Secretly, she'd packed her suitcases months before high school graduation and put them under her bed. Fortunately, she was going to be a freshman at Columbia and had signed up for early orientation and induction. She wanted to join a sorority in part to leave Indian Lake sooner.

Grandpa had put her on the Amtrak to New York and even now she remembered how tight his hug was. They hadn't shared deep sorrows or emotions since Bruce's and Jill's deaths, but Joy believed her grandpa had known she was running away.

She'd told herself the past was the past. She was running toward her future.

"But now…"

Now she remembered Adam's kiss and the way she felt his heartbeat through his chest. She felt a rush of caring that gave her chills.

"This is insane." She checked herself, hoping to shake off the goose bumps and erase the kiss. But it had happened.

His kisses now were filled with even more passion. At first, she'd thought his kiss was reactionary. Perhaps he was recalling the past and wanting to see if he could go back there. Maybe his kiss was an exploratory expedition—conducted like research. What she knew was that Adam's kisses past and present had the ability to keep her spellbound.

She swiped her face with her palms. "I can't let myself get pulled back here. Back to Adam." She'd told him she and Chuck were on hold. She was more than confused; she was conflicted. She'd worked diligently to build a career and life in New York. And she loved her life there.

Adam was a study in contrasts. One day

he was romantic and close and the next his barriers were back up and he kept his son and himself walled up. He was waiting for her to bolt again.

And she knew she could easily choose to go back to New York.

The fact was that since she'd left, she'd considered Indian Lake to be a town of enemies. People who didn't care for her or her family. Those opinions were twisted through her own guilts. Unraveling the past in the present was giving her an entirely new perspective.

She walked over to the grove of trees she and Sarah had decorated with the theme-oriented ornaments she'd bought from the supplier at the Merchandise Mart in Chicago. She reached out and touched a limb of the flocked white tree, decorated with white owls, reindeer, straw raccoons, squirrels, rabbits and white birds. White iridescent snowflakes and white glass pinecones sparkled against the crystal tree lights.

The next tree was lit with pink lights, pink angels, fairies, Victorian dolls, silk carousel horses from India and enormous pink glass balls.

The gold tree glittered with gold crosses, gold brocaded angels, pairs of golden angel wings, gold braided beads and twisted glass icicles.

The next tree was lit with blue lights, blue silk and white lace-edged hearts, blue birds, natural pinecones, crystal snowflakes and icicles and streams of silver-backed blue velvet ribbon. A blue star beamed from the top of the tree.

Joy's favorite was the red-and-green lit tree filled with red-and-white-striped candy canes, round peppermint candy ornaments, red and green glass balls, and red and green whimsical elves who danced, wore chef's hats, stood on little ladders or romped on sleds.

Around the base of each tree, Joy had placed a double ring of poinsettias. Pink flowers for the pink tree. Reds dusted with gold glitter for the gold tree, red and green flowers for "elf" tree, white for the woodland tree, white with blue glitter for the blue tree.

"Sarah designed these. She helped me order all these ornaments." She glanced back at the counter to the cupcakes and cookies. "And Maddie and Mrs. Beabots."

At the end of the room was a small wine cooler filled with wines that Liz and Gabe had brought. Next to that was a display case with gift certificates for the Book Shop and Java Stop, all donated by Isabelle and Scott

Abbott to give as raffle gifts each week to a lucky patron. Olivia had followed suit and donated a dozen gift cards to the deli for Joy to use at her discretion.

Granted, each owner benefited from the advertisement, but the gift cards were purely from the heart.

"My friends."

They were the people who had been her friends years ago. They had hugged her during and after the days of her parents' deaths. She, Sarah and Maddie had gone to the movies together. Had sleepovers at Sarah's house. They'd all spend lots of hours on Mrs. Beabots's front porch, helped her in the gardens or kitchen.

"I forgot how close we'd all been."

As she looked around at what her friends had done for her, she realized that she'd been the one to leave them. For too long she'd lumped her real friends into the twisted emotional ball she'd invented. She'd wanted to leave Indian Lake because she couldn't face her grief. She'd discarded love and friendship and told herself she wanted a new adventure. A new life. A fresh start.

She was young, she'd thought. She had her life ahead of her and she was going to make something of herself. She wouldn't be stuck in a small town with a small life. She wanted to see the world.

And she did.

The pulse of Manhattan had been beating in her veins for a decade and she hummed to it. She was accomplished. Even Glory said it. She was an integral cog at Newly and Associates. Chuck depended on her a great deal.

Perhaps their time apart was good for them both. Chuck should learn not to lean on her so much.

And she—

Needed to sort out her feelings for Adam. Indian Lake. And Chuck. If she really loved Chuck, she'd discover the truth now.

This decision to reopen the greenhouses had been hers, and from his perspective, it was a gamble. A shot in the dark.

She had to ask herself why she was taking it. Yes, she wanted to make her grandpa proud of her. She wanted his name and that of the Boston Greenhouses to last and be remembered. Whether the new buyer would see her vision, feel Frank's passion for this business, was yet to be seen.

As for Joy, the nagging voice inside told her that she was doing this for personal reasons. She felt regretful for leaving good friends all those years ago.

Of all the people she'd left behind, Joy realized the one she'd hurt the most was... "Adam."

CHAPTER SEVENTEEN

FAT SNOWFLAKES DRIFTED as Joy held the warm dish of candied yams smothered in marshmallows and pecan topping with oven mitts at Mrs. Beabots's front door, expecting to be greeted by her hostess.

"Hi!" Titus said, reaching for her arm. "I couldn't wait till you got here."

Taken aback, she stared at him. "Is that right?"

"Yeah! Dad said now the party can start!" He beamed. "Hurry in. It's cold out there."

Joy walked inside as Titus quickly closed the door. "Dad said I have to be careful with this door. It's really old."

"You're not careful with all doors?" she asked, following him down the hallway to the kitchen.

"Not really. I have a tendency to slam doors. Probably because I'm short."

Joy was glad Titus was in front of her and didn't see her smile at his response. She didn't think of Titus as short. She thought of him as a full-grown adult intellect stuck in a kid's body.

"Here she is!" Titus announced, as if he was the MC at a wrestling match. He even thrust his arm out toward her as she moved into the kitchen.

"Hi," she said, looking at Mrs. Beabots, who lifted a chef's knife and, in one smack, chopped off the stalk of a huge broccoli crown.

"Hello, dear," Mrs. Beabots said and waved the knife at Adam, who was sipping something from a massive mug and who eyed Joy over the rim. "Adam, take her coat, please."

"Sure." He placed the mug on the granite counter. He wore black jeans, black cowboy boots, a blue shirt under his navy cable-knit sweater, the sleeves of which were shoved up to his elbows, revealing his muscular forearms.

Arms that reminded her of the hard labor it had taken for him to install the geothermal heating system for Frank's greenhouses.

His blue eyes flashed and she got the distinct impression he was thinking about their kiss in the greenhouse, as well.

Joy cleared her throat and asked, "Where should I put this?"

"Right there is fine," Mrs. Beabots replied. "Do we need to put it in the oven?"

"Maybe on low. Two fifty?" Joy placed the casserole on the counter as Titus scrambled up on the stool near her.

"What is it?" Titus asked, trying to lift the aluminum foil.

"Candied yams."

Titus grimaced and made a contorted face. "Yams?"

Adam chuckled as he stood behind Joy, taking his time holding her coat, leaning his cheek close to hers and whispering in her ear, "Don't take offense. He's never had yams."

Joy couldn't help the shiver that scampered down her spine as she inhaled Adam's woodsy soap scent. She opened her mouth but she couldn't put two thoughts together in her brain. The only thing in her mind was how tender his lips had felt against hers.

He moved away and she felt an odd sense of loss.

Titus was still investigating the yams. "Looks like marshmallows to me."

"It is," Joy said, thankful for the opportunity to wrest her attention from Adam. "Pecans, brown sugar and my secret ingredient."

"Secret?" Titus's eyes looked enormous behind his glasses.

"Uh-huh. Brandy." She grinned.

"Brandy?" Adam asked. "Is that what your mom used?"

"Yup."

Mrs. Beabots smiled as she poured a bag of cranberries into a saucepan, adding water and sugar. "I gave Jill that recipe."

"You did?" Joy and Adam chorused.

"Will I get drunk?" Titus giggled.

"No, the alcohol bakes off," Joy said, walking past Adam to take an apron from the hook by the back door. She noticed he didn't move out of the way, so that she'd brush his arm as she passed. She took the apron and put it on. "Now, what can I do?"

"The turkey is huge!" Titus exclaimed. "Dad had to put it in the oven."

Mrs. Beabots smiled at Titus. "I always make sure I have a man around to do the heavy turkey lifting."

"Is that right?" Adam asked, picking up his mug again. "So, since this is our first Thanksgiving here, who's been the man of the house till today?"

"Luke usually. Before that, Austin Mc-Creary. His father died when you kids were in school. Remember?"

Joy paused. "I'd forgotten. Poor Austin."

Titus whirled around on the stool and

pushed his glasses to the bridge of his nose. "Mr. Austin's not poor. He's very rich."

"How do you know that?" Adam asked.

"Timmy. He tells me everything." Titus reached for a wooden spoon.

Adam grabbed the wooden spoon and put it back on the counter. "Leave cooking utensils alone."

"But you let me help at home."

"This isn't our house," Adam warned.

Mrs. Beabots handed Joy a stick of butter. "Melt this in the microwave, would you, dear? Pyrex dishes are over there." She pointed to an end cabinet, then turned back to Titus. "I always appreciate help in the kitchen, Titus. Why don't you take those silver saltshakers out to the table for me?"

"Sure, I can." Titus scrambled down, the stool tilting ever so slightly as he did.

"Be careful," Adam said, thrusting his hand out to hold the stool.

"I'm fine, Dad." Titus whisked the shakers off the counter and marched into the dining room. They heard the pocket doors slide open.

Mrs. Beabots's eyes shot to Adam. "I forgot I had the doors closed."

Adam started for the kitchen door and rushed to the hall.

From the hallway they heard, "Wow! This is awesome!"

Joy lowered her voice and asked, "What's wrong with the doors being closed?"

"Sometimes they stick and Titus got his fingers pinched in them a couple years ago. That kid can scream, I'll tell you." She laughed.

"But all kids get scrapes and bruises from time to time. It's part of growing up."

"Not like Adam's kid." Mrs. Beabots shook her head.

"But he's so…smart. So amazing. I'd kill for a child like Titus."

Mrs. Beabots's clear blue eyes scanned Joy's face. "You would, huh?"

Titus raced into the kitchen with Adam directly behind him. "What else can I do?"

"Butter sticks for the table. Joy, use those butter plates I put out there. Then, Adam, when you come back, you can mash the potatoes for me. Joy, the butter, cream and sour cream are in the fridge."

"Got it," Joy replied, taking an antique wooden-handled masher out of a blue-and-white china urn on the counter filled with spoons, spatulas and whisks. She held it out to Adam.

"Hand mashed? No electric mixer?"

"Aw, c'mon, Adam," Joy joked. "Put those muscles of yours to work."

He looked at Mrs. Beabots. "I suppose this was another of Luke's jobs."

"You got it."

"So, what's he doing today? Seems he's getting off easy," Adam said, as Joy stood next to him adding butter and cream to the boiled potatoes.

"He and Sarah were up till midnight making pies for the party later today."

Adam stopped midmash.

Joy let the dollop of sour cream drop from the spoon.

"What party?" they asked in unison.

Mrs. Beabots's eyes were curiously merry. "Didn't I tell you? The dinner is the warm-up. Sarah, Luke and the kids will be here in about fifteen minutes for our dinner, of course. But the real celebration is tonight for my annual Thanksgiving dessert party."

"Who's coming?" Joy asked.

"Why, Joy. All your friends."

Joy froze. Friends. If she was in New York that would be Glory—and Chuck, of course. There was Glory's "tribe" she hung with, but Joy didn't think of them as the kind of friends who would drop their work and life to come help her put up Christmas trees in a greenhouse. Or bake cookies or cupcakes for her store. Or give her free gift certificates for customers. Or a stocked wine refrigerator. "How many would that be?"

"Goodness," Mrs. Beabots said, checking the broccoli in the steamer. "I hadn't stopped to count. The crowd gets bigger every year. New marriages. New babies."

"Yeah," Titus said, reaching for a crescent roll in the bread basket on the counter. "Even Jules is flying in from Paris."

"Jules?"

"Mica Barzonni's son," Adam said, shaking his head at Titus, who was about to take a bite of roll. "Not till dinner, Titus."

"Mica is married? To whom?" Joy asked.

"Grace Railton," Mrs. Beabots said, handing Adam a pair of oven mitts. "Let's check the turkey. Take the aluminum foil off and baste it for me, would you?"

"Happy to."

"Do you remember Louise Railton, Joy? She owns The Louise House. Her niece, Grace, used to visit in the summers from Chicago and helped Louise at the ice cream shop. Best pumpkin ice cream in town, by the way."

"The pretty blonde girl who won Miss Teen Illinois or something? I remember she went to the Barzonni pool parties they used to have back then."

"That's right. Anyway, she married Mica and they live in Paris now. He's an engineer. She's a fashion designer." Mrs. Beabots winked. "I may have had a bit to do with her getting a job in Paris."

"You did?" Joy and Adam chorused.

Titus grinned. "I bet you can do just about anything, huh, Mrs. Beabots."

"Just about, Titus."

The tinny doorbell rang.

"I'll get it!" Titus scrambled off the stool, just as Adam placed the turkey on top of the stove.

"Slow down, Titus."

"It's Timmy and Annie!" Titus shouted from the foyer. "Hi, guys!"

Joy looked at Adam. "He's a ball of fire, isn't he? Does he ever slow down?"

"No. Not even when he sleeps." He lifted the aluminum foil off the turkey as she handed him the baster. "When he was younger he sleepwalked. I've gotta keep the doors locked from the inside so he can't get out."

"That's wise," she said, taking a whiff of the turkey, stuffed with apples, oranges and onions. "This smells so good."

"Hungry?" he asked, putting the turkey back in the oven.

"Almost as much as Titus." She laughed.

Sarah and Luke walked into the kitchen. Mrs. Beabots hugged both her guests and then went to the hall to hug the children.

Luke pointed at Adam taking off the oven mitts. "Sarah, I've been replaced!"

"I'll let you carve," Adam replied with a smile, walking around the island and to shake Luke's hand.

Joy hugged Sarah. "I can't thank you enough for all you did to bring the showroom to life. It's beyond beautiful."

She turned to Luke. "And thank you for getting those trees for us. That walkway feels like a real winter wonderland. Live trees made the difference."

Adam picked up a corkscrew and opened a bottle of white wine. "That was really thoughtful, man."

"You're welcome. I didn't live here back when you all were in high school, but I've been in Indian Lake long enough to remember going to the greenhouses the day after Thanksgiving when the kids were very young. We couldn't afford much back then, but every year we got an ornament for Annie and Timmy to put on our tree. Jenny always said her best ideas came from the Boston Greenhouses."

Joy watched as Luke's sad eyes went to Sarah. She'd told Joy that Luke had been a widower when he met Sarah. He'd been filled with grief and loneliness back then. Thanksgiving and Christmas brought back all kinds of memories for people. The happy ones, and the sad ones, too. She watched as Sarah mouthed "I love you" to Luke. He mouthed the same back to her.

Joy glanced at Adam, whose blue eyes were focused on her.

How many times in the past had he mouthed the same thing to her? How many times had she reciprocated? It was the most natural thing in the world to her.

"Glass of wine, Luke?" Adam broke the moment.

"Sure. I'll get the glasses."

Mrs. Beabots hustled the children into the kitchen, holding little Charlotte by the hand. "The children said they're starving."

"Me, too," Luke said.

"Okay." Joy went to the stove. "I'll get the broccoli. Sarah, you take the rolls. Luke is in charge of the turkey, and, Adam, you have more mashing to do before these are creamy enough to serve."

"And who made you the general around here?" Adam asked.

"I did." She smiled. "It's time that Mrs. Beabots sit at the table, have some wine and rest. We need to take over."

"I'll second that!" Adam said, taking up the masher.

"Joy, you are a blessing," Mrs. Beabots said. "Come on, children."

"I made the turkey place cards," Timmy said proudly.

Annie smoothed the skirt of her new bronze taffeta dress. "And I helped Mom make the centerpiece. It has carnations and chrysanthemums and pheasant feathers."

Joy put the cranberries in a footed Haviland china dish and poured the gravy into a silver gravy boat.

Joy helped Adam put the mashed potatoes in a covered dish with white-and-gold edges. They carried the dishes to the table.

Adam lit the candles as they all took their places. Luke poured wine.

They held hands and bent their heads as Mrs. Beabots said a Thanksgiving prayer. "Life is about friends and family and the love we share. Bless you all for being with me today to give thanks for everything we have, especially each other."

"Amen!" Titus shouted.

Charlotte clapped her hands and Timmy raised his water glass.

"Dad," Annie said, "can we have a toast?"

"Sure," Luke replied. "Good health and success to you, Joy, with your grand reopening. We're all here to help in any way we can."

"Thank you," Joy replied, as they all clinked crystal glasses and sipped. "You've done so much already."

Adam stood next to Luke as they both worked to carve the huge turkey. Adam passed the plates. "There's a long way to go. Don't stand on ceremony to ask your friends for help."

Joy worried her bottom lip. "I know I shouldn't, but frankly, I don't know what to expect."

"In what way?" Adam asked as he piled mashed potatoes on Titus's plate.

Joy noticed her place card positioned her between Adam and Titus—as if she was part of the family. She wondered if that was one of Mrs. Beabots's subtle "matchmaking" efforts. Smiling to herself, she said, "I know I have the radio ads starting this morning. And I took out a half-page ad in the newspaper, but that's not enough."

"I've distributed those flyers all over

town," Adam said. "They'll bring in a lot of people."

"Adam," Joy said, cutting Titus's white meat reflexively as if she'd been doing it all her life. She put cranberries on his plate, and as the rolls were passed, she gave him one. "You have hundreds left. I bet you didn't put out more than thirty."

"Thirty-six," Titus finished and shoved a roll in his mouth.

"You're right," Adam said, sitting down and putting his napkin in his lap. "We have to do something…dramatic. Get everyone's attention."

"And just how do you propose to do that? The grand reopening is tomorrow morning," Joy moaned.

Titus finished chomping on his roll, put the rest on his plate, wiped his hands on his napkin and said, "That's easy. We go house to house."

"Like politicians?" Adam joked.

"No." Titus looked at Annie. She winked back.

Timmy nodded at Titus, giving him the go-ahead signal.

"Dad," Titus began. "Me and Timmy and Annie—"

"Me, too," Charlotte interrupted, raising

her spoon over her head and dropping potatoes onto the table in the process. "Oops."

Sarah leaned over and scooped them up and put them back on Charlotte's plate. "Okay, what's going on here? All four of you—out with it," she demanded.

Titus put his hands on the table. "We've been wanting to have a caroling party. You know, singing from house to house."

"I know what that is," Adam replied, his eyes sliding to Joy.

Joy caught the excitement in the children's faces. The little stinkers had been talking and planning this for some time, she could tell. Sarah had told her that Annie would use any excuse to sing. School plays, church choir. Solos at church weddings. She'd burst into song walking home from school. And she was very, very good. "And you want to do this…"

"How about tonight?" Titus burst out. "It's perfect, Dad. Thanksgiving night starts the Christmas season. We can go to all the houses up and down Maple Boulevard. We sing and give the owners a flyer for the greenhouses."

Adam pursed his lips. "It's not a bad idea."

Joy felt like a child herself, as she caught their enthusiasm. "Why didn't I think of this?"

Titus shrugged his shoulders. "I dunno."

Annie smiled at Titus. "It was Titus's idea. He thought of it 'cause you and Mr. Adam were talking about advertising."

"Actually, Dad," Titus said. "Isn't this the personal touch you talked about?"

"When did I say that?"

"Uh, maybe I saw it on the web."

"You were on my computer?"

Titus slid down in his chair. "Maybe."

Joy laughed. "Oh, don't be mad at him, Adam. He wanted to help and took initiative. You all just said I should ask for help from my friends. Well, I am. This caroling party is just what I need."

"Okay," Adam said, sipping his wine. "Indian Lake is like no other place I've been or know about. The people here are a real community. They help each other like it's a life mission. You say all our friends will be here tonight, Mrs. Beabots?"

"Yes. All the Barzonni clan, wives and kids. Austin and Katia. Cate, Trent and Danny. Jack and Sophie Carter. Rand and Beatrice Nelson from the youth camp and their two boys will be here." She tapped her cheek with her manicured finger. "Oh, and I've invited all of Rand's family. All the Hawks family. Isabelle and Scott will bring Bella and Michael, and you do know that Violet is engaged to the famous Formula One race car driver Josh Stevens."

"Former racer," Adam corrected. "He's retired now, but he does a lot of commercials."

"Commercials?" Joy tilted her head a bit. It wouldn't be right to ask a stranger, and a famous one at that, to help her advertise the greenhouses. Would it?

Mrs. Beabots continued, "Connie Hawks's sons are so handsome and accomplished. I saw her at Jack Carter's insurance agency the other day and she said Dylan was moving back to Indian Lake from Chicago."

"No kidding?" Sarah asked, as she buttered a roll for Charlotte. "Isabelle said he liked the city."

Joy peered at Mrs. Beabots. "So, this is how you stay on top of all the local, er, doings? You have gargantuan parties and then work the crowd?"

Mrs. Beabots lowered her eyes coyly. "It's worked for fifty years. They all bring desserts and Gabe brought two cases of wine. I have plenty of cocoa for the kids. And this house is so huge, we spill from the library to the front parlor to this dining room and the kitchen."

Joy noticed there were tears in Mrs. Beabots's eyes. In all her life, she'd never seen the woman cry. But tonight was different. It was Thanksgiving and the house was filled with love.

"Thank you all," Joy replied, as chills of humility and the warmth of kindness enveloped her. "I didn't expect to enjoy Thanksgiving this much without my grandpa. But this…has been lovely. I don't know what to say…"

Adam reached over, took her hand, squeezed it under the table and said, "You already did."

Then he leaned over and kissed her cheek.

Joy blushed so hot she knew her face was crimson. Her eyes tracked across the table to Sarah, whose smile grew wider.

"Happy Thanksgiving, Joy," Sarah said as she lifted her wineglass. Luke leaned over and kissed Sarah's cheek.

Joy turned, and facing Adam, she said, "That was lovely."

"I thought so, too."

CHAPTER EIGHTEEN

MRS. BEABOTS WAS RIGHT, Joy thought as she helped to welcome the stream of guests to the enormous Victorian house on Thanksgiving evening. The fact that the snow had not abated didn't stop a single guest. This gathering was a tradition for Mrs. Beabots, and her friends didn't disappoint.

Joy and Adam had cleaned up the dinner dishes, Sarah had put away the leftover food, and the kids had taken the linens to the laundry room and then scrambled to the library to practice Christmas carols. Luke brought in wood and stoked the fires in the library and front parlor.

Joy had planned to return to the greenhouses and put out more inventory, but there was no way she was going to miss this party or Titus's advertising campaign.

Maddie and Nate Barzonni were the first guests to arrive. Maddie brought three boxes of red-and-green-frosted cupcakes. They were followed by Gina Barzonni Crenshaw and

Sam Crenshaw. Gina brought a tray of Italian cannoli. Olivia and Rafe Barzonni were next and arrived with Grace and Mica Barzonni and their toddler son, Jules, newly arrived from Paris.

"I'm so happy to see you, Grace. I don't know if you remember me…" Joy said, but a radiant smile filled Grace's face, and she pulled Joy into a hug.

"Of course I do, and Maddie and Olivia told me about your grandfather's passing. I'm so very sorry for your loss. I remember him from my summers here." Grace leaned forward. "He loved peppermint ice cream. I had to make it special for him in the summer."

"He did!" Joy exclaimed. "I can't believe you remember that."

"He was special, Joy. You were fortunate to have him as your grandfather."

Mica shook Joy's hand. "We were all sorry to hear about Frank, Joy. Mother called us in Paris when she heard the news."

"Thank you, Mica," Joy said, as she released his hand. It was then she remembered that Mica had suffered an injury on the farm and had lost the use of his left arm. However, he was an engineer and worked in Paris now. "How long are you and Grace going to be in town?"

"Until the New Year," he said.

"Adam Masterson is here and I thought, well, you being engineers…"

"We go way back," Mica said. "But truthfully, Joy, I design farm equipment for disabled folks like me. Adam, well, he's out of my league."

"He is?" Joy looked at Mica askance. She was about to continue when three-year-old Jules interrupted.

"Mama." Jules tugged on Grace's arm.

Grace hoisted him up. "Joy, this is our son, Jules."

Jules thrust his hand at Joy. *"Bonsoir."*

"English," Grace said.

Jules grinned. "Happy Thanksgiving!"

"What a gentleman you are, Jules. And so handsomely dressed." He wore a navy-blue wool coat, white shirt, red-and-white-striped bow tie and navy slacks.

"Merci. Mama made it. She makes clothes."

"I heard that." Joy smiled.

"So," Mica said, "Adam is here?"

"In the kitchen, I think. And, Jules, the children are in the library practicing Christmas carols." She looked at Grace. "We're planning a caroling party after dessert. If you're up for a walk down Maple Boulevard in the cold."

"Bien!" Jules scrambled down out of Grace's arms and took off toward the library.

Joy watched him leave. "He knows his way around."

"Uh, yeah. He does have a way of making himself at home wherever he goes." Mica chuckled.

The doorbell rang.

"Please excuse me," Joy said as she moved away. "I'll see you in a bit."

When Joy opened the door, there were over a dozen people on the steps. Isabelle Hawks threw her arms around Joy. "You're here! I thought I'd have to storm the greenhouses to find you! Sarah said you're working night and day!"

"Pretty close." She stood aside as Isabelle introduced her to all her family.

Violet Hawks and Josh Stevens. Isabelle's brothers: Dylan, Christopher and Ross. And her mother, Connie.

Following the Hawks family group was Beatrice and Rand Nelson and their adopted sons, Eli and Chris.

Rand explained that his family was following in the next car.

By the time all the guests had arrived, Joy felt like a politician at a rally, she'd shaken so many hands with old acquaintances and new faces, as well. They all knew who she was and they all congratulated her on her decision to reopen the greenhouses.

Sarah, Liz, Maddie, Olivia and Cate had taken over the task of arranging the desserts on the dining room table. When Joy saw the dazzling display of pies, cakes, cookies, cupcakes and Gina's cannoli, she couldn't help taking a photo and texting it to Glory, who had a penchant for sweets.

Gabe Barzonni had distributed glasses of champagne and his new ice wine. Mrs. Beabots rang a crystal bell calling everyone to the table.

Adam appeared from the kitchen, stood next to Mrs. Beabots and said, "After dessert, the children are going for a caroling party. Joy and I invite you all to come with us!"

Titus shouldered his way through the throng of adults and stood next to his father. "We're going to help Boston Greenhouses, too."

Joy smiled at Titus and looked at Adam. In that moment, she was struck with a romantic sense of belonging. They weren't a couple, but the shift inside her was undeniable.

"That's right, Titus," Joy said from the other side of the table. "I hope you don't mind, but

Adam has made up some flyers and we'd like to distribute them to our neighbors."

Mrs. Beabots held Joy's hand. "Frank would be very happy right now, Joy."

Gabe raised his glass. "To Frank Boston."

Joy watched as every eye in the room fell upon her, and she could see their memories of her grandfather etched in their expressions. The greenhouses weren't just a nursery or a retail establishment. They were that part of the past that settled into their hearts because her grandpa had appreciated and loved them. She felt her heart warm as it opened to their affection.

ADAM WALKED ALONGSIDE Joy as they made their way down Maple Boulevard. Because there were so many guests, they broke up into two groups, each taking a side of the street. Austin McCreary and his wife, Katia, spearheaded the group on the opposite side of the boulevard while he, Joy, Mica and Grace took their group.

The night was still, the traffic noises muffled by the white blanket of snow. The clouds had moved on, revealing an indigo sky studded with stars and lit by a full silver moon. It was the kind of night sky that brought back memories of Joy and the winter holidays they'd shared.

"Adam," Joy said with a smile. "I remember doing this with my parents. The night was just like this. You were with us."

"I was," he said. "We went to the nursing home and your dad gave them poinsettias he'd brought in the car. They were very appreciative."

"That was a good night."

"Yeah, it was." He would have slipped his arm around her shoulders, but Titus, Timmy, Annie and Danny dashed past them and raced up to the next door. Titus rang the bell, looked back at Adam proudly and held up a flyer.

A woman dressed in a sweatshirt, jeans and slippers came to the door. "What's all this?" she asked.

"Happy Thanksgiving! Merry Christmas!" Titus said.

Then Annie burst into "We Wish You a Merry Christmas."

Danny stood next to Annie singing at the top of his lungs, but he was no match for Annie. Titus sang along with them, but he was most intent on handing the flyer to the lady of the house.

When the children finished the song, the woman held the flyer high and looked over their heads to Adam and Joy. "Is this for real? Boston Greenhouses are reopening?"

"Yes!" Joy exclaimed.

"You can count on me to be there. I'll call my daughter. Thanks!"

The kids scurried down the steps, Titus leading the way to the next house.

"Titus…" Adam started in his warning voice, until Joy took his gloved hand and squeezed it.

"He's okay."

"But it's icy."

She smiled widely. "It's snowy, Adam. And he's having the time of his life."

Adam exhaled. "He is, isn't he?"

"Uh-huh," she replied.

Grace, who was walking behind Adam and Joy, carrying Jules, said, "I know just how you feel, Adam. I'm paranoid about Jules all the time."

"I wouldn't say I was paranoid," Adam protested, looking over his shoulder at Grace. Then his eyes went to Mica, who was stifling a laugh. "Okay. Maybe a little."

"Hey, Adam," Mica said. "Mind if I bend your ear?"

"Sure."

Mica put his hand on the small of Grace's

back. "Let Joy hold Jules for a bit while I talk to Adam."

Joy reached out for Jules. "Better yet," she said, "let's go sing with the kids at the next house."

"Bien! Bien!" Jules clapped his hands. *"Le chanson 'Noel'? Oui?"*

Grace touched his cheek. "English, Jules. We're in America."

"I can sing 'The First Noel' *en anglais et français.*"

Grace rolled her eyes. "I give up."

"C'mon," Joy said, as they went up to the next house and Titus rang the bell, ever ready with another flyer.

"What's up?" Adam asked, as they stood at the base of the house's newly shoveled sidewalk.

"I wanted to thank you again for putting me in touch with your patent attorney."

"Vince is the best, isn't he?"

"He sure is. I thought I had things well in hand, but he found two more operating systems I'd invented and had incorporated into my designs for so long, I'd forgotten that no one else knew of them, because they were mine. Vince ran the searches and then applied for the patents."

"So, you're covered."

"I am, thanks to you."

"And Vince." Adam smiled.

"Yeah." Mica exhaled a huge visible breath of air. "So, what are you up to these days? Last we talked, you were working on an anti-gravity drape. I mean, wow. Propulsion methods. Zero gravity…"

"Microgravity, actually. There're some physicists out in Altoona—self-funded, mostly—that I've been having conversations with. Actually, I've been approached by Hal Slade, who runs a think tank out there. He wants to fund one of my projects."

"That's fantastic, man. Knowing you, they're picking your brain more than you're picking theirs."

Adam faced Mica. "Look. Right now, everyone in this town thinks all I've done is some geothermal work. I've got an experiment going on at Frank's old greenhouses."

"Experiment?"

"I'm testing a new heating system. If I can prove this thing works, it could revolutionize energy usage in colder regions around the Great Lakes."

"You've gone a long way past your engineering degree. Unifying electromagnetic energy with gravity force? Working with these think-tank corporations keeps you busy, I bet."

"Very. I love it."

"What's not to love. Fascinating stuff."

"Yeah? Why don't you jump on board?" Adam asked.

"I'm not as smart as you."

"Yes, you are. Just maybe not as curious as I am."

Mica looked over at Titus. "He's like you, you know. Inquisitive. Never satisfied with a single answer. Always searching."

Adam followed Mica's gaze to his son. He looked at Jules in Joy's arms. "Because there's always a better way. There is so much we don't know. And I want to know it all. If I had my way, there'd be free energy for every living soul. Limitless drinking water. No one would go cold."

Adam turned back to Mica. "Is it wrong to want the impossible?"

Mica touched his paralyzed arm. "No. I never give up…on anything." He looked back at Grace, who had just turned to blow him a kiss. "I'd be miserable if I'd given up."

"I'm not going to stop, but I don't want anyone to know about my work. Not after my first projects were stolen before I could get them patented."

"Yeah, intellectual property theft is rampant. Trust is tough all around these days. So, that rule of yours—does that include Joy?"

"Absolutely. Why do you ask?"

"I dunno. Could be you look at her the way I look at Grace."

"I don't do that. Joy is engaged to a wealthy guy in New York. She's going back in a couple weeks."

"What? But she's reopening the greenhouses," Mica countered.

"I talked her into it. As is, they're nearly worthless. If she presents a profitable business…she gets a better price."

"I see." He rubbed his chin. "And you're doing this to…"

"To help out an old friend."

Mica snorted. "Ha!" He slapped Adam's back. "That's a good one." He shoved his hand in his jeans' pocket and shuffled toward Grace. "You keep tellin' yourself that, buddy. Often. Maybe you'll really believe it."

Adam scratched the back of his neck.

He and Mica had gone to Purdue together. Majored in engineering. They'd collaborated on several class experiments and enjoyed each other's company. Mica was about as close a friend as he'd had in high school.

Then Adam had moved away and Mica went to France.

But as close as Adam was to Mica, he couldn't tell Mica all the truth.

Being an inventor meant keeping one's ideas and experiments top secret. Adam kept his notebooks, flash drives and research in a safety-deposit box in the bank where they could not be stolen or lost.

Adam had to be careful.

His work could change the world one day.

Adam's real fear wasn't that his work would be stolen. It was that he'd be left behind. He didn't trust people a great deal. Amie had died. Frank was gone. And before all that, Joy had abandoned him. He still wasn't over the pain. Getting close didn't work out for him.

Joy still had a life in New York even though her engagement was "on hold." The problem was that Titus and Joy seemed to be getting attached. And there was the fact that Adam couldn't stop his own emotional reactions when he was around her.

His heart wanted her, but his head told him to back off. He was logical and practical, and Adam believed his head seldom steered him wrong.

CHAPTER NINETEEN

Joy walked across the snow-covered driveway to the greenhouses as the first light of dawn glistened across the snow. The Grand Reopening banner was tied above the front door, bookended by two enormous wreaths glowing with two thousand crystal lights each.

Joy had worked on the wreaths, making bows out of fat red and gold velvet ribbon while Adam had hung the banner. She'd walked out to the end of the expansive parking lot in front to see the effect. Gray skies were inevitable at this time of year, and the lights on the wreaths would sparkle day and night.

She opened the door, turned the Closed sign around and turned on the lights.

"Amazing," she said aloud, as the trees and garlands illuminated the showroom.

"Isn't it?" Adam said, walking out of the large greenhouse, wearing rubber boots, a rubber apron, and holding a box of flower food in his hand.

She drank in his smile and wondered why she didn't check herself. He never failed to surprise her with his magnetism. It was more than charm; it was innate charisma born of his intelligence. He'd always had it and it drew her to him now, just as it had years ago. "You're here."

"So am I!" Titus yelled, rushing from behind Adam's legs and into the showroom as if he were taking his cue for center stage. "We're gonna help!"

"But…" Joy looked from Titus to Adam. "I—I am…"

"Pleased? Overjoyed? Astonished?" Adam laughed as he walked forward. "All the poinsettias are watered, fed, and the heat's perfect."

"What time did you get here?"

Titus held up a Mickey Mouse watch on his wrist. "Five thirty. I couldn't sleep."

"Really?"

Adam untied the rubber apron. "It's true. We couldn't get out of the house fast enough."

Titus dropped his head down and yanked it up in a dramatic nod. "Yep. We had microwave oatmeal." He lifted his little palm to cover his mouth and said nearly in a whisper, "Not Dad's favorite."

"Also true," Adam said. "I asked Olivia to bring over some breakfast sandwiches when she comes."

Joy halted taking off her coat. "Olivia's coming?"

"She's gonna help, too," Titus said proudly. "It's arranged."

Joy was getting used to Titus's larger-than-expected vocabulary. "Arranged." She looked at Adam. "You did this?"

He shrugged his shoulders. "Didn't have to. Sarah started the scheduling at the party last night. Miss Milse is babysitting nearly every kid…"

"Except me," Titus chimed in.

Adam exhaled and pursed his lips. "Titus drove a hard bargain because he wanted to be here so badly."

"Why's that?" Joy asked.

"Because. My dad talks about when he used to work here. I never saw it with all these flowers. I only saw it with broken glass and weeds inside." He marched up to Joy and quirked his finger at her. She leaned down.

"What?"

"Dad said it was magic."

Joy sprang upright, surprised Adam would

use the same description he'd used back in high school. It was as if he was sharing his innermost feelings with his son. "Adam? You told him that?"

Adam walked toward her, took her coat and purse. "I'll put these away." He pointed to the register. "You need to get ready. Your public will be here in fifteen minutes. I'll turn on the cookie warmer." He started to walk away before saying, "Liz and Sarah are taking morning shifts. Olivia, Maddie and Cate the afternoons. Katia is every day, all day, except Tuesdays and Friday afternoons. Isabelle is every other morning. I think that about covers it."

Joy pressed her palms to her cheeks. "My gosh. I'll have more workers than I'll have customers."

"Nuh-uh," Titus said. "Dad had more flyers made. Mr. Carter and Dr. Barzonni said they're going to mail them to their personal friends." He turned toward Adam. "Right?"

"Yes. Everyone wants the greenhouse to succeed." He smiled.

Adam left the showroom to put Joy's things in the back-storage room.

When he came back he was wearing his cowboy boots, jeans and a red-and-green-plaid flannel shirt he'd had on under the apron.

With effort, she tore her eyes from his as he smiled at her. She looked down at her Boston Greenhouses sweatshirt and jeans. "Well, I guess we look Christmassy enough."

"I forgot about those sweatshirts," Adam said, coming over to her. "Hmm. I wonder if I can get more of those made up." He took out his cell phone and walked through the French doors. "Hello?"

Joy looked at Titus. "He's always like this, isn't he?"

Titus nodded. "He told me he's being… decided."

"Decisive."

"Yeah."

"Do you know how to make change yet?"

"Dad's teaching me. It's not hard."

"Really? I thought it was tough when I was your age."

"Nah. You just look at how much the register tells you to give back to them and then count it out."

"This register doesn't do that."

"Why not?"

"It's really, really old."

"Oh. But I can do credit cards with the square on my tablet."

"How did you learn that?" she asked.

"Timmy taught me. His dad taught him. He has one on his cell phone for when he gets paid for his carpenter jobs. It's easy."

"Well," she said. "For now, I guess I'll take care of the register and credit cards."

"Good," Titus said, running to the front door. "'Cause Dad said I could be the greeter."

As Joy looked up, she saw a young mother with two toddlers walk in. "My first customers." The words caught in a net of old memories and the vision of her grandpa standing at the door greeting customers. Her hand flew to her heart as an overwhelming sensation of pride filled her.

I'm doing this.

"Welcome to Boston Greenhouses!" Titus yelled at the woman, who chuckled.

"Why, thank you."

"Start here." Titus pointed to the woodland walkway. "It's a trip."

The woman laughed again, but her toddlers were clearly mesmerized by the trees.

Next, Sarah, Liz and Katia walked in. Katia, who was wearing a designer black coat with faux mink collar and cuffs, gaped at the showroom and then swept up to the counter.

"It's a wonder!" Katia said. "Sarah told me

I'd be surprised, but this…this is stunning. I need to get some reporters over here."

Liz put her hand on Katia's arm. "Isabelle told me Scott will be here at noon for photos."

"I meant the South Bend papers," Katia said. "Scott told Austin and my boss, Jack, he was planning several articles. Nothing but the best for our Joy."

The bell over the door rang again.

"Welcome to Boston Greenhouses!" Titus announced, as if he was a Victorian herald.

Sarah and Katia shucked off their coats. "Okay, where do you want us?"

"You all choose. But I think…"

The bell rang again and four women walked in. One came straight up to Joy. "We're here from the Methodist Church to place orders for our poinsettias."

Joy looked at Sarah and Liz. "Will you both help her to the greenhouse?"

"Absolutely!" Sarah smiled and led the way.

By eleven o'clock, there was a line at the counter. Joy was convinced her first morning of shoppers were die-hard Black Friday experts, because they all went straight for the poinsettias that sold for a discount.

To Joy's surprise, the white poinsettias were depleted by over half within the first few hours.

A representative from the Indian Lake Savings Bank came in, ordered four dozen red poinsettias and asked Joy to work up the cost of the gold angel tree, ornaments, tree, lights and all. The woman wanted the entire order delivered by the end of the day.

Adam promised the woman he would deliver everything personally.

Noontime offered no break. Adam called Olivia and asked her to bring more sandwiches and chips for everyone in the shop and two extra cartons of organic milk for Titus. Joy noticed that he placed the entire order on his credit card.

Tired of "greeting" so many customers, Titus took a break and sat on the stool behind the counter while Joy worked the register.

"You know, Titus, I may have to have you help me with the credit card orders this afternoon. Seems I get behind rather quickly." She handed him the tablet.

"Sure," he said.

After the next customer left, Joy glanced back at Titus. She noticed his fingers dancing over the tablet.

"What are you doing?"

"Checking your website."

"Of course. I worked on it every night."

"Dad said he helped a little."

252 HOME FOR CHRISTMAS

"It's a lot of work for one person with everything else we had to do."

Joy looked across the showroom to see Adam talking to an elderly woman considering a particular white-and-gold angel.

Titus thrust the tablet in front of Joy's face, cutting off her view of Adam. "Did you see these orders?"

Joy refocused. "Orders? I forgot to check it…"

"Look." Titus's little finger caused the screen to scroll. "This is good, right?"

She took the tablet. "These notifications were sent only minutes ago. Oh, my gosh." She jerked her head at Adam. "Can I see you?"

"Sure," he replied. After handing the angel to the old woman, he touched her shoulder and said, "Wise purchase." He walked to the counter. "What's up?"

"Look at this." She pointed at the screen. "If this is correct, we have more than that bank delivery we have to run today."

He took the tablet from her. "South Bend Public Library. Notre Dame Administration Offices. Saint Joseph County Bank. Joy, these are huge orders."

"How did this happen?" she asked, then halted. "Katia."

"What?"

"She said she was going to contact the South Bend papers. She must have done more than that."

"I knew I liked that woman." Adam laughed.

"But once we fill these, we'll nearly be out of poinsettias."

"No worries." Adam took out his cell phone and walked away.

"Hey! Come back here!"

The old woman walked up to the counter. "I want that angel," she said. "You know, that man is a good salesman."

Joy quirked a smile. "And sneaky, too," she said, as she watched Adam glide through the French doors while simultaneously pulling his wallet from his back jeans' pocket. He was putting the next poinsettia order on his credit card.

JOY TOOK THE ornaments off the gold tree and prepared them for delivery to the Indian Lake Savings Bank. Adam filled the back seats of his truck with the poinsettias, while Joy finished wrapping up the ornaments. The lights would stay on the tree, and fortunately, they had less than a half-mile drive to the bank. Adam said he'd place a tarp over the back bed.

Luke came at three to take Titus to his and

Sarah's house, where Miss Milse would watch the children until dinnertime.

As Adam drove them down Maple Boulevard toward the bank, she asked, "Just how often have you used your credit card to pay for goods and supplies for my greenhouses?"

"Um…"

"Truth, Adam," she demanded, narrowing her eyes.

"Are you mad at me?"

"I'd like to know in dollars and cents how mad I should be. I didn't authorize your spending."

"Spoken like a true accountant," he retorted. "At the moment, I don't have an exact amount."

"Fine. Ballpark then."

"Can't do that, either." He chuckled, but the laugh died as he glanced at her.

She glared at him. "I don't like owing people money. Debt is a sign of weakness."

"I'm not in debt. Not by a long shot," he said.

Her expression softened as her ire turned to curiosity. "I've never been the one to pry unless my clients are paying me to do so, but I've been very curious, Adam. Just how *do* you make your money?"

"Excuse me?"

"I mean, you have all kinds of time to help me out, order supplies, make deliveries for me, do everything from repairing broken pipes to scrubbing tiles. I don't see you punching anyone's time clock but mine. And I'm not paying you."

He glanced away for a moment, tapping his fingers on the steering wheel. "I'm doing what I love."

"And that is? Besides raising Titus, I mean."

"Ideas. I make money on my ideas. Besides my regular job, you'd call it, which I handle by email and phone with my colleagues in Indianapolis, I do quite a bit in astro-engineering. Most of my inventions and ideas have patents, and once they're up and running, I sell them. I have investors in Silicon Valley. Investors in Houston. New Jersey."

Joy's mouth gaped. "So, you did it? You made your dream come true?"

"For the most part. Yeah."

"And when do you do this work?"

"Nights when Titus is asleep and during the day when he's at school. Five or six times a year I have trips to Indianapolis for discussions. I tinker a lot on weekends. Titus likes to watch or help me. At least he thinks he's helping me."

"So…that means you're rich?"

"It's a living." He smiled.

Joy leaned back, staring wide-eyed at him. "Are you famous?"

"Only in very close physics circles."

She was speechless, but only for a moment. "And you didn't tell me this."

"You didn't ask," he replied with a sad edge to his voice.

"Sorry. Habit. I'm trained to be cautious. I don't pry. I don't ask."

"And being the accounting whiz that you are, you're worried I overstepped my bounds. Or is your concern really that being in debt to me would mean I could control you?"

"I didn't mean that."

"Then fine—I'll tally everything up tonight and give you a bill tomorrow."

"Fine." She folded her arms over her chest.

Adam exhaled. "I thought I was helping. You told me you don't have a lot of money. You said there was only enough inheritance to bankroll the poinsettias. I take responsibility for pushing you into this decision. And it was a big undertaking. I knew you'd need a little boost. I don't mind doing that. I'm not trying to hurt you. I'm trying to help."

"I feel like I've been duped," she groaned.

"It's not like that."

"You know—everyone has been so nice to

me since I came back. Overly nice. Maybe it's not about me. Maybe you all have your own agendas. I want to think that they all loved Grandpa so much that they wanted this for him, if not for me."

"In many cases, that's true."

"In yours?"

He pulled up to the bank. He put the truck in Park and turned to her. "What are you asking me?"

"Have you got an ulterior motive, Adam Masterson? Because if you do, it's time to lay your cards on the table."

"Initially, I wanted to show you that Indian Lake wasn't the hall of horrors you thought it was. That the people here were wonderful and loving and that maybe you could come to need them."

"I'm seeing that…" She paused. "You said 'initially.'"

"The more I'm with you, I have to admit, maybe my motives have changed." He unbuckled his seat belt and leaned forward to put his hand on the back of her nape.

When his lips met hers, she had every intention of pushing him away, venting more anger at him, but she didn't. This wasn't a kiss born of fond memories or a teenage crush; this was passion and eagerness. This was a kiss of now and his need for her in this moment. His fingers slid up into her hair, cupping her head, capturing her. He slanted his mouth over hers and deepened the kiss. He breathed her in as a faint moan hummed in his throat. Joy was lost like she'd never been, not even when they were kids. Back then, his kisses had been tender and playful. But this was desire and possession.

As she responded to Adam's kiss, holding him fast, she wondered if every decision she'd ever made in her life was a mistake.

CHAPTER TWENTY

ADAM BROKE FROM the kiss, reconsidered and kissed Joy again. Then he held her face in his hands, realizing she'd never taken her hands from him.

"I'm not gonna say I'm sorry. I've been wanting to do that since the day you came back here."

"You kissed me before."

"Not like this."

"No. Not like this," she replied in a low voice. "Adam…"

"Don't say it. Not right now. I don't want to think about New York or your other life. This is just us."

"But it's not," she whispered and dropped her hands.

He let his hands fall to her shoulders, still reluctant to let her go.

"I don't want to do anything that would make you distrust me or make you uncomfortable, and the fact that, apparently, empirically I've done both…" He sighed heavily. "I won't let it happen again."

"That a promise?"

"No. Yes." He laughed and fell back against his seat. He closed his eyes and leaned his head against the headrest. "You don't know what you've done to me."

"I wouldn't exactly say that," she replied. "As of two minutes ago, I have a much clearer picture."

He slid his eyes to her. "You kissed me back."

She hung her head and looked up at him with recalcitrant eyes. "I did."

He lifted his hand and tapped the steering wheel with his forefinger. "So, would I be out of line to ascertain that you might be feeling the same thing I'm feeling?"

She leaned against the door.

Trying to move away from him?

"Adam, I have to be honest. I don't know what I feel. I've gone from shock over Grandpa's death, to grief, which is almost choking me, to wondering why everyone here is so nice to me, to remembering you and me when we were in high school, discovering you have a son, whom I can tell you I love already."

"You do?" Adam was a bit surprised. Not that people didn't love Titus. He was a special kid. But Joy didn't have much exposure to children, not even a younger sibling.

And yet she protected and watched over her flowers. He'd caught her in the greenhouses talking to the plants, singing to them as if they could hear her and respond. Perhaps she had more motherly nurturing instincts than he gave her credit for.

"What's not to love, Adam? He's amazing. And so like you."

If she loved his son, did that mean she loved him again? He didn't want to hear her answer.

His world had been upended. If he were honest with himself, he'd needed her to re-open the greenhouses so that he could test his geothermal design for Hal Slade, his investor.

But even that wasn't the reason he'd cajoled her into this move.

If she'd left town, he would have paid to have the glass panes replaced anyway. He would have finished the system, turned it on without anyone's knowledge, read his results and sent them to the investor.

No, Adam was more underhanded than that.

He wanted Joy.

He'd needed her to stay in Indian Lake so he could win her back. And he was doing a lousy job of it. If anything, he'd played his cards too soon. She was right. She hadn't had time to digest Frank's death, let alone handle romantic advances from an old boyfriend while engaged to another man.

He'd done a bang-up job of confusing her. If she lasted the weekend, it would be a miracle. And if she packed up and left town, it would be his fault.

"I'd say he's smarter than me," Adam said, turning to look at the poinsettias in the back seat. "Tell you what. I won't push your buttons anymore. We'll put this in the past and just take care of business. That's what we're here for. Okay?"

"Uh. Yeah. Business," she stumbled. "And that's really fine with you?"

He pursed his lips. Of course, it wasn't, but he didn't have a choice. He wasn't about to give her an excuse to turn tail and run. "I did mean it when I said I wanted to do this for Frank. He was a real friend to me. I want you to have a thriving business to sell. Then you'll have money and you won't have to make decisions in the valley."

"The valley?"

"Yeah. There are two kinds of decisions we make in life. Those when we're on top of the mountain. We've succeeded. We're happy and then we choose. The other decisions are those made in the valley of despair. We're broken or near it. Maybe not quite as happy as we thought we were. Maybe our health is poor. Maybe our spirit is empty. Those decisions are never the right ones and it takes years and years to get ourselves back on the right path."

She leveled unwavering eyes on him. "And you know this…"

"Because I think we've both been to the valley."

"And?"

"I didn't like it," he said.

She clasped her hands in her lap, worried them a bit before she spoke, as if this decision was a great one. "Are you in the valley now?"

"No. I intend never to visit it again," he said earnestly.

"That's good." A pensive look remained on her face as she opened the truck door.

Adam was keenly aware as he got out of the truck that she would think about his words for hours to come.

He hoped she'd remember his kiss. He knew he wouldn't forget it.

WHEN ADAM PICKED up Titus from Sarah's house, it was after dinnertime. Titus rubbed his eyes and yawned.

"Dad," Titus said when Adam buckled him into his car seat. "Do I have to take a bath when I get home? Can I just go to bed?"

"Sure, if you take a bath in the morning. What happened? You're usually a bundle of energy."

"Dad. I'm a working man now." He yawned again.

"Right." Adam climbed in the truck and backed out the drive.

Once they were home, Angel met them at the door, and even she was surprised that Adam carried a sleepy Titus straight up the stairs to bed.

Angel waited patiently on her bed in the kitchen as Adam came in and scooped her meal into her bowl. As he refilled Angel's water bowl, his cell phone rang.

"California. Oh, boy." He felt his nerves jangle. His back went ramrod straight. He answered the call. "Masterson."

"Adam. Hal Slade here. Listen, I hate to call you over the Thanksgiving holiday, but I'm at LAX on my way to Aspen for the weekend. I wanted to get right back to you."

"That's quite all right, Hal. I didn't expect to hear from you until next week."

"I couldn't wait to ask. Those numbers you sent me—they're accurate?"

"They are. The last readings were taken this morning before dawn."

"Impressive. This geothermal system is everything you said it was. I'm all in."

"That's wonderful news, Hal."

"I'll get with my attorney and send over my offer. Probably not till middle of next week, if that's all right."

"Yes. I'll have my attorney go over it, as well."

"Great. I'll copy you on all the emails. Transparency. Right?"

"Always."

"Excellent," Hal said. "And as we discussed, once we get the contracts finalized, then I'll expect you out here the first of the year and we can get to work."

Adam swallowed hard. "Yes."

"Talk soon. I'm boarding," Hal said.

"Absolutely. Goodbye."

Adam ended the call, backed up against the kitchen counter and slumped into the kitchen stool. "First of the year."

Angel stopped eating, looked up at him and instinctively came over to rub her back against his leg.

Hal Slade was the CEO of three alternative energy corporations and was working in the cutting edge of space exploration.

Adam's geothermal unit was the tip of a very large iceberg of research and exploration he'd begun in college, when he'd started to explore the works of think tanks and learned more about Stephen Hawking and Elon Musk. Adam had always been obsessed with uncharted scientific realms as a kid, from the time he'd read about Nikola Tesla. Amie had encouraged him back then, challenging him to reach for the stars—in his own work. Now he was doing it…literally.

However, Adam's heart was in creating cheaper sources of energy and bringing them to Indian Lake. He liked his small town and wanted to make the lives of the people in his home better. His dream of worldwide cheap energy was not impossible. Adam didn't believe in "impossibles."

Joy was right. Her life was in New York. And perhaps Adam's future was in California. Maybe Adam was at the top of the mountain, after all. His geothermal theory was proving accurate and true. In weeks, he would have an investor. Not only would he have more income, but people would benefit.

So, he and Titus would move to California. Adam would continue to challenge himself and maybe he would reach a star.

He wondered what that would be like, looking back down on earth. Looking back and knowing he'd lost Joy a second time.

CHAPTER TWENTY-ONE

THE FIRST WEEK in December had flown by for Joy. Every waking hour was spent at the greenhouses, caring for the poinsettias, wrapping and delivering the gorgeous flowers across and beyond Indian Lake. As much as she groaned about year-end in the accounting world, it was no match for retail at Christmas. This was the time of year when most retailers made the majority of their profit margin, and she could see why.

Nights after closing were used to make lists of inventories her customers had requested and to calculate how much of those orders would sell. It had been a long time since she'd helped her parents and grandfather with wholesale buying.

She remembered accompanying her mother to the Merchandise Mart in Chicago, where they'd visited the wholesale gift showrooms to see the newest trends in home decorating, giftware, china and linens. In the middle of summer, she and her mother kick-started

Christmas by placing orders for decorations, garlands, wreaths, holiday pillows and bed linens, specialty foods, silk florals, ribbons, stockings and fun and funky gadgets, toys and games to fill those stockings.

"You know, Joy," her mother had said, "gifts are important. It's not the amount of money a person spends, it truly is the thought. It's the acknowledgment of the recipient's importance in one's life. Appreciation is like light and water to a growing plant. Without appreciation, given often, a human will wither—just like a flower without rain."

Jill had loved the people of Indian Lake and she'd worked hard to find unique, special items to stock the greenhouse shelves. She'd wanted the best for the townspeople.

Joy had forgotten that.

Unfortunately, Joy didn't have time to spend a day or two at the Merchandise Mart. She had to rely on Frank's contacts and representatives in the showrooms to advise her about orders.

Adam had been right about the impact of hand delivering the flyers he'd made up. And Titus's distribution scheme masquerading as a caroling party was not only effective, it bordered on genius. In the first week, she was amazed at the number of deliveries they made to Maple Boulevard residences.

The radio advertising campaigns she'd run had added to the need for the second shipment of poinsettias. Joy had agreed with Adam to send Lester MacDougal back to Dallas for another truckload.

Once Joy and Adam had set up the gold Christmas tree in the Indian Lake Savings Bank building, two more banks, not to be outdone by their competitor, ordered the rest of her "woodland scene" trees.

Before December 6, her "woodland walkway" had no "woods" and was down to baskets filled with ornaments, and the empty spaces were filled with poinsettias.

Joy was wrapping a large pink poinsettia with snowflake cellophane when Liz walked in with a group of her friends' children, along with her preschool-age son, Zeke.

Zeke was already a handsome boy, looking like his father, Gabe, more than honey-blonde Liz.

"Liz!" Joy said, coming around to hug her friend. "I thought all the kids were going to Sarah's house after school."

Titus raced up to Joy. "Miss Joy!" He tripped a bit on a rubber mat near the door, but, undeterred, flung his arms around her waist.

"We still are," Liz said, watching as the kids immediately began investigating the baskets filled with ornaments.

"Yeah," Titus said, cranking his head back to look at Joy. "We have to shop."

"You do? For what?"

Liz smiled. "Teacher gifts. Apparently, the school issued a letter to all the parents not to spend more than five dollars on a teacher gift. Also, due to dietary restrictions, no food, either."

"Bummer," Titus said. "I wanted to make Christmas cookies."

"Oh, Titus," Joy said. "That's a lovely idea. I bet your dad would have loved to help with that."

"Nope. He can cook. Baking is different," Titus replied.

Joy looked at Liz, who shrugged her shoulders. "Don't look at me. I do the slice-and-bake thing."

Zeke pulled on Liz's hand. "I love those!"

Liz ruffled his thick raven-colored hair. "Thank goodness."

"So," Joy said to Titus, "in the meantime, we have to find ornaments."

Sarah walked out of the back greenhouse with a customer who had filled two double carts. Annie saw her mother and rushed over.

"Mom!" Annie said. "Can I have my allowance early?"

"I guess so," Sarah replied, wheeling a cart to the counter as Joy went to the register and began counting the poinsettias and amaryllis. "Why?"

Joy tallied the purchase and took the woman's credit card. "The kids have to buy teacher gifts," Joy said.

"Oh, honey," Sarah said. "I'll pay for what you need."

"All of them?" Annie asked.

Joy halted as she handed the woman back her credit card. "Thank you so much." She looked at Annie. "How many teachers do you have?"

Timmy walked up at that minute, his hands filled with a miniature train, reindeer, a moose, a fire engine and a spaceship. "I have five."

"I have four," Annie said.

Charlotte skipped up holding an angel tree topper that looked half Charlotte's size. "I like this one."

Sarah rolled her eyes. "I need more hours on the clock," she joked.

Joy laughed, as did Liz and the woman customer.

Titus inspected Timmy's choices. "These are so cool."

As Joy helped the customer push the carts out to her car, Adam drove up from making deliveries to the courthouse.

He parked the truck in front and helped the customer load her SUV, then walked with Joy back inside.

When Adam saw all the kids, he held out his arms to Titus. "Hey, buddy. What's going on?"

"Dad." Titus walked up to him, glanced back at Timmy as if to get an affirmative nudge, then whispered, "Dad, we have a dilemma."

Joy's eyes widened. Children didn't usually have dilemmas. A problem maybe, but this sounded serious.

Adam squatted down and put his hand on Titus's shoulder. "What is it?"

"All of us need teacher gifts and we want to buy ornaments. But, Dad. There's no tree here to try them out on."

Joy's hand flew to her mouth as she wiped the smile from her lips. "Try them out?"

"Yeah. How can we tell if they're good or not if we can't see what they look like on a tree? That's the scientific method, like you taught me, right?" Titus asked seriously.

Adam chuckled as he stood and looked at Joy. "Well…"

"I'm sorry, Titus. We sold the trees."

"Aw, they weren't the right kind, anyway."

Joy's surprise rang in her tone. "What do you mean?"

"They were fancy trees. Not real Christmas trees," Titus informed her.

"I don't understand."

Adam rocked back on his heels as he folded his arms over his chest. "I know what he's saying."

"Good. Fill me in," she said.

"Better yet," Adam replied with a mischievous smirk, "I'll show you."

PINE COUNTRY TREE FARM spanned seventeen acres of rolling hills north of town. Marching up the inclines were blue spruce, conifer, Scotch pine, Norwegian spruce, Douglas fir and white pine trees. Encircling the farm was a split-rail fence decorated with live green garlands and enormous red bows. The wide parking area was filled with pickup trucks, minivans and SUVs. As Joy rode with Adam and Titus into the farm, she noticed that over half the vehicles bore out-of-state license plates.

As they parked, she saw a horse-drawn

wagon take a group of people out toward the forest. Two of the men in the wagon carried hatchets.

"You don't just buy a tree off the lot?" Joy asked.

"Not today," Adam said, unbuckling his seat belt. "Though you can do that if you want. But that's not the kind of tree we want."

"It's not? What is?"

He pointed to her green sweatshirt, which depicted the greenhouses at Christmas from their high school days. "We're going to do even better than that."

"Grandpa ordered our tree from Wisconsin," she said, opening the door. "I don't remember this tree farm."

"They were just getting started back then. I know the owner pretty well. He has to plant fifteen thousand trees every year."

Joy opened the back door to help Titus out of the back seat. "He sells that many?"

Titus put his arms out to grab Joy's hands and jumped down. "Thanks."

"He ships all the way to Florida," Adam said, going to the back bed and pulling out an enormous ax. He placed it on his shoulder.

She took Titus's hand and walked over to him. "With that plaid shirt and sheepskin jacket and that ax, you look like—"

"Don't say it." He laughed. "C'mon. I know just where to go."

"Who does he look like?" Titus asked.

"A mythical character," Joy replied, thinking of Paul Bunyan.

"Oh. 'Cause he doesn't look like a *Star Wars* guy."

Joy glanced at Adam as he walked in front of them. Adam had always been in tune with stars, interested in physics. "I'm not sure about that."

They walked up to a group of workers at a large red-painted baling machine. Adam turned to Joy.

"Keep Titus back here away from the machine. It can be dangerous," he said to her. "And there's so many people around, don't let him get distracted and take off."

"I'll watch him. We'll run reconnaissance in the gift shop. See what the competition is up to," she said.

"Great. I want to find out when the next wagon is due for a pickup."

"We're not going to walk out there?"

"It's too far to where I want to go," Adam said with a wink. "And we'll need a wagon to ourselves to bring it back."

Her eyes widened. "What are you up to?"

Titus shoved his glasses up his nose. "I know!"

Adam shook his finger at Titus. "It's a secret. Remember?"

"I don't know what's going on here, but it won't be a secret for long," Joy said. "Let's go, Titus."

She took the boy's hand again as they went to the log cabin gift shop. The long, wood-planked porch was draped with wide cedar and spruce garlands and enormous wreaths. A light breeze had picked up, causing the red ribbon bows to flap against the cabin's dark wood.

Inside, a potbellied stove heated the retail area. Interestingly, there wasn't a Christmas tree inside. The cabin was small, and the shelves were filled with pinecone ornaments, knit stockings, stacks of quilted place mats, Santa mugs and locally made jams, jellies and marinades. Fortunately, none were from her suppliers, which offered their customers and hers a variety. None of the wreaths outside or inside were lit. She noticed that the rest of the gifts were rustic in nature, small replicas of horse-drawn wagons, woodland creatures or miniature trees. There wasn't a Santa or crèche to be seen. Her first thought was that perhaps they'd sold out of product already.

Then again, their focus was selling live trees, garlands and wreaths. Decorating them was why people would come to Boston Greenhouses.

"Miss Joy," Titus said, as they made their way through the groups of customers, "I like our place better."

Our place. Joy felt her heart swell. Titus was at home in her shop, and that gave her enormous comfort. Her reaction was unexpected, but as he looked up at her, his sport strap askew and a clump of dark hair sticking out over his ear, emotion gripped her. She knelt down, put her arms around him and said, "Titus, that's the best compliment I've had in all my life."

"It's true," he said and hugged her back. "I like being there very much."

"You do?"

"Uh-huh." He smiled, looking at her through his glasses' lenses. "You're there."

Joy exhaled deeply as her heart swelled. This kid rocked her to the bone.

It was all she could do not to burst into tears. She rose. This was the craziest thing. She held out her hand and he slipped his into hers.

Joy's emotions were altering her perspective. She was tied in knots of accomplishment, pleasing Frank, grief over losing him, and the myriad of feelings involving Adam and his kiss that had turned her world upside down.

The kiss had been a mistake—or so she'd told herself all week. It should never have happened, but it had.

Should she talk to him about it? Admittedly, if she had a moment alone with him, she'd be the one to make another kiss happen. And would it be as shocking as the last? What if what had happened had been an anomaly? Shouldn't they find out?

And what if they discovered this attraction was more than some touchstone to the past? Would he be willing to delve further? Would she?

Titus still stared at her with one of his penetrating gazes. Knowing this was one kid who hadn't lost his childlike intuition and probably read her thoughts, she said, "And you're the best part of the new Boston Greenhouses."

"You mean that?"

"I do," she affirmed. "Best greeter I've ever seen."

"Thanks. I practiced what I saw in movies," he replied proudly. "Things like that are always correct in movies."

"I never thought of it that way, but you're

probably right," she said, as they walked out the gift shop door.

Adam was just outside on the porch steps. "There you are! The wagon is here to take us out to the grove."

"Hey!" Titus thrust his fist in the air. "It's snowing!"

"It is," Adam replied, reaching in his jacket pocket and pulling out a pair of mittens. "You left these in the truck. Put them on."

As Titus wiggled his hands into the mittens, Adam helped Joy up into the wooden horse-drawn wagon.

There were benches along each side. The area in the middle was wide, which Joy guessed was to load the trees in.

She used a green plaid wool blanket to cover Titus. As they rocked from side to side as the wagon climbed over the frozen hills, Adam kept his arm around his son, who sat between the two adults. Joy noticed that Titus kept his mitten-covered hand on her thigh, not for stability…but for comfort.

They passed rows of six-, seven- and eight-foot Douglas fir trees. Then passed ten-foot and taller blue spruce trees Joy knew had been growing for over a decade, yet the wagon kept rolling.

"Where are we going and what are we looking for?" Joy asked.

"The best!" Titus exclaimed.

"It's not much farther," Adam replied.

"Do you come here every year?"

"Since we moved back, yes," Adam replied. "Titus likes the wagon ride."

"Yep. And Dad likes to chop down the tree." Titus nodded.

She pursed her lips and said, "You'd think that with all Grandpa's focus on Christmas, I would have had a similar experience to this. But I never did."

"So, we're changing your life?" Adam grinned.

Before Joy could answer, the wagon stopped.

The driver pointed to the east. "Over the top of the hill is where you'll find them. I'll wait here, and I do have a chain saw under my seat if you need it."

Adam jumped down from the wagon and hoisted Titus to the ground. Joy started to jump, but Adam caught her and lowered her gently in turn. Snowflakes fluttered between them and one landed on her eyelashes. She blinked. For a split second she imagined Adam's lips on hers again and almost felt her heart hum.

"C'mon, Dad! Let's go!" Titus broke the moment.

Adam's eyes still held Joy's gaze as he answered his son. "Yes." He didn't move.

Joy knew he was considering kissing her, but this wasn't the time or place. "Better get that hatchet."

"Ax," he said. "No mythical character should be without the proper tools."

"Right."

Leaning into the wagon, Adam handed a tarp and some rope to Joy and a ball of twine to Titus. He picked up the ax himself.

She walked over to Titus. "So, how do you know what kind of tree to get?"

"Easy. I measure for Dad."

Joy looked back at Adam, who was chuckling. "This I gotta see."

They walked up the hill, past very tall Fraser fir trees that looked to be at least fifteen feet tall. "These are amazing," she said, touching a bough.

"Nope. Not good enough," Adam said. "Too skinny."

Titus stood still and looked straight up. "Too short."

They continued through four more rows of dense Douglas firs. "What about one of these?"

Adam stopped at a very wide, deep green, fat tree. "Titus, come here."

"Sure, Dad."

Titus stood next to the tree. Adam stood behind him. "Okay, son."

Titus cranked his head back as far as it would go until Joy thought the boy would topple backward. What were they doing?

"Can you see the top, Titus?"

"Nope."

"That's it, then," Adam said, taking a pair of buckskin leather gloves from inside his jacket and putting them on.

"That's how you measure a tree?"

"Yup. We worked this out earlier. I figured when Titus can't see the top, then I know we got a really tall one." He leaned closer and whispered, "It makes him feel involved. Know what I mean?"

"I do." She smiled.

"We have to have the best tree the greenhouses have ever seen. Those glass ceilings are twenty-five feet high. So, we want a twenty-two-foot tree. Plenty of room for an angel."

"Or a star, Dad," Titus said.

"A star would be good."

"Right, we can put angels all over the tree," Joy said. "I just ordered another two dozen."

Adam smiled winsomely at her and she

didn't miss the sincerity in his eyes. "I like angels."

Joy glanced at Titus and saw his wide smile.

"Joy, will you unfold the tarp and put it on the ground there? Positioned correctly, the tree should fall right on it. If I have to, I'll roll the tree over, if it falls to the side. Then we'll tie the rope around the trunk and pull it to the wagon."

"What about the twine?" Titus asked.

"We'll tie two pieces of twine around the trunk, as well. Each of you will take a side. I'll pull from the middle. If we need to tie up some of these branches, we will, but I think we'll be okay."

Adam lifted the ax. "Titus, you and Joy stand back. But first…" Adam knelt down and lifted the bottom branches to look at the trunk. "It's straight. No bends. That's good."

First Adam cut a row of branches off the bottom for easier access.

Joy moved Titus far out of the way as she saw how wide a swing Adam was about to take against the monster tree. With his long, strong legs braced against the frozen ground, he swung hard and true. Then again. Again. And again.

Crack!

"She's ready to fall!" Adam shouted. He shoved his arm into the middle of the tree and pushed it away from Titus and Joy, toward the wide alley space between the rows of trees. The trunk cracked loudly and a slow splitting sound signaled the tree had finally given way. The air whooshed around them as the long limbs stirred the cold air. Snow whirled up into Titus's face as the first branches hit the ground.

"Timber!" Titus shouted and laughed and wiped snow from his cheek.

They went to work preparing the tree. Adam put the rope over his shoulder, as Joy and Titus took up their stabilizing pieces of twine.

With three people pulling the slick tarp over the frozen ground, it moved easily. Once they got to the wagon, the driver helped them slide the tree up a slanted board that was fitted under the wagon bed.

On the way back, the snowfall increased. Titus stuck out his tongue to catch fat snowflakes. Adam laughed and hugged his son close.

Once they reached the main area, workers hauled their tree off the wagon and took it to the baling machine. Joy, Adam and Titus went to the truck and waited. It took two men to haul the big tree to the truck and secure it in the truck bed.

One of the workers came over carrying another, shorter tree that was also baled with twine. "What's this?" Joy asked.

"Oh." Adam grinned. "We picked that tree out for our house a couple days ago."

"Yep!" Titus said.

"But today is your day, Joy. I figured I'd bring them back together."

"Hmm," she mused. "So, the trip to the tree farm was all about me, er, rather the greenhouse? Why do I feel I was set up?"

"You weren't," Adam replied and winked at Titus. When he looked back at Joy, he took a deep breath, then leaned over and kissed her cheek.

He took her hand and walked her to the passenger seat as Titus climbed in the back.

Joy couldn't stop smiling. It was cold outside, but Joy didn't feel it. Just looking at father and son, she was warmed feeling their love for each other. It was a perfect day. A lovely experience. Joy had had the time of her life.

CHAPTER TWENTY-TWO

BY THE TIME they arrived at the greenhouses, it was nearly closing time. Sarah and Olivia had checked out the last customer as Joy walked in with Titus. Adam backed his truck up to the middle greenhouse to unload the Christmas tree.

"Sarah, Olivia. Thanks so much for taking the shift today. You guys are the best," Joy said.

"No worries," Olivia replied. "I had a blast. Plus, I went Christmas shopping and filled a basket with things I want to give as gifts. Sarah promised not to tell Maddie or Liz what I got them. But I will tell you I bought that dark-haired angel in the sky blue organza gown for Gina. That elegant dress is so her."

Sarah took off the green apron with the Boston Greenhouses logo. "It was a good afternoon. Not too busy, but enough that we could handle it. There're some phone messages with delivery orders for tomorrow."

"Poor Adam," Joy said. "He never thought he'd be stuck doing my deliveries for me."

"Uh, I don't think he minds." Sarah smiled.

Olivia caught Sarah's eye. "Me, either."

Joy cleared her throat and glanced at Titus. "Hey, could you do me a favor while I help your dad with the tree? Would you check the website for orders like you did earlier?"

"Sure." He scrambled behind the counter and climbed on the stool, taking Joy's tablet from the countertop.

"Hey," Joy said. "Do you both mind helping us get the tree inside and up? We had a stand put on it at the tree farm, but it's really big."

"Absolutely," they chorused.

"Titus, you stay here. We'll be right back."

He didn't look up from the tablet. "Sure."

Joy led the way and saw that Adam had lowered the tailgate and propped the door open. "Is it going to fit?"

"Sure," he said. "They did a great job of baling it. We'll take it in by the trunk and stand first. I laid some clear plastic sheeting near the windows. I thought we should place it where you guys used to put the tree."

As Adam's blue eyes rested on her, Joy felt a shower of tingles trickle down her spine. She remembered that Christmas all those years ago when he'd told her under the tree that he loved her. Apparently, so did he.

"Joy," Adam asked. "Where's Titus?"

"In the showroom, checking the website. Is that okay? I thought it would keep him busy for a few minutes."

"Yeah, but only a few minutes." He chuckled.

"That's all we'll need," she replied.

"Good night, Adam!" Sarah exclaimed, breaking the moment. "How big is this thing?"

"Dunno. Twenty feet plus."

Olivia shook her head. "Oh, boy. Maybe I should call Rafe."

"Nah, we can do it," Adam said. "It's all a matter of weight distribution."

As Adam guided them, they slid the tree through the door and around the corner another three feet. Adam came to stand by Joy, put his hands in the middle of the tree and picked it up. With a groan, they all hoisted and pushed.

The tree settled perfectly in the stand.

He took a pair of snips out of his jacket pocket and cut the cords, allowing the limbs to fall in a beautiful cascade of green.

"It smells divine!" Joy said, looking up at the tree.

Titus came in from the showroom, holding

the iPad over his head. "We got six orders for flowers!" Then he halted, stared at the tree and approached reverently. "Gosh, Dad. That is the best tree ever."

"Told you." Adam beamed proudly and put his hand on Titus's shoulder.

"Hold on!" Titus scurried into the retail area and in a flash was back, holding a little train engine ornament in his hand. "I have to see." He went up to the tree, carefully chose a branch and slipped the gold ribbon around the green needles. He stood back, observed for a thoughtful moment and pronounced, "I'll buy it.

Joy burst into laughter and everyone joined her. Adam picked Titus up, hugged him and kissed his cheek. "All that for a three-dollar sale, Joy."

"Adam, I'm truly impressed with your salesmanship."

"Thanks." He looked at Sarah. "Did a delivery addressed to me come today?"

Sarah snapped her fingers. "Yes, it did. I put it over here under this first table like you asked me."

Joy shot Sarah a curious look. "Secret Santa?"

"Hardly." Adam went over and opened the large cardboard box. Inside were dozens of boxes of new multicolored lights. "I didn't

"Since last week when you put that sweat-shirt on." He looked up. "It felt important."

She knew exactly what he meant. He was drawing her in closer and tighter by the day. She knew he knew that she knew it. And she couldn't let it happen.

"Why's that?"

He opened his mouth to speak, stopped and exhaled through his nose, like he used to when he was reconsidering options. Paths. Making decisions. "It's advertising. I realize it's not as big as Rockefeller Center, but for Indian Lake, it'll do."

"And do quite well," she said, looking up to the tip. "You and Titus measured this per-fectly. There's plenty of room for a star. But we sold out.

"I'll order one tomorrow," she said, taking one of the boxes of lights. "We should get to it. I'll start on the bottom."

"I'll get the extension ladder."

"Ooh. That thing always scared me. Too high."

"Yeah?" he said, walking away. "I thought angels were impervious to heights."

Joy lowered her head as his words drifted across the room as he left.

How could he think she was an angel after

everything they'd been through? When she was marrying another man?

Each time he paused, took a breath or cast one of his longing gazes at her, she melted. Like the teenager she once was.

She must have missed some important phase during her evolution to adulthood, because something in her psyche was stuck back here in this small-town world. Adam's world.

What would have happened if she hadn't gone to New York? Would she have married Adam? Then again, if she hadn't left, Adam would not have married Amie and Titus wouldn't exist, and for Joy, she'd have been robbed of knowing a most wonderful and endearing little boy.

Or would she have allowed her bitterness toward the people who caused her parents' deaths to destroy all her chances at happiness? As it was, she'd run away and buried her grief and anger— "In my work."

Adam walked in with the ladder. "What's wrong? The lights don't work?"

"Uh, no. I need to get some extension cords. I have some under the front counter. Be right back."

"Okay," he said and set up the extension ladder, the top of which he propped against the center beam in the glass-paned ceiling. "I haven't done this for a long time," he called.

After retrieving the cords, Joy walked back into the greenhouse. "Getting a tree this tall was your idea."

"I know" He beamed, taking the long green wire extension cord she handed him up the ladder with him. "I'll run this one through the center so we can hang the lights straight down in a line from the top. It'll be too difficult to go around the tree."

"Hmm. Second-guessing your choice?" she teased.

"Hey, my kid wanted this tree and it's the one he's gonna see. I want to knock his socks off."

"I think you already did."

"Yeah? How's that?"

"Oh, Adam. Anyone can see he idolizes you."

"You think?"

"He works so hard on his vocabulary. It's got to be hard for a little kid to keep up with a genius like you. I know I had a hard time measuring up back when..." She unboxed another string and handed it to him.

"That's not true. You always measured up."

"Maybe that's not the right choice of words. It was, well, you were so—advanced. You talked about machines and propulsions and free energy. You sailed through physics and advanced science classes like they were child's play."

"They were," he said, reaching for another string and plugging them in.

"I always wondered why you didn't become an astrophysicist or a theoretical physicist like Stephen Hawking."

"You saw that?" He paused, then took another string and hung it.

"I did."

"I got a scholarship for mechanical engineering."

"Wait—is that why you went to Purdue?"

"I thought you knew. Or I told you. Maybe I was too embarrassed to tell you. I didn't have a family to pay for my education. That was the best I could get and I took it."

He climbed down the ladder. "Okay," he said, moving to the other side of the tree. "I'll take four strings up with me this time."

Joy unboxed the lights and handed him the bundles of strings. "I'll plug the lower strings into these. They should reach to the bottom."

"Without a problem," he said, as he continued working.

Joy plugged in the second tier of lights as Adam worked from the very top. In another thirty minutes the boxes were empty and they stood back to critique their creation.

"It looks like a waterfall of light," she gushed. "It's magnificent, Adam. A wonder."

"It is different." He snapped his fingers. "I just remembered," he said, rushing away.

"Where are you going?"

"I found something… Be right back."

Joy picked up the empty light boxes and tossed them in the larger cardboard shipping box. The tree shimmered.

"Here!" he said proudly, walking in with an enormous glitter gold star. It had a metal corkscrew attachment at its base.

"Grandpa's old star!" She reached for it. "Where was it?"

"In the very back of the storage room. I was looking for more lights, and when I realized there were none, I ordered the new ones. But I found this in a crumbling box under an old bag of glittered cotton batting."

"Can you reach the top and put it on?" she asked. "I mean, if it's too dangerous, don't do it."

"I can try," he said, going back up the extension ladder. At the very top, he had to reach with every inch his long arm allowed, but he managed it.

He looked up. "Oh, Joy, I wish you weren't afraid of heights."

"Why?"

"Wait." He hustled down the ladder, then went to the far wall and turned out the overhead fluorescent lights. He took her hand and they went over to one of the poinsettia tables where their successful sales had cleared a portion of the tabletop. "Sit here."

Joy sat on the table and Adam stood next to her. "Now what?"

"Look up." He pointed. "No place else in town can you see a crystal clear winter sky like that and without freezing outside!"

"So many stars." She sighed as they looked through the glass. The sky was nearly black, the half-moon to the east. The greenhouse was warm, thanks to Adam's invention. As she looked at the sky, she could see the Little Dipper, the North Star. Venus.

"Galaxy after galaxy and on and on to infinity," he said. "Worlds beyond worlds."

Just then two shooting stars whisked across the expanse, their tails streaming glowing light behind them.

"Did you see that?" she gasped.

"I did." He turned to her. "You know what that was?"

"No." She gazed up at him.

"That was your grandfather telling you he loves you."

Joy's eyes filled with tears. She threw her arms around his neck. "Thank you, Adam."

"For what?"

"Being you—never changing."

He pulled her close and let her cry into his shoulder.

CHAPTER TWENTY-THREE

JOY WAS HOLDING Titus's hand, but he shot away, up Mrs. Beabots's shoveled sidewalk, past the lit garland-draped wrought-iron handrails and up the steps to the front porch. Then he put his hands on his cheeks and said, "Wow! She decorates more than you do."

Joy looked up at half a dozen lit wreaths suspended between the Victorian porch posts, yards and yards of red-ribbon-wrapped and lit garland strung along the entire expanse of porch ceiling, and glimpses of more lights inside beyond the beveled glass doors. "All this wasn't here yesterday when you were at Sarah's house next door?"

"Nope!"

"Then Mrs. Beabots must have found some elves to help her." Joy walked up to Titus, leaned over and shook her finger at him. "And don't run away from me like that again. What if you fell?"

He smiled impishly. "I'd get up. Like always," he said, putting his hand in hers. "Can I ring the bell? I love this bell."

"So do I. It reminds me of when I was your age and came to this house."

"You did?" He looked up at her, pushing his glasses in place.

"Uh-huh. But you go ahead."

"Thanks!" Titus proudly went to the antique door and twisted the hundred-plus-year-old pewter bell. "This was really nice of her to invite us for dinner."

"It sure was," Joy replied, as Mrs. Beabots opened the door. Though she wore a pink-red-and-white toile apron with pink-and-white candy cane striped straps and ruffle at the bottom, Joy's eyes caught her Chanel logo gold earrings. Her platinum hair was meticulously styled, as it always was, and her makeup just as expertly applied.

"Come in!" Mrs. Beabots smiled as she opened her arms for hugs. "You're just in time to help," she said to Titus.

They walked in and Joy shut the door as Titus shucked off his hooded jacket, boots and scarf.

"I'd like to help with dinner," Joy offered, taking off her coat and boots. She put on her shoes, which she'd carried in a shoe bag.

Mrs. Beabots hung their coats in the closet

and said, "Oh, dinner is ready. Macaroni and cheese with bacon. I hope you like it."

"No vegetables?" Titus asked. "I have to eat something green, Dad says."

"I know," Mrs. Beabots confirmed. "I'm steaming organic green beans. How's that?"

"Cool," Titus replied.

Joy gaped as they entered the kitchen. There wasn't a bare surface anywhere. The island, the counter around the sink, the stove and the long side serving counter were filled with cookie sheets; tiered pie servers bore plates filled with cookies. Several boxes of plastic wrap were piled next to a cardboard box that held paper plates with assorted cookies.

"What is all this?" Joy asked. "And how long have you been at it?" She spied two large mixers, eggs, boxes of butter, a twenty-pound sack of flour, brown sugar, and large containers of spices sitting on the windowsill, apparently because there was no room left on the counters.

"Days, actually," Mrs. Beabots replied.

Titus's eyes were huge, reminding Joy of those cartoon characters with the massive goggles and big eyes. "Is this for our supper?"

Joy couldn't help her giggle and hugged Titus. "No, honey."

"They're for my charities," Mrs. Beabots answered. "The Recovery Alliance downtown. The Fireman's Christmas Gala. Your children's Christmas pageant at Saint Mark's."

As Mrs. Beabots spoke, Joy was suddenly aware of the number of community projects seemingly the whole town supported. A new Community Center on Gina Barzonni's land. A safe and maintained winter skating rink for the kids, rather than old Craven's Pond, which was all they'd had when she was a kid. The City Council's Father's Day Pancake Breakfast to support Hungry Child efforts. The list went on.

These were not the efforts of an apathetic community she remembered.

Mrs. Beabots was still chatting away. "Some of these cookies are for—" she shot Joy a smile "—the Boston Greenhouses…"

Joy put up her hand. "Stop right there. I had no idea so many people depended on you. I can't accept these cookies anymore. You're doing too much."

"Joy Boston, don't you dare tell me I'm too old to do this work."

"I wasn't gonna say *that*."

"You were thinking it."

Titus's gaze tracked from one adult to the other. "Are you arguing?"

Joy laughed. "I should argue with her, but I'm not. She's always been this stubborn. And energetic."

Mrs. Beabots ended the birth of the argument and said to Titus, "Your dad told me he had work to do tonight. More deliveries for the greenhouses?"

"No," Titus answered, rubbing his nose. "He has to work on the computer. He does that a lot after I go to bed."

"That's right," Joy said. "I volunteered to bring Titus with me over here so Adam could have some time. He's done so much for me. First fixing up the greenhouses. Helping with supplies. The deliveries."

"Don't forget the tree!" Titus grinned.

"I can't forget that. I can't wait for you to see it." Joy stared at her hostess. "Speaking of which, who put up all those decorations for you?"

"Lester MacDougal. His landscaping company puts up lights all over town. I have a standing commitment from him."

"He told Adam he wasn't all that busy and we're sending him back to Dallas for more poinsettias."

"Lester never turns down work," Mrs. Beabots said, brushing her palm over the back of her silky hair. "Someday, I've got to find the right girl for him. He's such a loner."

"Matchmaking again?" Joy accused.

"When did I ever?"

"What's matchmaking?" Titus asked, scrambling up onto his usual stool and placing his elbows on the granite counter.

They stared at him.

"It's okay if you don't tell me. I'll just look it up on the internet."

"Fine!" Joy interjected. "Mrs. Beabots has always had a penchant— You know what that is?"

"A proclivity." Titus ratcheted up his eyebrow challengingly.

Joy exhaled. She could see she would seldom ever fool this very bright boy. "She likes to meddle—"

"Help," Mrs. Beabots corrected. "I help boys and girls, men and women, in their romantic relationships."

"So, are you helping my dad?" Titus asked boldly.

"Uh…"

"No," Joy interjected quickly. "Your dad appears to be quite happy in his life. After all, he has you."

"Yeah," Titus said. "He told me he has a lot to do with his life. That's why he has to concentrate on his work." Titus nodded to himself as he reached toward a lopsided gingerbread man. "Can I have this one?" he asked.

"Dinner first," Joy said.

He pulled the gingerbread man toward him, patting the cookie. "You'll be dessert."

Joy rubbed her hands together. "Where do I start?"

"A big plate for Titus."

"Yay! I'll have extra green beans, please. Do you have milk?"

"I do. Organic."

Joy went to the refrigerator. "I've noticed you, Sarah, even Grandpa had organic milk. Is it because the kids are in and out of all your homes?"

Mrs. Beabots pulled a casserole out of the oven and put it on top of the stove, where she'd cleared a space big enough for the round blue-and-white-painted dish. "I would, certainly, but the truth is, Adam buys it and drops it off."

"That's thoughtful," she said, taking a glass out of the cabinet for Titus and pouring his milk.

"Oh," Titus began. "Dad does that so I won't eat the wrong thing no matter where I go."

Mrs. Beabots scooped a large ladleful of

beans from the saucepan on the stove. "How's that, Titus?"

"Perfect. I'm hungry. And after I eat, can I help decorate some cookies? I told Dad I wanted to make Christmas cookies, but he doesn't make them."

Joy took a small plate and placed a spoonful of macaroni and cheese on it. "I guess he thinks it's too much sugar for you, huh?"

Titus put a long green bean in his mouth and chomped on it. "He doesn't like baking. He said it's not creative and it takes too long. He cooks dinner for me every night, except for when we have leftovers."

"Not creative?" Mrs. Beabots exclaimed. "I need to talk to that boy." She waved her hand over the array of lemon bars, chocolate-iced cherry cookies, powdered-sugar-covered snowballs, peppermint-candy-filled puffs, butter cookies in the shapes of green wreaths, green trees and white snowmen, all decorated with cinnamon candies. "What would he call this?"

Joy speared a forkful of macaroni. "Delicious, I'm guessing."

"Well," Mrs. Beabots said, "I'll just have to make a plate for Titus to take home. I'll show him."

Joy glanced at Titus and saw the smirk on

his lips as he ate. She couldn't help wondering if Adam had made that comment or if Titus had just wrangled a plate of cookies for himself.

After they finished their dinner, Joy cleaned up. Then she said, "I'll make the icing for the sugar cookies."

Mrs. Beabots placed plastic and paper plates of cookies in the large cardboard boxes she had stacked by the back door.

"Titus, would you take these boxes, one by one, to the dining room table for me?"

"Sure," he said, getting down from the stool and taking the first box from Mrs. Beabots.

Joy noticed that the stool teetered slightly. It amazed her that Titus climbed up and down stools like that, seemingly unaware of his imbalance, and yet he managed to right the stool every time. She looked into the large mixer bowl. "What's this?"

"Oh, my gosh, I forgot. I need to make another pan of lemon bars. I started that before you got here. The recipe is there on top of the flour canister. Do you mind finishing up that filling? That's the lemon juice and sugar. You'll need to melt the butter in the microwave and go from there. I made the cookie crust bottom. It's in the nine-by-twelve pan there next to the date pinwheel cookies."

Titus came back into the kitchen, took another box and marched it to the dining room.

Mrs. Beabots filled another box. "I promised Beatrice Nelson I'd bring some cookies out to her youth camp. There aren't any campers around in the winter, but I wanted Chris and Eli to have some cookies. I suppose I could drop them off at the fire station with her husband. Do you mind driving me over there, Joy?

"Of course I will. And every other place you need to go."

Titus came into the kitchen and got another box, then turned back toward the dining room.

Joy smiled at him. "You're such a good helper, Titus."

"It's important to stay busy," he said from the hallway.

Joy looked at Mrs. Beabots. "That sounds like something you'd say."

"I do remember saying that to you when you were young." She smiled.

Joy measured the rest of the ingredients, turned on the mixer and scraped the sides of the bowl. This time when Titus returned, he went up to Joy and asked, "Can I lick the bowl?"

"Sure."

He started to reach up, with the beater still going, and Joy snatched his hand away. "Not yet, Titus. After I turn the machine off."

"Oh." He pulled his hand back and looked down.

Instantly, Joy knew she'd hurt his feelings. "Titus, sweetheart. I didn't mean to snap at you. Haven't you ever worked with a mixer before?"

"No. We don't have one," he replied and looked up. "Dad has an immersion blender he uses for sauces and soups."

"I see. But you've licked a cookie dough bowl before."

"Uh-huh. Miss Milse makes all kinds of sugary stuff at Miss Sarah's house and she gives us the bowls to lick. That's where I learned it."

Joy pursed her lips. "I see," she said again. "So does your dad know you have treats at Miss Sarah's house?"

Titus glanced at Mrs. Beabots. Then slid his eyes back to Joy, fiddling with his sport strap. "I think I forgot to mention it."

"I'll tell you what," Joy said. "I won't tattle on you and neither will Mrs. Beabots. But you should tell your dad. It's not a bad thing, and I'm sure Sarah watches how much sugar she allows."

"Yes," Mrs. Beabots interrupted, "but Miss Milse is the best pastry chef this side of Berlin."

Joy sighed. "I remember."

"She uses cage-free eggs and organic milk," Titus said brightly. "That's a good thing, right?"

Joy laughed along with Mrs. Beabots. "Most certainly."

Joy turned off the mixer and prepared the lemon bars. "Is the oven preheated?"

"I never turned it off. I may need more date bars before the night is over."

"Good heavens. You really do feed the town."

Mrs. Beabots lifted her chin proudly. "It's my town and my honor."

A surge of regret hurled through Joy. Her town. Joy had run away because she'd hated too many of its residents, and she'd pushed away the love offered to her by people like Mrs. Beabots, Sarah, Maddie, Olivia—and Adam. Times had changed. Old Wilma Wilcox was long buried. The town council had new members. People had changed.

Joy wondered what Adam was working on

tonight. He'd told her about several patents he'd applied for.

All this time that she'd been back, Joy had concentrated so much on building the greenhouses back to their former successful state that she hadn't questioned Adam's participation. Had he put his work aside to help her and was it costing him? She hoped she hadn't jeopardized his career in any way. Typical.

It was Joy's fault she didn't know more about the adult Adam. Was she wrong to have parked her heart back there in her memories of high school? Were Adam's feelings for her now real, or was he doing the same jog down memory lane?

Were they both guilty of resurrecting the greenhouses to keep a past romance alive?

Or was there something more? Something real?

And did she even want to know? Wasn't it safer to stick to the plan and then go back to her life in New York?

Wasn't it safer to choose Chuck and the career she'd worked so diligently for and keep her errant heart and romantic dreams locked in the past?

Titus stepped back while Joy put the pan of lemon bars into the oven and set the timer.

Titus looked up at her, smiled and, without

a word, put his arms around her waist and hugged her.

"I like you being here with me," he said and squeezed his little arms tighter.

Joy rested her palms on the top of his head, leaned down and kissed his crown. "I love it," she said, feeling every space inside her glow.

Titus tilted his head back, stared up at her and said, "My mom used to kiss the top of my head. She said all her love would go straight into my heart from there."

"It sounds like she was a wise woman."

"So are you," Mrs. Beabots said softly as she poured more milk for Titus. "Come eat your gingerbread man, Titus. That bowl can wait."

Joy rubbed Titus's back before he walked to his stool and climbed up.

The whorl of longing, caring and, yes, love that overtook Joy left her light-headed. She grasped the edge of the counter and realized her eyes had filled with tears.

She loved little Titus, who reminded her every second of the kind of young person Adam had been long ago.

It had been only a few hours since she'd seen Adam at the greenhouses and she missed him already. She knew there was at least another hour or more of work to do here with

Mrs. Beabots, but all she could think about was the opportunity to see Adam when she took Titus home.

She wondered if he would kiss her good-night. Or give her a hug. Would he ask her in? Would it be wrong to tell him about her feelings?

Maybe Adam did care for her now, but the harsh fact was that he didn't know the adult Joy any more than she knew what he was like.

Adam didn't trust her.

And he had good reason. She was here in Indian Lake for another ten days. By Christmas Day, she'd be off to New York and out of Adam's life forever.

He was right to protect his heart. His child. His future.

She should do the same for herself.

CHAPTER TWENTY-FOUR

JOY STOOD OUTSIDE the main greenhouse, huddled in jeans, a pair of broken-in cowboy boots she'd found in the very back of her closet and her grandpa's sheepskin-lined leather jacket. Snow whirled around her feet and her teeth chattered as she tried to smile for Scott Abbott's DSLR camera.

Scott waved his left hand at her. "A little to the left, Joy. I want to get all the tree in, but with you out here, it gives a flavor of how huge the tree is."

"Couldn't we do this inside?" she groaned, her smiling lips feeling as if they'd frozen to her teeth.

"I got those, but this is epic!" He took a few more shots. "Done."

"Oh, thank goodness. Trust me, there's not enough hot cocoa to warm me up." She laughed as they hustled through the showroom's front door.

Adam was at the counter checking out a customer whose double-tiered cart was piled with Sonora Marble poinsettias. Joy loved the pink-and-cream-splattered bracts and smaller leaves. They were part of the new shipment from Dallas.

"How'd it go?" Adam asked.

"Freezing," Joy said. "I need a warm drink."

Scott went up and shook Adam's hand. "I'd stay, but I want to get this in for this evening's edition. They're literally holding the presses for me." He took the memory card out of the DSLR and plugged it into a laptop he'd opened up. "I gotta email these ASAP." He typed the email address and uploaded the pictures. "Okay, photos sent. I'll write the copy on the drive back to my bookshop."

"You're amazing," Joy complimented him.

"Ain't me." He held the phone up. "Technology. Much of it, I love. Some, I hate. Gotta run." He started to jog to the door and halted. "Hey, you both going to the kids' pageant at the school?"

Adam beamed. "Absolutely. Titus is a shepherd and he has a couple lines to recite. He didn't get to write the play this time."

"Yeah? Don't tell my daughter. Bella wanted to be the angel. She's a townsperson instead. Isabelle convinced her it was a good gig because she still got to wear a costume." Scott went to the door and helped the lady customer out with her poinsettias. He waved to them as he shut the door.

Joy laughed. "He's such a neat guy."

"The best," Adam replied as his cell phone rang. "Masterson."

Joy watched as Scott helped the woman load her car and then put the cart in the bin near the front door. She was still surprised how these little exchanges about school plays, cookie baking and Christmas decorating reminded her of her mother. Jill had made certain that Joy participated in school events, invited her friends over to share in holiday activities. She and Sarah had made ornaments together. And Sarah carried on the tradition for her kids and included Titus. Jill had told her, "The greatest gifts, Joy, are the memories we make with our friends."

Joy hadn't made much of Christmas at all since she left Indian Lake. And her life lacked a great deal of her mother's kind of loving sparkle. "Nobody's fault but my own."

As she took off her jacket and headed to the greenhouse, Adam waved to her. "I just took care of the watering. I have to take this call, so do you mind watching the front?"

"Of course not," she said, putting her jacket

under the counter as some patrons walked in. "Go!" She waved him away.

Adam pushed through the French doors. "Yeah. I'm here. So, what did he say?"

Joy knew the kids were at school, probably rehearsing for the pageant. She'd forgotten how important play parts, leading roles and being chosen for school teams, bands and choirs were to kids. She'd won the parts she wanted back then, and if a role was truly challenging, she didn't try out for it. Acting, singing and music had never been her forte the way it had been for Sarah, who always seemed to do everything exceptionally well.

Come to think of it, Adam hadn't been much for group activities, either. Except for his participation in science fairs, he'd been a loner back then.

Another big change for him in adulthood. He was very much the joiner now.

Sarah came through the doorway to the middle greenhouse with a customer who was wheeling a double-tiered cart filled with the new Cortez White poinsettias that were also part of the shipment from Dallas. Sarah pushed a second cart and pulled a third filled with an assortment of poinsettias, including Winter Rose, an odd-looking flower, half ruffled rose and half poinsettia. Joy loved it. Adam couldn't stand it.

This late in the season, Joy had been able to garner only the more interesting and expensive poinsettias, since the mass retailers had already spoken for the traditional reds, whites and pinks.

"Joy," the seventyish woman in the long camel coat said, "I can't tell you how thrilled I am with what you've done. When I got back to town from my cruise, everyone at my church and book club was talking about the reopening. I was so late getting here, I was afraid there'd be nothing left. But these poinsettias! I've never seen anything so exotic." She touched the bracts of a Winter Blush flower with pink-and-cream blossoms and green-and-white-veined leaves.

"Thank you so much," Joy said.

"I'm having forty people on Christmas Eve and these beauties will be banked around the fireplace and up the staircase." She leaned forward. "I'm going to knock their socks off this year," she murmured, smiling broadly.

"I'm glad you feel that way. I was worried because there's nothing traditional about any of the flowers in this shipment."

"I love them. And I'm going to send my friends from the book club over, if they haven't been here already," she said, handing Joy her credit card. "Why, with flowers like these, who needs any other decorations?"

"That's a lovely compliment," Joy replied. "But I have to say, it's not Christmas in Indian Lake without a tree."

"Oh, absolutely."

Sarah pushed one of the carts toward the door. "I'd have a tree in every room if I had the time."

"And the decorations!" the woman said and took another cart as Joy came around the counter and took the third.

They filled the woman's SUV with the poinsettias, placed the carts in the bin and rushed back inside, hugging themselves.

"Wow! I forgot how cold and snowy it gets here," Joy said.

"And it's only December. Wait till late January." Sarah laughed.

Joy's smile vanished as she looked at her friend. "I'll be back in New York…" Joy said, feeling a distance between her and Sarah as the realization settled into Sarah's expression.

"Yes," Sarah replied slowly. "I forgot. You will."

"That is, if everything goes well and I get a good price." The words felt bitter and raw as she spoke them aloud and saw disappointment fill her best friend's face. Joy was responsible for shoring up everyone's enthusiasm and hopes for the greenhouses. Sarah, Maddie, Liz, Olivia, Katia, Mrs. Beabots and Adam had gone to great lengths to help her. They believed in her.

But, Joy realized now, they'd all hoped she would stay. And when she left Indian Lake, she'd be disappointing a lot of people.

Sarah clapped her hands, breaking the mood. "I forgot to tell you—Katia is on her way over. She's bringing a group of people from Austin's car museum. Then she wants poinsettias for the museum and her house."

"Katia is going to love these designer hybrids." Joy pressed her hand to her cheek. "That reminds me. I told Daryl I'd call her about now to see what she thought about Grandpa's Frankincense poinsettia."

"You have a poinsettia that smells like frankincense? We'll make a killing."

Joy smiled as she took her cell phone out of the back pocket of her jeans. "No fragrance, but boy, wouldn't that be something? It is Grandpa's hybrid poinsettia. Finally!" She punched in Daryl's number.

"Oh, Joy! I've been meaning to call. In a word, it's fabulous. It's got a good woody stem and I can do some cuttings right away. I found how he cross-pollinated with Lemon Drop poinsettia and a softer red, almost pink, variety to get this tangerine color. It wasn't easy. But just having this original plant, I can start cuttings this winter and propagate that ad infinitum."

"Are you sure?"

"I am. But I need legal permission to do this, Joy. You most assuredly have something amazing here. I had a similar situation a couple years ago when I propagated for another hybridizer. You keep the rights and pay me for my services. However, I would like to advertise Frankincense on my website. I'll email the document to you, but the sooner we sign, the better."

"Tell you what. Email the papers to Kyle Evans, Grandpa's attorney. I'll text you his information. I'll ask him to read them over ASAP, and if he says everything looks okay, maybe I can drive out there tonight after closing here."

"That would be great, Joy. I'm really excited about this. It's such an unusual flower."

"A showstopper?"

"Most definitely."

"Talk soon."

Joy hung up and looked at Sarah's anxious face. "Daryl can do it!"

Sarah jumped with glee and put her hands on Joy's shoulders. "Oh, my gosh! This is—is earthshaking! I'm so happy for you."

Joy sent a quick text to Kyle and he texted back that he'd received the papers and was reading them over. He cautioned that this was a preliminary agreement and he would draw up formal documents over the next few days.

Adam walked in through the French doors, and having overheard their conversation, he joked, "Whose earth is shaking?"

"Joy's!" Sarah pointed.

Joy knew her smile was wide. This was what she wanted for her grandpa. This was the recognition he deserved, and if all went well and Daryl could indeed continue propagating until next Christmas, she could fill the greenhouse with tangerine-colored poinsettias.

Like a banging gong, Joy's thoughts clashed.

What was she thinking? She wouldn't be here.

"Are you gonna tell me?" he asked.

"I talked to Daryl. She wants to propagate and breed Frankincense."

"No kidding?"

Joy rushed on. "She's sent legal papers to Kyle Evans for him to go over. If all is good,

I'll drive out there tonight and sign. Daryl will start immediately."

Adam pointed to the whirling wind outside the greenhouse. "That bit of winter storm in town is nothing compared to the open road."

"It's not that far," Joy said dismissively. Knowing that she was leaving in ten days, and with all the work she still had to accomplish before her flight to New York, she needed to take care of this right away. Her cell phone pinged with a text.

"It's from Kyle. He says the paperwork looks good. I can sign. So, it's done. I'm going out there."

"Not without me," Adam said. "We'll take my truck."

WHEN KATIA ARRIVED at the greenhouses and heard of Joy's plans to visit Daryl that night, she offered to walk Angel and feed her in addition to cooking for all the kids, Sarah, Luke and Mrs. Beabots at her house, taking some of the burden from Sarah and Miss Milse, who'd been watching Titus nearly every afternoon after school since the greenhouses reopened.

Adam had thanked Katia profusely before Katia showed her friends around the greenhouses. By the time they all left, their cars filled with flowers and gifts, Adam looked at his watch.

"We need to hit the road. I should get gas before we leave town."

Joy had quickly closed up the greenhouses, leaving on the Christmas lights and the stunning lit tree. She'd checked her cell phone, saw that the battery was low, but other than calling Daryl to announce their ETA, she didn't expect to need the phone.

After fueling the truck, they headed east out of Indian Lake. They'd passed the county courthouse, the enormous Santa, and the lit spruce on the lawn that was now at least twenty-five years old and three stories tall. Three enormous lit wreaths hung over the two-hundred-year-old entrance.

Once away from the town lights, Joy was surprised how dark it was.

"It never gets this dark in New York," she said, looking at the falling snow in the glow of the headlights.

"And if we're lucky, we may even drive out of the snow. The storm is coming from due north and this snow is lake-effect."

Joy leaned forward and peered out the windshield. "Those aren't snowflakes. Those are feathers, they're so big."

"From angel's wings. I remember Frank

saying that," Adam mused, keeping his eyes straight ahead.

"When I was little, I believed him."

"I never stopped believing him."

Adam gave her a brief and deeply sincere gaze that went straight to her heart. She said, "Adam, I owe you so much for what you've done. You've been…"

"Still your best friend?" He smiled.

"Yes. Best ever." The words had come out without thinking. They were there, in her heart, and she wanted him to know that.

"Yeah?"

"Uh-huh."

"Well." He lifted his chin as a slight but satisfied smile drew his lips up. "That's good to know."

They rode in silence for a bit, when Adam asked, "Tell me, what do you like best about your life in New York?"

"Seriously?"

"It's not a trick question."

"From you? Sure it is."

He laughed. "C'mon."

"It's my dream come true," she replied.

"Is it?"

"For me, it's everything. I have a job that I love and I'm good at. I have respect from my colleagues, clients and the partners. I have

Glory, whom I love. Then there's the city it-self. Broadway. Restaurants. Museums. Radio City Music Hall at Christmas. The Statue of Liberty, for goodness' sake."

"Yeah. I see what you mean. You should love it."

"I do," she replied. She hadn't mentioned Chuck in her list. With each day, he was fading from her conscience—and she hadn't missed him.

He glanced at her and then away. "I have to say—I liked climbing all those stairs."

"You...went to New York?"

"Yeah."

"When was this?"

"Summer after college graduation."

"Why?"

He gripped the steering wheel. "Isn't it obvious? To see you."

Joy had to close her mouth, she was so surprised. "But you never called."

"I, er, didn't get that far," he confessed.

She turned in her seat and stared at him. "Just how far did you get?"

"I found out where you worked. Frank told me, actually. I saw you coming out of the building. Getting into a limo. With someone."

"Probably Chuck."

"I figured," he said, gripping the steering wheel even tighter.

Joy felt his discomfort and yet this was a revelation to her. She wondered what she would have done back then if she'd known Adam had come to New York. While Chuck had always pursued her, they hadn't been in a relationship then. Over the years, she'd broken down; now she'd committed to him. Hadn't she? She rubbed her forehead, as if wiping away visions of Chuck and the Newly office. "Turnabout is fair play. Why do you like Indian Lake so much?"

"The people. Frank."

"Yeah," she replied sadly. "But he's gone now."

She noticed Adam lifting his chin and grinding his jaw. He was holding something back, but what?

"Life is about people. Loving. Sharing. Look at today. Katia canceled her plans, even took care of Angel, and brought everyone to her house for dinner so that you and I could make this trip. She wanted to help. And Sarah…"

"Has been a godsend. I couldn't have done all this without her help."

"That's what I'm saying. All your real friends were there. I've been trying to show you that

Indian Lake is where you belong. They're here for you."

"And so are you," she said softly.

His blue eyes slid to her with fierce earnestness. "I am."

The truck swerved slightly.

"I better concentrate on the road," he said.

They both watched the highway, looking for the sign that marked the turnoff to Daryl's nursery.

"There it is!" Joy pointed as the headlights lit up a snow-covered but distinctive royal-blue-and-white-lettered sign with a reflective painted arrow pointing to the right.

"I see it," Adam replied, as he turned off the highway and onto the county road.

It was only a mile to Daryl's farm. They followed silver reflective markers topped with bright red bows that led up to the drive. There were solar lights on tall poles at the entrance and leading up to the house and the massive greenhouses.

Adam honked the horn as they drove up. The front door of the house opened and Daryl, dressed in jeans, a hooded parka, gloves and snow boots, waved to them as she approached.

"I figured you'd call and reschedule," she said, holding Joy's door.

"I was persistent."

"And daring," Daryl added, hugging Joy. "Well, c'mon in. I have everything in the kitchen."

"Something hot?" Adam asked.

"How about some hibiscus tea? I dried the petals myself," Daryl said.

Joy looked at Adam, who shrugged his shoulders. "Of course you did," Joy said.

Adam rubbed his chin as they walked. "Do you do a lot of that? Make flower teas?"

"Yeah. After the summer season, I cut back the rose petals, hibiscus and violets and dry them. I have to do that to pollinate and hybridize the roses, especially. I have barrels of dried flowers." She held the door open for them. "Why?"

Joy went inside, careful to keep her snowy boots on the rag rug to the side of the foyer. She took off her coat and caught Adam's eye. She knew just what he was thinking. "Because we might want to package them and sell them at Boston Greenhouses."

Daryl smiled at Joy. "I love this idea! I don't reopen till the last week in April, to the public, I mean, and all I've done with them is to mix them and sell as potpourri. Not such a big call for that anymore," she admitted. "I never thought of selling them for teas."

Joy followed Daryl to the kitchen, where

the papers rested on the wooden table. Daryl put a teakettle on the stove to boil. "You look those papers over."

Joy started reading.

Adam quickly moved over to the stacked teacups. "I'll fix the tea while you two discuss business. You want sugar, Joy?"

"Yes, thanks."

"Adam, I have some local honey there for mine. Thanks." Daryl sat next to Joy.

"To save time, I can write that provision here." Joy pointed to the signature page. "We'll both initial and date."

"Okay. Anything else?"

Joy read the points. "This is very specific."

"I know. Kyle rewrote the contract on my request. If you'll notice, he has a clause that if either of us decline to do business together, or upon my death, neither I nor my heirs can use the name Frankincense for a poinsettia."

"He told me he researched it and the name hadn't been taken."

"That's right," Adam said. "Actually, I did the research and I sent him an email."

Joy and Daryl turned around and said at the same time, "You did?"

He put their tea in front of them, leaning so close to Joy that their noses nearly touched. "I wanted you to be safe."

Joy had to drag her eyes from him. She felt uncomfortable, as if Daryl were witnessing an intimate moment. Maybe she was.

Joy quickly took a gulp of tea. Anything to avoid the twist of warmth in her belly and the distinct hammering of her heart. "I'll sign," Joy said, picking up the ballpoint.

"I'll do the same."

Adam drank his tea. "You should have it notarized. And a copy in Kyle's office."

"It's kinda late for a notary," Joy said.

"There's one at the library," Adam said. "This is good for now, but once the weather breaks, and you can get to town, Daryl, I could cover at the greenhouses for Joy while you two take care of business," he said.

"I'll do that," Daryl agreed and finished her tea.

"I'd love to sell the tea before Christmas, but that's a lot to ask."

"Not really. I can use my business card as the label. It's cute, with a blue ribbon at the top. I'll use clear food-safe plastic bags. I'll have them for you in two days." She glanced up at the kitchen window. "As long as the snow abates."

Joy followed her gaze. "We should go." She picked up her copy of the contract and held out her hand. "Partners."

Daryl shook her hand. "Frank would be proud. I promise to do my best by him…and you. This flower is unique, Joy. And, Adam, thank you for working with Frank on it all this time."

Joy walked out of Daryl's house feeling an unfamiliar sense of true accomplishment. In all her years in accounting, no matter how difficult the client or precarious their situation, when she'd righted their corporate ships, she'd only moved on to the next problem. The next file.

This was vastly different.

She was creating something that had never existed before. She was carrying on Frank's legacy just as Adam had said.

She reached for Adam's hand as they walked to the truck. But instead of holding her hand, he put his arm around her shoulders and said, "I've never been so proud of you."

"Thank you, Adam." She looked up at the snow falling in her face. The sky was heavy and gray.

But even without the stars and moon, she felt her grandpa around her. As Adam pulled her a bit closer, she felt love from both of them.

CHAPTER TWENTY-FIVE

SAINT MARK'S AUDITORIUM was standing room only for the children's Christmas pageant. There was a single adult role in the entire play and Adam volunteered.

"Dad!" Titus ran up to him in the school hallway where kids were dressing in the classrooms for their appearances. "How do I look?"

"Genuine."

"Huh?"

"Like an honest-to-goodness shepherd boy. I like the crook."

"I thought it was a staff." Titus looked at the Irish shillelagh Timmy's dad had let him borrow for his premier acting role. He flipped the ends of the scarf under the kippah he wore on his head.

"Where'd you get that head covering?"

"Mrs. Beabots had it. She said the scarf is from Paris. I gave Miss Sarah a thank-you note for making my tunic." He lifted his sneaker. "We didn't know what to do about the shoes."

"It's okay. The tunic covers them."

"Timmy has burlap sacks over his shoes and tied them with twine. But Miss Sarah said she ran out of material."

"I'm sorry, Titus. I've been so busy with all this work that I didn't realize how much you needed my help. You didn't say anything."

Titus pushed his glasses up. "Actually, I figured I better not have bags on my feet. In case I trip."

"Really?" Adam put his arm around Titus's shoulders. "You're aware of the danger. You must be growing up."

"I am, Dad." Titus wobbled his head and rolled his eyes. "I'll be six in two weeks."

"I remember," Adam replied with a smile. Then thrust his tongue against his lips as a clump of white nylon hairs got caught in his mouth. He patted down the white beard and adjusted the wide black belt on his Santa costume. "So, what do you think of my, er...suit? How do I look?"

"Fat."

"That's the point."

"But awesome, Dad. Totally." Titus grinned.

"I've never been dressed like Santa before. This beard is really long."

"So, why did you do it?"

Adam's smile pinched his eyes as they misted. He put his hand on Titus's shoulder. "I did it for you, Titus."

"Thanks, Dad. And Miss Joy knows you're Santa?"

"I thought it should be a surprise."

Titus laughed. "Well, at least she'll know what you'll look like when you're really, really old!"

"Oh, thanks a lot."

The intercom sounded a bell. Titus jumped, his anxiety rising to the surface. "It's time! I hope I remember my lines. It's hard when you don't write them yourself."

"You can do anything. You remember that and you'll be just fine. C'mon. I'll walk you to the stage. I don't go on till the last scene, so I'll watch you from the wings. Okay?"

"Okay." Titus playfully banged the shillelagh against the floor as they walked, reminding Adam that his son, as brilliant as he was, still was a child filled with wonderment and blind faith.

The play was true to the Christmas story, but the spoken lines between the shepherds, angels and the wise men were contemporary, and when delivered by nervous, nonprofessional children, the murmur of laughter from the audience and the continued flash of cell phone cameras made Adam proud.

Adam's role was as simple as one could be. After the children sang "Silent Night" and then hummed the tune, Adam walked on stage, reached in his sack and started handing candy canes out to all the kids there.

The curtain fell to thunderous applause as all the parents shot to their feet, clapping for their kids.

"Bravo!"

The curtain parted and Titus took his bow, along with Timmy, Annie and Danny. Then the kids playing other parts joined them. Adam stood behind all the children and bowed, as well.

Watching from on stage, he saw Joy next to Mrs. Beabots, who pointed to Adam, whispered something that caused Joy to gape at him, then smile broadly. She clapped even harder.

"Uh-oh. Busted," he said, as the kids started off the stage. He then went down the steps and to the kids who had gathered at the bottom, eager for their own candy canes.

Backstage again at last, he took off the hat, long white wig, and the beard that had been hooked around his ears.

"Dad!" Titus rushed up, the shillelagh pointed not up in the air, but straight ahead.

"Titus! Be careful with that thing," he said as he grabbed it. "You could hurt someone with it."

"Sorry." Titus dropped his chin to his chest. "I forgot. I just wanted to tell you how great you were."

"Thanks, son, but I didn't have a speaking part like you."

"I know," Titus replied.

"Adam!" Joy shouted, as she walked down the hall with Mrs. Beabots. She waved.

He waved back, then lowered his arm.

It had been a long time since he'd seen her face light up at the sight of him. Was he dreaming? Was she this happy to see him or was it simply that his Santa role had surprised her?

"Adam!" Affectionately, she put her hand on Titus's shoulder. "You were both great." Her eyes lifted from his son to him. His blue eyes held hers.

Suddenly, he remembered they were not alone. "I, uh, better get this back to Mrs. Cook. She has to return it by the end of the day. Probably being used again tonight by someone else."

"Right," Joy said, looking at her watch and

then at Mrs. Beabots. "I'll drive you home and then go back and open up the greenhouses. I hope not too many people were disappointed I was closed for an hour."

Mrs. Beabots chuckled. "They'll come back."

"I hope so. Well, see you later, guys," Joy said as she walked away.

Titus shuffled to Adam's side and took his hand. "She looked really pretty today, huh?"

"Mrs. Beabots always looks elegant."

"I was talking about Miss Joy."

"I know who you meant," Adam said. Joy always looked lovely to him, even with smudges of humus on her cheeks. He'd tried, maybe in vain, to show her that not just her friends wanted to support her, but more important, he did. Yes, he'd pushed to help her out revamping the greenhouses. Yes, he'd made himself available to her—maybe too often. But, darn it, he wanted her to see what she was missing.

He knew she had to make a lot of choices if there was anything that could happen between them. Her fiancé. New York and putting her grief and anger in the past, where it belonged.

But in the end, Adam had decisions, as well. Since Amie died, he'd closed his heart down to new love. Until recently, he'd been successful teaching Titus to keep his distance from others. But Titus's friendship with Annie and Timmy and even Danny Sullivan had opened Adam's eyes. Perhaps he'd been wrong.

If he took a chance with Joy, would she hurt him again? Or would she surprise him? Adam wished he could be sure.

"Let's go change. Then we'll go home."

"You aren't going to the greenhouses?"

"Not today. I have a lot of other work to do."

They walked into Titus's classroom. Adam helped Titus take off his tunic, kippah and scarf. Adam helped Titus into his jacket, put up the hood and then helped with his boots. Adam lumbered out of the Santa costume and gave it to Mary-Catherine Cook, Titus's teacher.

"You were terrific," Mary-Catherine said.

"Wasn't much to it," Adam replied.

"But you did it with spontaneity and, well, fun!" She looked at Titus. "You have a happy vacation, Titus. I'll see you in the New Year."

Adam's smile vanished. He'd been so immersed in Joy's world at the greenhouses and recording the results of his geothermal heating system, he'd actually lost track of time.

Christmas was nearly here. The kids were on vacation as of the end of the play today. The New Year was almost upon them.

Last night, Hal had called and pressed him about the California job. Adam turned him down, believing that he and Joy were finding their way back to each other. Hal had been disappointed, naturally, because he believed in Adam.

Admittedly, Adam wasn't all that keen on moving Titus from his friends. And he still hoped that Joy would give him a signal that she'd found happiness in Indian Lake. He'd hoped, foolishly, that she'd see her fiancé was not the kind of guy who would make her happy. Yet, when they'd discussed her early career, Chuck had been there. She'd known him a long time. Were they romantic all that time? And if so, what chance did he really have with her?

Their kiss that afternoon before going into the bank building had been premature. If anything, he'd probably frightened her.

He'd certainly caused enough consternation in his own heart and mind.

After their breakup, he'd found happiness again with Amie. They'd been of like mind and the thrill of Titus was incredible. He would always be grateful that Amie had been a part of his life, but the truth was, Joy had never left his heart.

Apparently, his heart was still Joy territory.

He wished he knew how to cross into that country again.

It was time he'd have to force the situation to a conclusion.

CHAPTER TWENTY-SIX

IT WAS NEARLY eleven o'clock as Joy checked out her customers, wrapped their poinsettias and bagged their gift items. She wished them a merry Christmas.

"I guess we should have shopped earlier," the twentysomething young woman said to her mother.

"I've been fortunate that my inventory has sold well."

"I'll say, though I do like these unusual poinsettias. Quite honestly, I got tired of the same old thing I could find at the Tractor Supply." The mother laughed.

"I aim to please," Joy said.

"So, next year, can we expect more of the same?" the blonde daughter asked.

She'd been focused on the present circumstances since she opened the greenhouses. Make the business solvent. Sell. Go back to New York.

But she'd put Chuck on hold. In fact, he'd taken her very seriously and gone radio silent on her since they'd had that conversation. And she'd thought about no one but Adam.

But next year?

Joy could only stare at their curious faces. "I, er, don't know what I'll find next year," she replied honestly. In more ways than one.

"Maybe something more exciting?"

"You never know," Joy replied, thinking about the tangerine Frankincense poinsettia Daryl was already propagating.

The ladies left just as Adam walked in.

"Hi!" she said. "Where have you been all morning?"

"Missed me, huh?" His smile was mischievous.

"I know that look. You've been up to something."

He reached in his jeans' pocket and pulled out two tickets. "I had to stand in line for over an hour to snag these."

"Theater tickets?"

"Front-row seats for the symphony Christmas concert tonight."

"They still do that?"

"Absolutely. It's tradition. So, you'll go?"

"I'd love to."

"I'll pick you up in front of the greenhouses at seven." He leaned over the counter and kissed her cheek.

"Thanks," he said.

"For what?"

"Making another dream come true."

She hadn't been to the concert since they were in high school. She remembered that last Christmas and the long black skirt and burgundy blouse she'd worn. She glanced down at her jeans. Glory had sent her an infusion of her clothes once she knew she was staying in Indian Lake for an extended period. However, Joy hadn't asked for anything dressy. She held up her finger. "Oh, Adam. Is this still a dressy affair?"

"It is." He grinned and left.

"Oh, boy. I need help." She yanked her cell phone from her back pocket and dialed. It was answered on the first ring. "Mrs. Beabots? I need you. Again."

Joy stood at the doorway to the largest personally-owned closet she'd ever seen. Of course, living in Manhattan, few people had room for a walk-in closet, much less one that could have housed all their friends and then some. "Is this for real?"

"Of course." Mrs. Beabots put her hand on Joy's waist. "You're about the size I was back when I wore some of these creations, so we should find something that fits."

"Cate told me you had this treasure-filled closet," she said, looking at floor-to-ceiling lit glass shelving that held dozens of Lalique perfume bottles and velvet-lined boxes displaying jewels the likes of which Joy had seen only when window-shopping on Fifth Avenue. "These are real?"

"Well, they're old. Like me. A few baubles I picked up at Harry Winston and Boucheron in Paris. Nothing like the pieces Elizabeth Taylor wore, or Audrey."

Joy held up a voluminous aqua skirt embroidered with butterflies and dragonflies. "This is incredible."

"No, it's Balmain. Here's the white organza-and-silk blouse that goes with it. It would look lovely on you." She went to the far-right side, where a rack held coats and jackets. "It's in here somewhere. Ah!" She pulled out a long, heavy satin theater cape, aqua lined in black wool, with a wide hood. "You'll need this."

"But it's too much," Joy protested.

"Not for the Christmas concert. Besides, don't you want to create a bit of shock and awe?"

Joy's eyes shot to her friend. "Why would I want to do that?"

"Why, to get Adam to come out of his shell, of course."

"That's not it. He knows I'm going back to New York."

"Are you?"

"Why…yes."

Mrs. Beabots stared at her with piercing blue eyes.

"He's afraid, all right. He lost Amie. He goes into panic mode watching Titus in my kitchen. He's terrified of losing someone again."

"He lost me once before. And now…"

"Now you both need a bit of a push." Mrs. Beabots went to a gilt-edged built-in drawer and pulled it out. The drawer was black velvet lined and filled with ropes of pearls, diamonds, rubies and sapphires. She held up a pair of aquamarine chandelier earrings that were a good four inches long. "Only someone with your long neck can wear these," she said, holding them up to Joy's face.

On each wall was an inset of mirrors so that one could see every angle of the chosen ensemble. Joy held up the earrings. They sparkled in the light of the crystal chandelier overhead.

"These are amazing," Joy gasped, holding her hair back from her ears.

"You're like these aquamarines. Timeless. A jewel of the ocean. And you're no more in love with this man in New York than pigs flying."

"How can you say that?" Joy gasped.

"You're settling," Mrs. Beabots said boldly and sat on the pink silk pouf in the middle of the closet. "You ran away to escape the pain of your parents' deaths and you still haven't dealt with that, if you ask me. You left Adam behind when you left town. Maybe you're just like he is now. Afraid of losing."

"Wow. You don't pull any punches."

"Somebody around here has to knock some sense into the two of you before you mess it all up again."

Joy held the gossamer-sleeved white blouse and the aqua skirt, admiring the workmanship. "I don't know. I've been nothing but confused since I came back here. What I do know is that when I'm with Adam I feel happy and enthusiastic, which I now realize hasn't happened for a long time. I'm proud of what we've accomplished in such a short time. If it weren't for him and his geothermal heating system, I'd be stuck with a useless property and never would have reconnected with Grandpa's spirit, our precious memories or my endearing friends."

"And you certainly would never have realized its potential, would you?"

"No."

"And why do you think he did all that?"

"Because of Frank…" she answered hesitantly. "And because he wants me to stay."

"He does, but I also know Adam plays his cards close to the chest. He's not going to announce his intentions until he gets a little push from you."

"And you think tonight's the night?"

Mrs. Beabots rose, went to the shoe rack and withdrew a pair of aqua leather pumps. "Even Cinderella needed a shove."

Joy took the shoes, leaned over and kissed Mrs. Beabots's cheek. "I bet her fairy godmother could take lessons from you."

"I taught her everything I knew."

JOY STOOD OUTSIDE the greenhouses. With no wind and no snowfall, the sky was crystal clear ebony studded with stars. The moon was nearly full, casting silvery light across the snow.

Joy heard the sound of horses' hooves against the snow-packed street.

A white-painted open carriage festooned with spruce and cedar garlands and drawn by two white horses pulled up. The driver was dressed in Victorian costume complete with a black top hat. Adam stood, dressed in a black tux and black wool coat.

"Your carriage awaits, milady." He bowed, then jumped down from the carriage.

She noticed he wore black cowboy boots. She smiled. He was still all Adam and she'd never seen a more handsome man, whether he was in a tux or his familiar jeans.

She walked up and took his hand. He kissed her tenderly. "You look beautiful," he said. Then he kissed her again.

"Shouldn't we go?" she teased.

"Oh, yeah!"

He helped her into the carriage. He took out a faux fur blanket. "To keep us warm on the drive," he said, taking her hand.

"It's not even a mile to the Civic Auditorium," she said.

"I know." He put his arm around her shoulders and pulled her close to him. "You should be able to keep me warm."

The driver whistled to the horses and they drove away from the greenhouses.

"Adam, this is too much," she said.

"I figured you did this all the time in New York City."

"No. Never."

"Aw, c'mon. Even I did this in the Big Apple."

"With whom?" she asked, feeling a twang

of jealousy for the woman who'd shared any time with Adam.

"Myself," he replied.

"Really?"

"I wish I hadn't been so chicken and actually reached out to you on that trip."

When he looked into her eyes, she almost winced at the hope she saw there. "But you're not now..."

"No," he said, moving closer, their noses nearly touching. "I'm not."

His lips against hers should have been cold, but they were warm and filled with the tender passion she'd come to expect from Adam. Maybe Mrs. Beabots was right. Maybe they both needed a push.

But was she brave enough to provide it?

The carriage halted, and when it did, Joy realized she'd been kissing Adam nearly for the entire journey. Short as it was.

"I'll be here to take you back home, sir," the driver said as Adam rose and helped Joy out of the carriage.

"That'll be great."

Joy took Adam's arm as they mingled with the throng going into the auditorium.

Once inside, Joy realized Mrs. Beabots was right. Everyone was dressed as if they were attending the Met. The auditorium held over three thousand people and it looked to be sold out.

Folding chairs had been set up on the main floor to resemble auditorium seats. The orchestra was warming up as they took their seats. Adam helped her with the cape.

"I bet you have awesome concerts in New York."

"I've been to a few and they were incredible. Mostly, though, my life is my work."

"I see," he said, as the overhead chandelier lights dimmed and the orchestra began.

THE RIDE BACK to Joy's house was equally magical, though a light snow fell. Adam kept his arm around her and she wasn't about to take her head from his shoulder.

Joy was sad to see the evening end. "This has been a wonderful night, Adam. Thank you."

"The concert always puts me in the Christmas spirit."

"I've never met anyone who keeps Christmas all year like you do."

"Most of our friends do."

"That's true."

"Your New York friends. They're not like that?"

"Glory is," she said, thinking fondly of her wacky friend.

"I'd like to meet her."

"You'd love her."

"Joy, you have to know, it's you I—"

A car came speeding down the street. The horses whinnied, one rearing up as the driver shouted, "Whoa! Whoa, girl! Take it easy."

The carriage lurched forward before the driver had the horse under control.

"Sorry about that, folks."

"It's okay, man," Adam said, a look of disappointment on his face.

She said, "I have an idea. Titus doesn't have school tomorrow, right? Wouldn't it be fun to take him sledding? Just the three of us. I can break away from the greenhouses for a few hours. Liz is planning to work the register and Katia will be there. The crowds are starting to dwindle a bit this close to Christmas."

"Everyone is busy wrapping and cooking, I suppose."

"So, what do you think?"

"Sure. Titus would love it. I have a sled in the basement. Not a toboggan."

"Don't worry about it. I have my old toboggan in Grandpa's basement. We'll go out to the golf course on the west side."

"Deal," he said, pulling her close for one last kiss. "This was special."

"I'll never forget it."

"Joy," he said. "There could be more moments like this, if you'd stay."

She froze. "Stay?"

"Yes. With me." He kissed her cheek. "You aren't the only one who's been looking at their choices differently. I'm as guilty as you—holding back, I mean. For years, I've kept my work a bit under wraps, bottled up my feelings and focused on Titus. I did all that to avoid looking at the past. That past is where you lived. But now you've come home. When I told you about my work, I didn't tell you all of it."

"No?"

"I've been offered a very lucrative opportunity—in California."

"California?" She was stunned. He had other options. Serious ones.

"That's the place. I turned the job down. It's not what I really want. What I want is you."

"Adam…" Her breath caught in her throat. He wanted her. She hadn't been imagining it when he nearly told her that he loved her. "The truth is, I have thought about what it would be like to stay. The best part would be working with you just as we always did. I've been so happy these past weeks. Watching the greenhouses thrive. And thanks to you, there's a future for Frankincense. I can't tell you how I'll miss you and Titus. But I have commitments in New York. I've made promises."

"And you need to deal with those," he replied sadly.

"I do."

His crestfallen expression broke her heart. She was hurting him again. She couldn't let it end like this. She had to find a way, but at this moment she didn't know how she could do that.

"I want to be honest with you, and right now, that's the part that hurts us both."

His gaze probed her. "You're right, you know. I hate it, but you are. You have obligations." He jumped out of the carriage and held out his hands to help her down.

She felt his hands around her waist as he lifted her down. She wanted nothing more than to stand in the circle of his arms—forever.

He dropped his hands and she looked into his eyes. Seeing lost hope gathering there pained her more than losing her grandpa. Was she doing the right thing? She hadn't a clue how to sort out her entangled choices. Her own heart mystified her.

"I can't let this be the last time I see you. You've been the world to me. I meant it about tomorrow. Let's take Titus out for some fun. Please."

He glanced back at the greenhouses.

Were those tears welling in his eyes? She thought she saw regret. Or was it simply nostalgia for a dream lost once again? It took him a moment to answer.

"Okay," he muttered as he walked her to the door of Frank's house. He turned to her. "Titus would like a fun day of tobogganing. I'll see you tomorrow."

"Tomorrow," she replied, as hope sprouted in her heart. She nodded toward the driver. "You need to get home and let that man and the horses warm up."

Adam walked away and climbed into the carriage.

He didn't turn around to wave as they drove off.

Joy had never felt so cold in her life.

CHAPTER TWENTY-SEVEN

JOY WAS DETERMINED to end her time in Indian Lake on a good note with Adam and Titus. She needed to find out if she had the kind of feelings for Chuck that she should have for a fiancé. Or was the love she felt for Adam the real thing?

She found Frank's old toboggan, a knit cap, mittens, scarf and a pair of her old ski goggles in the basement. When Adam pulled up in his truck, Titus was securely strapped into his car seat, but the boy was all smiles. As Adam put the toboggan in the back bed, Joy opened the door and gave Titus a hug.

"Are you all set for our adventure?"

"Boy, am I! I helped Dad make hot cocoa and we brought a whole thermos. We can sled all day practically."

"Practically." She laughed.

Adam came around to the passenger side. "Listen, I have to run to the back for a minute. You get in and settled."

"Can I help with anything?"

He shook his head. "Won't take a minute."

"Okay." Joy got in the truck, buckled her seat belt and said to Titus, "I thought you were so good at the school play. Do you think you'd like to take up acting?"

"No way." Titus flapped the air with his palm. "I'm thinking about being a playwright. But maybe Dad's right. I should be a physicist like my mom. Dad says I have a proclivity for it."

"Proclivity?"

"Yeah. It means I was born with a talent for it."

Joy stifled her laugh. Titus amazed her. If she did stay in Indian Lake and watch him grow up, she couldn't imagine the challenges he would throw her way.

And if she stayed in Indian Lake—with Adam—being a mother to Titus would be real. In that instant, her dreams and needs to be the career woman in a major New York accounting firm crumbled. True, running the greenhouses was a businessperson's dream. She smiled. All these years she hadn't really thought about what it would be like to have real love in her life. Or be a mother. She'd pushed those ideas out of her mind because they'd been too painful. But they weren't now. Had she already blown that chance with Adam last night?

"Here comes Dad." Titus pointed to Adam jogging up the drive from the back of the greenhouses.

Joy saw that he was on his cell phone and was shoving a small notepad into his sheepskin-lined jacket pocket. He looked worried.

"You okay?" she asked.

"Yeah." He shut the door, buckled his seat belt.

"Was that California?"

"Yeah."

"They must really want you. What did you say?"

He avoided her eyes and glanced into the rearview mirror at his son. "All set, Titus?"

Right, she thought. *None of my business. Not after turning him down.*

Titus tossed his head back on the headrest. "This is so cool. I love sledding. Now a real toboggan."

Joy knew to leave well enough alone. The distance she felt from Adam was tearing her in two. She turned her head and looked at Titus. "You've never been tobogganing?"

"Dad went over all the rules with me."

"Well," Joy said. "There's not much to it.

Get on, sit down, hands and arms in, and go down the hill. Yelling in delight is optional."

Adam started the engine.

He checked the mirrors and backed up the truck. His face was still rigid. "So, did Titus tell you we brought cocoa?"

"Yup," she replied. "Good thinking. It can get cold out there."

"Well, the minute it's too cold for Titus, we'll call it a day, right, sport?"

"Yes, Dad."

The drive out to the hilly golf course was beautiful. They drove around the lake so that Titus could see the beaver dams along the marsh areas. The lily pads were frozen and covered in snow, but Joy remembered how she and Adam used to drive out to the lake in summer and sit in her grandpa's truck and watch the sun go down.

Back then, they'd talked about the future and what it would be like to spend all their time together. Those memories hurt now. Adam had told her how important family was to him, since he'd never had one. In high school, she and her parents and Frank were his family.

Joy's hand went to her heart, empathy for the loss Adam had felt when she'd left Indian Lake raking her. For so long, her need to survive, get past her grief and succeed in college, then in the business world, had consumed her, to the point that she hadn't thought about Adam...or anyone but herself.

She'd been self-indulgent. And wrong about so many things.

Regrets were prickly, unrelenting things. She would have given anything to have one more day with Frank. And she wanted to apologize to Adam for hurting him. Now she'd done it again.

"Here we are," Adam said, driving up the steep paved hill where skiers and sleds were allowed. He pointed to the right. "We'll try that smaller hill first."

"But, Dad. That big one is meant for toboggans. See? Look at all those people."

"Precisely my point. Too many people can cause accidents. They can crash into you, and you're a novice."

Titus unhooked his seat belt. "True. But you'll teach me."

"We both will," Joy said. "Your dad and I used to come here all the time when we were young." She hoped her statement would bring up a fond thought for him, at the same time hoping he didn't resent her for last night.

"That was before he knew my mother," Titus said matter-of-factly, taking Joy's hand.

"Yes." She looked up at Adam, who smiled at her, mouthing "It's all right."

Adam went to the back and lifted the toboggan out of the bed. "Yep, this old thing has seen better days."

"But it's still good," Joy said.

"I checked the riggings. We're fine."

"Yay!" Titus yelled, thrust his arms in the air and raced ahead, up to the base of the hill.

"Titus! Take your time and watch where you're going."

"Oh, he's fine, Adam."

"Trust me, that kid is never fine. So far today, he slipped on Angel's doggy blanket. Spilled his cereal because he wasn't paying attention, talking too much about our adventure today. He put his boots on the wrong feet and tumbled down the front step."

"My gosh! Was he hurt?"

"No."

She exhaled. "Kids. They're resilient."

"Yeah, but I'm not. My blood pressure soars when I see him fall."

"Honestly, so does mine."

"You do care about him, don't you?" Adam asked.

"More than you know," she admitted as she trudged up the hill. Her own words ping-ponged in her heart. What was she doing, thinking of leaving him? Them?

They made it to the top of the hill, though Joy was surprised that Titus didn't appear to exert half the effort she did lifting her legs in the snow.

Adam put the toboggan on the ground and checked all the ropes. "These are a bit dry," he said. "I wonder if they're safe."

Joy looked down the hill. "It's a straight shot. And as I remember, we never used ropes. We hung on to each other."

"So, let's do that, Dad!" Titus scrambled over to the toboggan. "Me first." He snuggled his legs into the bow. "C'mon, guys!"

"Okay, you next. I'll take up the rear," Adam said.

"And we hold on to each other," Titus said, as Joy slipped her arms around him. He felt so good. So trusting and openhearted in his love. Then Adam looped his arms under hers and she felt a familiar zing go up her spine. She blinked back her regret.

"I'll push us off," Adam said, as he placed his long legs alongside Joy. With his gloved hands, he pushed the toboggan.

It barely moved. "Push again," Titus ordered.

Joy laughed and kissed Titus's head. She

was having the best time holding Titus, feeling Adam's chest against her back. She felt safe. Loved.

Adam pushed again. Nothing.

"Okay, everybody wiggle," Adam said.

"Done." Joy moved her hips from side to side as Adam pushed and...

Whoosh!

The toboggan flew down the steep hill. It wasn't a long run, but it was enough to exhilarate.

"Let's do it again!" Titus shouted, as Adam got off and held out his hand for Joy.

"Okay, sport."

Once at the top again, they got back on the sled. Now that they had the rhythm, they flew easily down the hill.

"Again!" Titus jumped off the toboggan, clapping his hands. "I could do this my whole life."

"Tell me he knows nothing about the Olympic luge runs," Joy said.

"I wouldn't dream of telling him that," Adam groaned.

By the time they'd finished their fourth run, another group of tobogganers came to the hill.

Adam walked back to Titus and Joy. "Okay. One more run and then we'll call it a day."

"Thanks, Dad," Titus said as he scrambled to the bow. Joy got in behind him and Adam behind her.

They had no more than set off when one of the boys jumped onto his toboggan, belly down, and took off down the hill.

"Hey, man!" The boy waved. "Race you to the bottom."

Because there were no brakes on a toboggan, Joy knew they had no choice but to finish out the run.

"Oh, crap!" Adam exclaimed.

Joy saw the boy had lost control of his toboggan and was headed straight for them. She didn't know what to do, so she leaned to the left, getting out of the way of the boy. Adam leaned with her and brought their toboggan onto its side, spilling them all onto the snow.

The boy kept laughing all the way to the bottom. "Sorry, man!"

Adam got to his feet and glared at the boy. Joy grabbed his hand. "Not now."

She leaned down and picked up Titus, who had a cut on his forehead where he'd hit the edge of the bow. Joy held Titus's face between her forefinger and thumb.

"He's bleeding," Adam blurted.

"I am?" Titus said. "My face is cold. I don't feel anything."

"We should take him to urgent care. He may need stitches."

Joy inspected the cut. "I don't think so. A butterfly bandage is all it looks like to me."

"Oh, yeah?" Adam picked up Titus. "What makes you an expert on my child? Get the toboggan. We're going to the hospital."

Joy felt her heart ice over. Adam's rigidity struck her to the bone. Adam had been keeping his real feelings and distrust of her hidden all this time. In fact, his true colors had come out at the incident at the trenches. He'd never forgiven her for leaving him. She'd rejected him and he was biting back.

As well he should.

She'd told him she didn't want to be part of his family and now he was showing her precisely that.

As they drove back around to the road, she glanced over at Adam, who ground his jaw enough to break teeth. This sledding party had been her idea, and then when the crisis came, she'd butted in with her opinions.

Looking past Adam's hard expression, she saw the north side of the road. The same road where her parents had been killed.

Dead Man's Tree was gone. Cut down and Mrs. Beabots had said that Wilma's brother's remains and dog tags had been properly buried. However, there were still wooden crosses of others who'd died in car accidents at this site.

Was it telling that she was this close to Dead Man's Tree and didn't notice because at the time she felt whole while she was with Adam? And was it some twist of fate that little Titus had been injured this close to Dead Man's Tree? Or was this a warning to her that she'd made the right decision when she'd run from Indian Lake? And now she was leaving him again.

Maybe she was never meant to be with Adam.

Maybe love just wasn't enough.

Twenty minutes later, Joy waited in the reception area of the hospital ER as Adam made it clear she would be in the way back in the examining bay.

It had all happened so quickly.

Every bit of it.

Adam's kisses had turned her head, confused her and caused her to rethink every priority she'd set for herself over the last ten years. He showed her how wrong she'd been not to spend time with her grandpa. He'd shown her how to dream the impossible. He'd trotted out all their old friends, who'd been wonderful and given of themselves and their time, when she'd given nothing in return.

She'd been insular, self-centered and wrong, all these years.

And last night.

He'd asked her to stay in Indian Lake—with him. Be a family with him and Titus.

She'd wanted to believe that dreams could come true. She wanted to believe in a love that never died.

Childhood dreams were just that. Meant for children.

Titus came rushing out of the ER's double doors. "Miss Joy!"

"Titus. Slow down!" Adam barked.

Joy looked at Titus and at the butterfly bandage on his forehead. Her eyes tracked to Adam. "He's okay, then?"

His expression was granite, his lips pursed so tightly they looked white. "He is."

"Thank goodness."

Adam reached for Titus's hand. "We'll drop you at the greenhouses."

"Right," she whispered. "I have packing to do and I need to relieve Liz. She's taking Pye and the kittens to the vineyard. Zeke loves the kittens."

"That's good. She's a special friend."

"She certainly is." Joy nodded.

"C'mon, son. Let's go home."

CHAPTER TWENTY-EIGHT

"Angel!" Titus yelled. "We're home!"

Adam shut the door behind him and took off his coat, his mind still on Joy. It was clear that he'd read everything wrong. He'd misjudged her smiles, her hugs and her kisses. He'd read love in her eyes when she was still thinking about New York.

It had taken every ounce of courage he had to ask Joy to stay in Indian Lake with him. He'd held his heart out to her, and she'd refused him.

What an idiot he'd been to think that after a decade in New York and all the work she'd put into her career, she'd be happy in slow-moving Indian Lake—with him. He was a "mental" kind of guy. Tinkering. Thinking. Creating. Not much exciting about Adam Masterson when one got down to it. He didn't mountain climb. Didn't scuba. Didn't even golf.

What he did do was see people in the world living better due to his inventions.

It was time he rearranged his priorities and put himself and Titus first. Pride swelled in him as he looked at his son.

Titus shucked off his parka and hung it on the hall tree. "Angel? You in the kitchen?" Titus called as he walked down the hall.

Adam took out his cell phone and called Hal.

The call was picked up on the second ring. "Hal. Glad I got you."

"Please tell me you called to say you've reconsidered."

"I'm doing just that," Adam replied confidently.

"Excellent. Is there any chance you can fly out Christmas Day? We really need to meet with the team on the twenty-sixth."

"I'll check flights as soon as we hang up and email you the flight itinerary."

"Adam, this is the best Christmas present I could have received. Thanks."

"Merry Christmas."

Titus raced back to Adam. "Dad! Come quick! I think Angel is having her babies!"

"Oh, my gosh!" Adam shoved his cell in his pocket and rushed after Titus.

Angel was lying on her doggy bed, panting and moaning. She barely lifted her golden head to see them as they hovered over her.

"Titus. Get me a pan of warm water and towels from the bathroom. The first pup is about to be born!"

JOY HADN'T HEARD from Adam since the day of the accident, and now it was Christmas Eve.

She hadn't expected to, but she'd hoped.

As the hours passed, she couldn't help the barrage of Adam thoughts. Adam's smile as he showed her Frank's poinsettia and pressed her to move forward with Daryl to have it hybridized. His helping with the grand re-opening and corralling her friends. The day at the tree farm. Decorating the huge Christmas tree. The symphony night. The carriage ride.

The kisses.

More than anything, she would never forget sitting in the greenhouse after they'd put up the tree and watching the shooting stars. "See that, Joy? That's your grandpa telling you he loves you."

Joy stood up and went to the closet. She carefully packed her business suit, pumps and the dress she'd worn for the funeral.

"What kind of guy would do those things if he didn't love me?"

She sank onto the side of her bed and pressed her palms to her temples. "I hope I'm doing the right thing."

Joy had come to town with a plan. Sell the greenhouses and Frank's house and return to New York.

But she was a different Joy now.

The New York Joy had been afraid. Afraid to love. Afraid to risk just about anything in her life. She chose an accounting career even back in high school hoping to help her parents and Frank. All she did was add up dependable numbers. She chose a man she didn't love in order to be safe.

Adam hadn't broken her heart when she left Indian Lake all those years ago. She'd broken it herself.

She hadn't risked anything. She had pushed the fear button all her life.

"No more."

She picked up the black jewel box and lifted the lid. Her engagement ring sparkled in the light. Last night she'd taken the ring off her finger and put it in the box.

Next, she grabbed her phone.

"Hi, Chuck. We need to talk."

IT WAS SUNSET WHEN Joy stood at Mrs. Beabots's front door and turned the tinny bell. Over her arm she carried the dress, cape, shoes and jewels she'd borrowed.

"Joy! I'm happy to see you. Come in and share a glass of champagne with me."

"Thanks," Joy said and entered the house.

They sat drinking their champagne in front of her Christmas tree.

"You don't look all that merry," Mrs. Beabots said.

"I haven't heard from Adam in two days and I think he's done with me."

"What happened?"

"He asked me to stay—here in Indian Lake. I turned him down—again."

"When was this?" Mrs. Beabots put her champagne down and leaned forward.

"The night of the concert."

"Ah! Then that explains it," she replied with a knowing gaze.

"Explains what?"

"Adam's leaving for California," Mrs. Beabots said.

"He took that job?"

"Apparently. I couldn't figure it out. He was so happy being with you and Titus."

Joy stared at her glass. "Well, he's apparently a darn good physicist, as well as a mechanical engineer. He's the kind of guy who can not only figure out how to create advanced propulsion engines, he can build them."

Mrs. Beabots put her hand over Joy's. "But I know that's not what makes him tick."

Joy nodded. "Family. He's always wanted a family."

"I have a suspicion that's what you want, too."

"I do."

"Then follow your heart."

Joy smiled. "I should."

"What have you got to lose?"

Joy took out her cell phone. She punched in Adam's number. Titus answered.

"Titus, hi! Whatcha doing?" she asked, expecting to hear how he was waiting for Santa Claus.

"Dad's putting our suitcases in the truck. We're leaving for the airport."

"Now? On Christmas Eve?" She rose, nearly spilling her champagne.

"Uh-huh. It was the only flight we could get."

"Tell him to wait…" She hung up immediately and handed her glass to Mrs. Beabots. "I gotta go!"

"Hurry! And merry Christmas!"

ADAM SMOOTHED A lightweight sweater over a half-dozen shirts he'd packed.

He supposed he should be ticked off at

himself for letting his barriers down and falling in love all over again with Joy. But he wasn't. They'd both changed since her return. He'd found that he could never keep his heart closed off to Joy. He'd succeeded in showing her that so many people in Indian Lake loved her and missed her. She could have a life here.

He picked up his sneakers. People ran in LA, right? He didn't need boots. Or did he? "Am I running away just like Joy did all those years ago? Am I guilty of the same wrong choice?"

No. He'd done it all. Put his love on the line. Asked her to stay, and she'd chosen her other life. Another guy.

"Not me."

Again.

How many times did he have to go through this heartbreak to get it? They weren't as right for each other as he'd thought.

If he'd been selfish to want a life with Joy in Indian Lake, then perhaps this was fate showing him there were other options to consider.

Like the pounding of a jackhammer, someone banged on the front door.

"What in the—? All right already!" Adam yelled, coming out of the bedroom with his duffel. "Titus. Get the door, willya?"

Titus stood at the entry to the kitchen and put Adam's cell phone in his pocket. "I can't… Uh, Angel has to go out. Really bad."

"This must be the dog sitter. She can take Angel out. Did you finish packing?"

"Not yet."

The banging continued.

Adam dropped his duffel and opened the door, ready to read the dog sitter the riot act. As the door flung back and he opened his mouth, he saw Joy. "Joy?"

"Can I come in?"

"We're on our way out."

"Please," she said, pushing on his chest and closing the door behind her.

"I guess, okay," he replied. "I thought you'd be halfway to New York."

"I'm not going to New York."

"No?"

She shook her head. "It's over. I'm staying here. I'm going to ask Glory to move out here to help me with the greenhouses. She'll love it. Most of all, I'm hoping you'll rethink California."

Titus snickered in the background. "Dad, I should watch the puppies nurse."

"Puppies? Angel had her pups?"

"You wanna come see them, Miss Joy?" Titus asked.

"Of course." Turning back to Adam, she said, "But first I have to tell your dad that I love him."

"You do?" Adam asked.

"Yes, Adam. I love you—with my whole heart. And I can't let you leave without you knowing that. Even if you never speak—"

Adam clasped his hands to her cheeks and touched her nose with his. "That's all I wanted to hear."

His kiss was born of thousands of days apart. Years without her. Memories of being in love. The past spun to the present and created a whirlpool of love and longing around them. "Joy, I never want to be away from you again a single day."

"Then you love me, too?" she asked, placing her hands over his.

"More than you can imagine."

"Dad—the puppies!" Titus's frustration ripped across the room. "I wanna show Miss Joy the puppies."

"Yeah? I want to show her something just as important."

Adam kissed Joy again, and this time she put her arms around his neck and leaned close.

Titus turned around, went to the kitchen and came back with three newborn puppies in his arms. He walked up to his father. Following behind him was Angel, who kept a very focused eye on her babies.

"Are you gonna come to California with us now, Miss Joy?"

"I'm staying here."

Titus pushed his glasses up to the bridge of his nose, not an easy feat with one puppy licking his cheek. "I'm gonna miss you. And my new puppies, too."

Adam put his arm around Joy's shoulders and laughed. "I have a better idea. What if we forget about California and stay here?"

"Adam? Can you do that? I mean, this is important," Joy countered.

"I was only taking the job because Indian Lake would be empty without you. California is just a job. It's not my life here with you."

She snuggled closer.

"It's Christmas Eve and we're all home now."

"Yes, Adam. We're home. We're right where we should be."

Joy reached up, touched Adam's cheek and kissed him again. "I'm never leaving you, Adam. Or you, either, Titus."

Titus handed Joy a puppy, then gave one to his father. He held the largest puppy to his heart as he put his other arm around Joy's waist.

"I knew my Christmas wish would come

true," Titus said. "I just had to believe extra hard."

Adam smiled softly at Joy. "I think a lot of wishes came true."

Adam hugged Joy, and she laid her head on his shoulder. Through the window behind him, she saw a single shooting star sail across the sky. Tears sprang to her eyes. "Grandpa's wish for us was the best of all."

* * * * *

THE CHRISTMAS ROMANCE COLLECTION!

'Tis the season for romance!

You're sure to fall in love with these tenderhearted love stories from some of your favorite bestselling authors!

YES! Please send me the first shipment of three books from the **Christmas Romance Collection** which includes a FREE Christmas potholder and one FREE Christmas spatula (approx. retail value of $5.99 each). If I do not cancel, I will continue to receive three books a month for four additional months, and I will be billed at the same discount price of $16.99 U.S./$22.99 CAN., plus $1.99 U.S./$3.99 CAN. for shipping and handling*. And, I'll complete my set of 4 FREE Christmas Spatulas!

☐ 279 HCN 4981   ☐ 479 HCN 4985

Name (please print)

Address   Apt. #

City   State/Province   Zip/Postal Code

Mail to the Reader Service:
IN U.S.A.: P.O. Box 1341, Buffalo, NY 14240-8531
IN CANADA: P.O. Box 603, Fort Erie, Ontario L2A 5X3

---

*Terms and prices subject to change without notice. Prices do not include sales taxes, which will be charged (if applicable) based on your state or country of residence. Offer not valid in Quebec. All orders subject to approval. Credit or debit balances in a customer's account(s) may be offset by any other outstanding balance owed by or to the customer. Please allow 3 to 4 weeks for delivery. Offer available while quantities last. © 2019 Harlequin Enterprises Limited. ® and TM are trademarks owned by Harlequin Enterprises Limited.

Your Privacy—The Reader Service is committed to protecting your privacy. Our Privacy Policy is available online at www.ReaderService.com or upon request from the Reader Service. We make a portion of our mailing list available to reputable third parties that offer products we believe may interest you. If you prefer that we not exchange your name with third parties, or if you wish to clarify or modify your communication preferences, please visit us at www.ReaderService.com/consumerschoice or write to us at Reader Service Mail Preference Service, P.O. Box 9049, Buffalo, NY 14269-9049. Include your name and address.

XMASR19

ReaderService.com has a new look!

We have refreshed our website and we want to share our new look with you. Head over to ReaderService.com and check it out!

On ReaderService.com, you can:

- Try 2 free books from any series
- Access risk-free special offers
- View your account history & manage payments
- Browse the latest Bonus Bucks catalog

Don't miss out!

If you want to stay up-to-date on the latest at the Reader Service and enjoy more Harlequin content, make sure you've signed up for our monthly News & Notes email newsletter. Sign up online at ReaderService.com.

RS19